T0272500

HOLLOW BONES

HOLLOW BONES

Erica Wright

**SEVERN
HOUSE**

First world edition published in Great Britain and the USA in 2024
by Severn House, an imprint of Canongate Books Ltd,
14 High Street, Edinburgh EH1 1TE.

severnhouse.com

British Library Cataloguing-in-Publication Data
A CIP catalogue record for this title is available from the British Library.

ISBN-13: 978-1-4483-1394-5 (cased)
ISBN-13: 978-1-4483-1395-2 (e-book)

All Severn House titles are printed on acid-free paper.

Typeset by Palimpsest Book Production Ltd.,
Falkirk, Stirlingshire, Scotland.
Printed and bound in Great Britain by
TJ Books, Padstow, Cornwall.

Praise for Erica Wright

"The action builds to a thoroughly satisfying and exciting finale"
Publishers Weekly Starred Review of *Famous in Cedarville*

"Wright provides it all: clean prose, captivating characters, a gripping mystery, and a wry look at Hollywood glamour and decay"
Publishers Weekly Starred Review of *Famous in Cedarville*

"Wright successfully combines small-town sensibility with the money and glitz of twentieth-century Hollywood in a suspenseful mystery populated with winning characters"
Booklist on *Famous in Cedarville*

"A clever little whodunnit"
The New York Times on *Famous in Cedarville*

"A twisty and engrossing thriller, one of those rare page-turners that you have to force yourself to slow down and savor the lyrical prose and atmospheric scenes . . . It's the kind of book that stays with you long after you've read it"
Daniela Petrova, author of *Her Mother's Daughter,* on *Famous in Cedarville*

"A gripping addition to the recent trend in crime fiction of portraying the dangers facing America's immigrants"
Booklist on *The Blue Kingfisher*

"Fascinating and fully developed characters . . . Wright's vividly told tale is studded with wry wit"
Publishers Weekly on *The Blue Kingfisher*

"Readers will want to see more"
Publishers Weekly on *The Red Chameleon*

About the author

Erica Wright is the author of seven books, including the essay collection *Snake* and the crime novel *Famous in Cedarville*. She is a former editorial board member of Alice James Books and was the Poetry Editor at Guernica Magazine for more than a decade. She currently lives in Knoxville, Tennessee with her family.

for Arthur

'. . . thy bones are hollow; impiety has made a feast of thee.'

– Shakespeare, *Measure for Measure*

A WEEK BEFORE THE FIRE

The camera switched on, the recording light a watchful eye, a witness even, and the preacher thought about mercy before he pulled the snake on to his lap. The trick required steady hands, yes, but your heart had to be still as well, unburdened. Pastor Micah stared at the animal as it coiled into a thin circle, almost an ouroboros eating its own tail. Forever and ever amen. The color shone in the bright light as if the scales had been anointed in oil, the black iridescent next to the reds and yellows. He knew the old nursery rhyme couldn't be trusted – red next to yellow can kill a fellow – but he also knew this one was the genuine article, not some kingsnake picked up by accident. No, he held life and death in his hands, and he felt no fear. When he smiled at the reporter, his face opened like a curtain.

Merritt Callahan crossed her legs and leaned forward, licking her lips.

'You'll ask me if I've ever been struck. That's natural curiosity is what that is, and I welcome it. You can't save people with all the doors shut, you know? You got to let a little light inside.'

'Is that what you're doing here? Letting some light inside?'

Pastor Micah made a show of looking around New Hope. The wooden pews from 1952, the plastic paneling meant to imitate oak. The linoleum floor had been replaced, but otherwise, the place looked a step away from being condemned. Not exactly the kind of church you'd put on a postcard, and he knew when folks arrived for the first time that they weren't impressed. They wanted the holy dust of cathedrals. They wanted the awe of stained glass crafted by artisans who worked until their hands buckled from arthritis. Here, they didn't even have a pulpit. The preacher preferred it that way, everybody equal. He had been called, but that didn't make him better than anyone who stumbled through the front door. And stumble they did.

'She's a looker, right?' Pastor Micah lifted the coral snake, let it wrap around an outstretched arm – the most vibrant thing in the whole building except for the reporter's pink lipstick. 'How else would sin tempt us if it weren't beautiful? If it were easy to resist? No, the devil knows his work, sure enough.'

The reporter glanced at her notes even though she didn't need them and shifted uncomfortably at the word 'sin'. Pastor Micah had a talent for reading people, and this one had chosen ambition over everything else. Why else would a woman be on her own in middle-of-nowhere West Virginia – hauling her own equipment, doing her own makeup – if not for a story that would propel her to a better time slot, a better show, a better network. Oh, those never-ending ladders. To say nothing of her cheap heels but tailored blazer, the part that would be seen by viewers. Greed, plain and simple, with a side helping of vanity. Once you knew what vice somebody favored, you knew everything you needed to manipulate them. A different sort of man could make a fortune as a motivational speaker. Pastor Micah led a church.

'Can you tell me about your Narcotics Anonymous group?' she asked in a brisk, clipped voice.

Pastor Micah ran his free hand through his black curls, as dark as the snake's darkest stripes, and looked at her with his pale green eyes. He figured the Lord had made him handsome for a reason too.

'Let me tell you a story instead about a man who'd given up. Lost his job, his family, his mind. Found him collapsed on the side of Packer Road, a bundle of clothes more than flesh and blood. Half-ghost already.' Pastor Micah felt the snake begin to move over his arm, looking for a way down. 'Another overdose.'

'Nearly a hundred deaths in West Virginia already this year, and it's only January.'

'I always liked a smart lady.'

The reporter responded with a close-mouthed smile, and Pastor Micah knew the comment would be cut when the interview aired. For the best.

'This state's opioid problem is the worst in the nation,' she said a little louder, getting the conversation back on her terms.

'Now, is that a problem or an opportunity? I ask you. For somebody who wants to help, this state – this town – is paradise. Or could be.'

The snake slid back on to Pastor Micah's jeans and tried to escape down his leg. The reporter flinched, and Pastor Micah gripped the animal gently behind the head like a cat carrying a kitten. It was so small that too much pressure would snap its vertebrae.

'But why snakes?'

'Not snakes, serpents. "They shall take up *serpents;* and if they drink any deadly thing, it shall not hurt them." If God tests your faith, and you pass? Whew, I'm telling you, praise Him, there's no drug can compete with that rush.'

'And the man you found?'

Pastor Micah squeezed a little, feeling the sliver between life and death. People call it a veil because there's so little fabric separating life from the afterlife. They can even see it sometimes if they're looking, a shadow moving in their periphery, a figure in their bedroom as they wake from a dream.

'That man should've been dead, and I thought he might be. But as I touched his forehead, I felt the spirit move between us. Electric. God had a plan for him yet.'

The snake wrapped its tail around the preacher's arm, desperate to flee. Pastor Micah pressed a little harder – then released. The snake slithered on to the floor, causing the reporter to scoot her chair back. Pastor Micah could see the realization in her eyes – that she was alone, that she'd been foolish. That her ambition might cost more than she wanted to spend. Pastor Micah looked directly into the camera, not bothering to keep track of his pet. He trusted in the Lord. It wasn't his fault if his guest didn't feel the same.

'There's only one question worth asking,' he said. 'When you get up in the morning, when you tuck yourself in again at night, and all the long hours in between. How's your faith today?'

ONE

Essa learned to appreciate the taxidermied animals, especially the red-tailed hawk with her curved beak hovering over a disapproving little frown. After everyone left for the day, she would try to guess the bird's grievances. She'd wash the forceps, inventory the pins and think of a list of possibilities: the raptor didn't like sitting next to the lynx, or the air conditioning was turned up too high, or somebody had left the hall light on overnight. That somebody would be Essa of course, who'd been locking up the Vintera Wildlife Investigation Laboratory since she turned sixteen. The red-tailed hawk was a bit of a mystery, neither endangered nor what experts called 'ecologically significant'. She'd never asked why the old girl stayed in the display room, but then again, she'd never asked about the timber rattlesnake either, and she knew the snake didn't belong there. The species was native to the area, of course, and thriving. She tried not to think about that one, pointedly ignoring its extended fangs each time she passed. Oh, it couldn't hurt her. But she'd rather not look at it all the same.

The day of the fire, Essa assisted Dr Kester with the necropsy of a *myotis septentrionalis*, a long-eared bat, by cataloguing the contents of its tiny stomach. The other employees resented that Essa got to help so often, especially considering that she had an online associate's degree and they had fancier academic pedigrees. But Essa had a quality that nobody else possessed; she could be silent for hours. Not simply quiet but silent. Not a murmur or squeaked shoe. Rarely a cough. At first, people noticed her odd clothing, her long-sleeved blouse and floor-length skirt. Sometimes they might comment on her thick brown hair, which fell below her waist. But if you'd grown up anywhere near Vintera, you knew about the insular community over by Tyson's Creek. And anyway, Essa wasn't one of them anymore. When she stilled herself, you could forget she was in the room at all.

She watched Dr Kester create two straight incisions in the bat's abdomen and peel back the skin. Before he could ask for them, Essa handed him pins for the mat. He used a probe to move the animal's organs around, looking for anything unusual. He made a tsking sound, and Essa could see that he wasn't happy about the discolored lungs. There was a new manufacturing plant a few towns over, and lately the local flying species had been coming in with similar symptoms.

'That's the problem right there,' Dr Kester said. 'Nobody worries about the long-term consequences. It's a cheap buck, and that's the end of it.'

The town liked Dr Kester well enough, but he wasn't from around there. He'd been recruited from some state-of-the-art facility near Atlanta. He'd been all but retired, then the opportunity to run his own lab had been too much to pass up, even if from time to time he had to assist the local police department, a group he considered a step up from ghouls. 'Sentient cinder blocks,' he'd been known to say. Essa worried about him – the way his hands shook a little by the end of a long day. But Essa was only twenty and her legs hurt too sometimes. It wasn't easy standing on a concrete floor for hours.

'Do you know what a group of bats is called, Essa?' He never expected her to answer, so she didn't acknowledge the question. Instead, she took the probe from her boss and handed him some forceps. 'A colony. So assertive, don't you think? They claim their territory. And they're wildly successful. Wildly. Heh.' Dr Kester removed the stomach and placed it on a tray. He stretched his fingers three times, holding them out as far as they could go before letting them return to their natural curl, then he cut into the organ with a scalpel. 'They hunt together, you know.'

Essa did know. At dusk in summer, they would swarm up over her house. They stayed in the oak tree she'd climbed as a kid, racing to the top. The bats would swerve and dive, feasting on mosquitoes. She'd lived in the same place her whole life, though everyone had expected her to leave when her older brother Clyde moved out. He'd raised her after their parents died, but as soon as Essa turned eighteen, he'd shacked up with his girlfriend. Clyde had adapted to life outside the community better than she had. After all this time, Essa thought her best shot was starting over somewhere else, somewhere nobody knew her past. Somewhere she wouldn't be one of the serpent orphans. So she'd been saving every penny and applying for jobs, trying not to get discouraged by the string of rejections.

'Not much here,' Dr Kester continued, using tweezers to move some half-digested bugs on to the table. Essa wrote it down all the same, using a notebook because Dr Kester didn't trust technology. She'd type an official report later. 'We'll have to look at a few more to be sure, but I'd say there's no outside interference here. I'd testify to that. They'll have me back out next week though – you mark my words.'

Dr Kester nodded once at the notes Essa had taken then peeled off his plastic gloves. He barely checked her work anymore. When he started whistling, Essa knew his mind had turned to the weekend. When he wasn't at the lab, he and his wife went on road trips to nearby towns, taking their dogs with them and buying jadeite pitchers and glasses. They didn't have any children, so who knew what they'd do with all their stuff when they passed, including their bevy of pets. Essa had lost count of how many they'd rescued or rehabilitated. Their latest was a grey squirrel with a broken foot and a penchant for walnuts.

Essa organized the space for Monday morning while Dr Kester washed his hands and put on his tweed sports jacket. He always dressed impeccably while everyone else preferred casual, comfortable attire. There was no dress code besides closed-toed shoes. Essa's least favorite co-worker Karl wore boots, hoping to get into the field. He preferred the cases outside, animals that needed to be examined where they'd been found. And when he spent all day cooped up inside, he got a little mean. Essa stayed out of his way. Essa stayed out of everyone's way.

Dr Kester didn't say goodbye when he left, but she knew he was gone. When she'd started, being left alone with all the dead animals had bothered her. She'd had nightmares about them all coming to life, trapping her in a corner and eating her guts out. After a while, she'd grown used to them, even naming a few. There was Greta the red-tailed hawk of course, but also Lionel the vulture and Tanya the tortoise. She knew their lab's reference collection was small compared to the larger facilities, but she thought it impressive enough. Their taxidermy guy lived nearby and was known as something of an artist, east of the Mississippi at least. Not a single specimen had crossed eyes or visible glue.

Essa washed the equipment they'd used and disposed of the bat in one of the sealable plastic hazard bags. She said a little prayer over its body out of habit then swept the floors and turned out the lights.

It was dark when she stepped outside, and only her rusted Honda Civic remained. As she moved toward it, red and blue lights flashed, and she shielded her eyes from the glare as they turned into the parking lot. Essa had never been pulled over, never even had a parking ticket, and her heart started to pound when the car jerked to a stop in front of her, blocking her way. Every nerve in her body told her to run, but she knew that was a way to get shot in these parts. Instead, she stayed as still as one of the dead animals inside as two cops approached her, walkie-talkies squawking and hand-cuffs jangling. Her keys slipped out of her hands, but she didn't dare retrieve them.

'Essa Montgomery,' one said. She couldn't see his face, but that didn't bother her as much as not being able to see his hands.

'Yes, sir,' she said. She hadn't spoken in hours, and her voice came out weak as a leaking faucet. 'Yes, sir,' she tried again.

'I'm Lieutenant Barnes, and this is Sergeant Sallis. We need to speak with you a moment. About the fire.'

The lieutenant and sergeant had the better of her because they could see her face.

'I don't think she knows,' said Sergeant Sallis, and Essa was surprised to hear a woman's voice. There weren't too many lady cops in Vintera.

Essa hoped somebody would tell her what was going on before her heart burst out of her chest. This must be what it felt like to be hunted.

'What were your whereabouts this morning between, say, six and seven a.m.?'

It took a moment to understand the question. Essa gestured to the building behind her. 'I was here.'

'That early?'

Sergeant Sallis sounded suspicious, but Essa came in before everybody else to clean. It didn't take her three hours, that was true, but she didn't have anywhere else to be.

Lieutenant Barnes reached for something, and Essa closed her eyes. When nothing happened, she opened them again, seeing the silhouette of a notebook not a gun. The cop cleared his throat as if preparing for a monologue.

'Sometime between six and seven a.m. this morning, a fire was set at New Hope Pentecostal Church on Pine View Road. The fire consumed the steeple, roof and better part of the walls before the fire department arrived.' Lieutenant Barnes looked up. Or at least, Essa thought he did. His tone changed. 'They tried their best.'

Essa couldn't care less about the church. No, that was a lie. She'd wanted the place gone for years. All it had brought her was misery, and she'd hoped it would collapse. She'd hoped it would be struck by lightning or run through by a lost tractor trailer. She'd hoped to wake up one day, and poof – it would be gone. But the rectory? The rectory had remained her home even after her father died.

'You telling me I'm homeless?'

'No, your house's still standing. By the grace of something. But we need to know if you've seen your brother today.'

'Clyde?'

'You got another brother?'

'I haven't seen Clyde in—' Essa paused to think. They weren't exactly estranged, and Essa didn't like that word. It sounded too much like 'strange', and she knew people called her that. Essa saw Clyde from time to time. They'd say hello. 'Not since September maybe?'

The two officers turned away from her for a few seconds, and Essa thought about how information was power. Power that could be hoarded or shared. She would fixate on that moment often in the days and weeks that followed. But power was power too. The ability to make people do what you wanted. So when Lieutenant Barnes told Essa to get in the patrol car, she didn't hesitate or protest. They said, 'Come with us,' and she obeyed.

Essa tucked her hands under her skirt, shivering from the cold but not daring to ask if they could turn up the heat.

'Maybe you could tell me what's going on,' she said to the back of two heads.

The officers spoke their secret, silent language again, deciding what the girl could be told and what she couldn't.

'We think your brother burned down a church,' Sergeant Sallis said. 'And it wasn't empty.'

Lieutenant Barnes took over. 'We think your brother killed two people.'

TWO

Juliet preferred a new moon to a full one, a darkness like ink pooling over an ancient contract, erasing history so that it could be retold, reshaped even. But this was the only night she could complete her task, and she stared at the sky, daring the stars to challenge her. A new year, a new opportunity.

She stacked the seven flat pieces of limestone around her, sizing them up. If she rushed, she would fail, and she didn't intend to fail. Not this time. Not when it mattered more than ever. Her fiancé didn't exactly endorse her nocturnal excursions, but he'd brought the stones back to her all the same, one each month from June through December, always from the same hiking trail. Could there be a clearer sign of love, these slabs of stone? This steadiness? They meant more to her than the small garnet ring he'd held out to her over pancakes one morning, although she would never say as much aloud. It hardly seemed like a secret even, her preference for something solid rather than pretty.

Juliet picked up the largest ragged rock and positioned it over the dried grass, sage and dandelion root. In this way, she began her offering, a cairn stable enough to hold her weight.

When she'd turned eight, Juliet had noticed that she could read people's emotions. As the candles on her cake burned, the room had seemed to freeze in time, and she'd taken her time peering at each face. They'd all smiled, but her father's eyes had remained steel, unhappy, dreaming of someplace else. Her mother had radiated annoyance and something underneath that had taken Juliet longer to pinpoint. Perhaps she hadn't known the word for it at the time, but she'd known it was something akin to stubbornness, what she felt when told to clean her room or go to bed early.

A few weeks later, her mother had packed her bags and taken Juliet out of her third-grade classroom early, marching them both into a new life with fewer toys but less yelling. Still, the change had fractured something inside of Juliet, and she believed that if she could have seen the change coming, she would have been better prepared. She could have said goodbye at least. And so, once a year,

Juliet walked into a clearing far from town and asked for the gift of precognition. The rituals varied, but her intentions never did. She wanted to see what lay ahead.

She dreaded this part, slipping off her shoes and socks to feel the frozen ground, but she hummed with an internal heat. She felt on fire, and the frost soothed the burn, melting under her skin. A branch nearby cracked, and she tensed, wondering if an animal or spirit watched, wondering if she would be judged – finally – worthy. But she was too far from the trees to see anything, and she crouched to scrape the frozen earth with a stick, carefully drawing a square around the largest of the wide and thin rocks, her base. She stepped up, satisfied by the nearly imperceptible wobble. Six more to go.

By the time she got her driver's license, Juliet could concentrate on someone's face – or palm if offered – and see glimpses from their life. She'd stare at her high school English teacher Miss Savry and know that the woman had credit cards frozen in blocks of ice to keep from using them. Her biology teacher Mrs Balcones had a secret girlfriend that she'd meet when her husband worked late. She wished she didn't know about how her mother rifled through any bags left unattended at the laundromat, how she would pilfer quarters to put into her own machines. And she'd once seen such a violent image from a man at a gas station that she'd vomited in the middle of the floor. Her mother had insisted she take a pregnancy test even though Juliet had tried to explain. Nobody believed her. Or they didn't want to believe her, saying they'd pray for her soul.

It wasn't enough. When she'd met Madame Clarita, she'd jumped at the opportunity, ingratiating herself to the woman who'd given her access to bookshelves brimming with texts on astrology, divination, meditation. Her teacher had cobbled together her own kind of psychic understanding, which she'd passed along willingly, almost eagerly.

Madame Clarita had agoraphobia and hadn't left her home in a decade or more, so the place smelled like spoiled cabbage, and even as a teenager, Juliet had seen opportunity. Her teacher's client list shrunk a little each month, because Juliet would slip them her number. A girl had to look after herself. She hadn't intended to take advantage of the woman's loneliness, but Juliet couldn't remember a time when she didn't want more. It couldn't be helped, she figured. What choices did she have? She could count them on one hand, and she wasn't lining up for grease burns if she could help it.

Something like a bee sting brought her attention back to the stones, and she saw that one of her knuckles had split open. She didn't remember scraping it on anything, but her hands were chapped from winter. Maybe it was a sign – the night asking for blood. Maybe her body and mind were ready, and she whispered into the wind what she wanted.

She placed the second and third stones more quickly than the first, tested them, her bare toes curling around the edges for balance. She was only a few inches off the ground, but she felt nervous. No, not nervous. Agitated. It should have felt desolate out there in the wilderness, a West Virginia terrain as hardscrabbled as its people. Her people. But Juliet liked the severity of the season even as she longed for the languid, green days of summer, when anything seemed possible. No, the cold kept her awake, and by the fifth stone, her confidence returned. She stepped up to test her makeshift platform again, and even the shaking below her feet didn't bother her.

The years after she discovered her ability to peer into strangers' minds – or loved ones' for that matter – were hardly worth recounting. She'd gotten straight Cs at school, preferring to spend her evenings studying Madame Clarita's texts rather than algebra or literature. She'd never use those subjects. What was to be gained from equations when she could make star charts and charge classmates five dollars a pop? By the time she'd met Clyde, she'd siphoned off enough of Madame Clarita's clients to rent her own place, hang out her own shingle. But she also knew her checking account balance down to the penny.

Juliet didn't like the looks of the sixth rock, and she turned it by degrees, hoping that it would find a groove. When she stepped back, it turned a fraction of an inch without her, from the wind or something else. A shiver ran down her spine that had nothing to do with the temperature. She glanced again at the trees, squinting in the bright moonlight. Did her ancestors want her to fail? Was she doing something wrong? No. She pushed on, not bothering to test the penultimate one. It would hold or it would fall. Juliet had to try.

Another crack of a branch nearly derailed her, but she bent at her knees to bring the final one up as she chanted, '*Thoir dhomh sealladh, leig dhomh fhaicinn.*' The words were familiar but the feeling alien.

An unease settled into her bones as she eyed the two-foot cairn.

It was hardly Mount Everest, but her legs trembled as she pushed herself up, realizing too late that the structure would never hold her. She flailed back to the ground, her body aching as the pieces of limestone tumbled around her feet.

After a moment, she opened her eyes to see the moon mocking her. She wasn't alone, she told herself. And she'd never be alone again.

THREE

When they pulled up to the police station, Essa felt as if her spirit left her body. She'd heard of that phenomenon, the spirit and body severed by shock. But in her case, it lasted only a few seconds before she felt utterly, disappointingly human again. Was she being arrested? It had been a normal work day. She'd cleaned like she was supposed to clean. She'd stayed quiet like she was supposed to stay quiet. Essa was good at rules, written and unwritten. And she had followed the rules. Her day shouldn't have ended at the Thorngold County Police Station.

She ducked her head as Lieutenant Barnes and Sergeant Sallis led her through a crowded lobby. Two men argued at the top of their voices about a stolen motorcycle, and a woman wearing a bathrobe and rain boots gripped a television remote even though there was no television in sight, only drab, beige walls decorated by a Heimlich maneuver poster. There were two doors marked 'Security Required', and Essa walked through one of them like a rat following her pipers.

'Friday night,' Lieutenant Barnes said.

Now that Essa could see his face, he was less intimidating. Freckled with red hair, he looked more like a kid than an authority figure. Sallis had the swagger of a middle-aged woman who knew her worth and knew she wasn't being fully appreciated for it. A swagger with a chip thrown in for good measure. They both radiated heat, couldn't disguise their excitement. They'd landed a big case, and they'd wrapped it up in twenty-four hours. Almost. They wanted a confession, salivated after it, and they'd decided the long-lost sister could deliver unto them what they wanted.

Essa watched her brother from behind two-way glass, happy at least that she'd learned to disguise her emotions years ago. She wanted to weep at the sight of him. Not because he looked distraught. No, Clyde looked calm, all things considered, and the spitting image of their mother with those unnaturally long eyelashes over hazel eyes. He wore a clean white T-shirt and dark-washed jeans. Essa guessed that he'd come home from work, scrubbed the grease from his fingers and gotten ready to take his fiancée out. Then the knock at the door. Would a killer look like that? Essa didn't want to believe it, so she didn't believe it.

Before she could prepare, she sat in front of him. Her instructions were simple: Get him to tell you what he's done. Get him to ask for forgiveness. No, beg. They'd said 'beg for forgiveness'. All Essa could think about was that he must be cold in his short sleeves. That she hoped they heated the cells at the correctional facility if they transferred him. She'd rather not dwell on that place's reputation for making gang members out of first-time offenders.

'I wish you hadn't come.' Clyde glanced at his handcuffs. Essa could see that they were tight enough to leave ugly red lines. Clyde had once had a snake tattoo on his right wrist, its triangular head resting on his palm. Somebody had turned it into a dragon, and now the beast's tail swished down the length of her brother's arm.

'Didn't have much choice.'

'They hurt you?'

Essa shook her head. 'They say you burned the place down finally.'

'Finally? You think I did this?' Clyde's eyes turned darker, even under the bright fluorescents. 'Shit, String Bean. If you think I'm guilty, who's gonna believe me?'

'I believe you, Clyde. Whatever you say, I'll believe.'

'I was at home this morning. Same as always.'

Essa didn't relax, but she didn't feel as nauseous either. 'That's settled then. You got an alibi.'

Clyde pushed back his hair from his forehead, and Essa remembered when he'd let it grow long after their parents died. For a while, they could have passed for twins. Then one night, they'd taken kitchen shears to Clyde's mop. They'd done such a poor job that it looked like his hair had fallen out in clumps from some disease. Like the tattoo, somebody had fixed that for him too. Juliet maybe. They'd started dating around that time, and if Clyde had been a girl, people would have said he blossomed. Got promoted to manager at work, went to poker nights with friends and took his girlfriend out to the movies from time to time. He'd even gotten a little meat on his bones. He looked like a man, Essa realized. Capable of anything. Capable of things she didn't want to think about.

'Naw, Juliet was sleeping. Works late, you know.'

Essa didn't know but nodded.

'And I thought maybe I could get a hike in before the shop opened.'

Clyde got into hiking after meeting Juliet too. She'd encouraged him 'to get in touch with nature', and instead of laughing at her, he'd followed her advice, taking rambling trails through the nearby Alleghenies when he had the time. Said it cleared his head. And they'd never slept well, Essa or Clyde. That much remained the same.

'So you weren't at Juliet's?' Essa wondered if she was allowed to move around. She hadn't been told not to, but it seemed like she was supposed to sit here, and Clyde was supposed to sit there.

The room consisted of three concrete walls and one glass with starburst scratches as if a suspect had thrown a chair against it. What would that feel like – to get so angry you wanted to break something?

'They say there were folks inside,' she said. The words came out as a whisper.

Clyde didn't respond at first, and when he did, his voice was quiet too. 'I don't know about the boy, but you remember Sara Beth Booth?'

Essa felt a jolt of recognition. She'd assumed the victims were strangers. When a flashy new preacher had taken over the church a year after their father died, he'd attracted a new congregation. Only a few of the old families had remained, and that didn't include the Booths. Sara Beth wasn't exactly a friend – Essa didn't have friends – but she was friendly enough when they happened to cross paths.

Sara Beth now looked like any other young woman in town, with curled hair and leggings. For the past year or so, the girls had been using eyeliner to make little seventies-style cat eyes, and Sara Beth had the look down pat, her points never smudged even at the end of her shift at the Dollar Tree. Nobody would ever know that she'd grown up passing copperheads around while singing hymns. She'd blossomed too.

'She's a kid,' Essa said.

'Same age as you. Eighteen.'

'I'm twenty now.'

Clyde shrugged as if he didn't care that he'd forgotten her birthday. Two birthdays. Under the circumstances, she could forgive him.

'Make him beg for forgiveness,' they'd said. Essa turned to stare at the two-way glass, knowing Lieutenant Barnes and Sergeant Sallis watched. She felt a flicker of something in her belly. Not a fire, but a little bit of heat. The afternoon had been a blur, and she'd been in shock, first at the news of her brother being held then at the role the detectives expected her to play. A girl and boy had gone to their eternal resting places. But she was starting to thaw out and realized with some surprise that she held more anger than sadness.

She turned back to Clyde, raising her voice. 'You didn't do it?'

'I didn't do it,' he said.

'Good enough for me.'

Clyde grinned as if he'd won a goldfish at a fair. 'So you'll help me?'

The flicker of anger sputtered.

'I'll ask about bail.' She knew even as the words left her mouth that she couldn't afford it. She had some savings, sure, but it wouldn't be enough.

Clyde shook his head. 'Don't waste your money. The shop'll hold my job for a few days. I've not been charged with anything yet, so they can't keep me here forever. No, you go talk to that son of a bitch preacher. Tell him it wasn't me.'

Essa felt cold all over when she thought about the new preacher; how much he'd scared her when he first arrived. Still scared her, if she was being honest with herself, and she tried to be honest with herself. She figured Pastor Micah would demand the rectory, and she didn't know if her family ever legally owned it. Her father never showed her a title or made a will. He felt himself above those sorts of worldly matters and didn't trust lawyers to boot, saying 'they trust in vanity, and speak lies. Isaiah 59:4'. But weeks passed then months with the new preacher waving at her as he went inside his church. A year. Essa celebrated the anniversary by buying a little wreath and hanging it on her front door. *Her* front door. But the fear never went away that he might one day take her home.

'Pastor Micah? I don't know. Maybe Juliet—'

'He won't listen to somebody like her. But maybe somebody like you.'

Clyde tried to gesture with his right hand, forgetting about the cuffs. He meant how Essa looked, meek and humble. A natural supplicant.

'Why's he think you did it?' she asked.

Clyde's gaze darted to the two-way glass, and he didn't respond right away. Essa knew he was keeping something from her – or from the cops listening to them anyway.

'Does it matter? He says I did it, and bam.'

Clyde held up his wrists for emphasis, and Essa's eyes went back to the red lines, raw enough to bleed. What would life in prison do to her brother? He hadn't been around lately, but there was a time when he'd been her sole protector, her only family. Even so, she wanted to say she couldn't talk to the preacher. She wanted to say it was pointless. Clyde's girlfriend may have worn revealing clothes and heavy makeup, and believed in horoscopes more than the Bible, but she'd probably never passed out in freshman orientation either when asked to introduce herself. Essa didn't look directly at Clyde, staring instead at the scratches, how they seemed to split the dragon in half, one part still a snake, the other part bigger and deadlier but imaginary. Dragons couldn't hurt you because they didn't exist.

But this? This cinder-block room, the cold floor under Essa's feet. Her brother's request. This was all snake, no dragon.

FOUR

Merritt Callahan had sworn she'd never return to Vintera, West Virginia. As far as she was concerned, the whole state could be swallowed by a sinkhole, may it rest in peace, etc. She'd shelved her story about Micah Granieri's groundbreaking addiction program after he'd let that coral snake loose during their interview. A little digging around had told her that the preacher donated heavily to local political campaigns, maxing out the monetary limit for judges in particular. He was likely dipping into church funds, but Merritt didn't have proof. He'd even finagled some sort of grant for the police department to update their computers. But her viewers were used to that kind of corruption; would yawn in response. No, she'd decided, Vintera, West Virginia could be marked as a mistake in her mental index before being filed away for good. Then she'd heard about the fire over her scanner app and been on the road before WTGX-Roanoke switched to the mid-morning crew. She'd beat the other reporters there by an hour. Merritt Callahan liked to beat the other reporters. Merritt Callahan liked to win.

Her producer had left a string of expletives on her voicemail, but she'd grown accustomed to his overreactions and the word 'unauthorized' rolled off her like water from a duck's back. Since being hired, she'd sent him dozens of pre-recorded interviews, and he would begrudgingly air them on slow news day. Over the course of her three years at the station, she'd racked up nearly as much airtime as the anchors. Initiative. She had initiative. And, perhaps more importantly, didn't care that much about pissing people off.

By now, most of the other crews had left for the day. Merritt swayed back and forth, trying to stay alert and warm. She wasn't standing close enough to the church – to what used to be the church – to get any residual heat from the smoldering ashes. A fire crew had been working fourteen hours now and showed no signs of stopping. She'd spoken with a few of them, their names carefully recorded and spelled correctly in her notes. They said the big concern with a fire like this on such a dry January day was it reigniting and burning other buildings.

'The rectory?'

'The rectory, sure, but if those trees catch fire? This is the kind of animal that can spread to town before you can say boo. Before you can say run,' said Tim Guthrie. He'd removed his goggles and looked like a raccoon, the red rings around his eyes in stark contrast to the rest of his sooty face.

Merritt hoped her cameraman had captured the intensity of Tim's expression. But 'cameraman' was a stretch. 'Cameraboy' would be more appropriate, and Merritt knew why the undergrad had been hired. He was cheap. Her producer had sent him without her approval. She would have picked Yarrin or even Doug. Anybody else. But the station always sent her P.J.

Merritt thanked the firefighter for his time as well as his bravery, and Tim's serious expression turned softer for a second or two. Merritt winked at him, which made him smile. Then he returned to his duties and, to his credit, only glanced back at her once or twice.

'You thinking about wrapping up, Ms Callahan?' The cameraman was dressed in a seasonally appropriate parka and leather boots with fur at the ankles. He'd tied the hood of his coat so tightly that his face was barely visible. He peered out at her now like a puppy eager for a walk, his breath making clouds.

'You can go home, P.J. I've got this.'

'You sure,' he said, but he was already folding his tripod.

Merritt briefly wondered what P.J. stood for – certainly not 'Persistent Journalist'. Then she got distracted by Granieri pulling up. He'd been at the site on and off all day. He'd let her record a second interview, as camera-ready in a crisis as he had been for their pre-arranged conversation a week before. If she had to guess, his disheveled curls were created with a little pomade, his disheveled clothes chosen from a walk-in closet. She'd found his house title with a little digging, and the riverside place was no shack. The words he spoke were the right ones: tragedy, faith, prayer. But she trusted the man about as far as she could throw him. Still. A scoop was a scoop.

Granieri noticed her staring as soon as he climbed out of his car, but Merritt didn't flinch or look away. Instead, she nodded and received a nod in response. He'd have all the money he needed to rebuild and then some. She knew the right words too: tragedy, faith and domestic terrorism. And she'd dropped them the first time the station let her go live around 8 a.m. Now everybody was yammering about this 'unimaginable act of domestic terrorism'. She should sue them for copyright infringement.

Nobody from the police department would speak with her, repeating 'No comment' as if they'd been threatened within an inch of their lives not to reveal anything to the press. But if you lingered long enough, you caught snippets of conversation. You saw the body bags too. So far nobody had dropped the victims' names, but Merritt could wait. Vintera had a motel, bedbugs be damned. She'd sleep in a hazmat suit if she had to.

When she thought nobody was paying her any attention, Merritt walked to the property line, following the bank of a little creek until she was behind the church and away from the tumult. The steeple had fallen to the ground nearby and shattered on impact. With some effort, she wove through the debris. Her heels didn't sink into the frozen ground, and Merritt thanked her guardian angels for small favors. She'd had her eye on a little shed all day, curious about the deadbolt. You didn't lock up rakes and shovels in a town like this.

She had bolt cutters in her car, but somebody would stop her if she fetched them. Instead, she pulled a flathead screwdriver from her shoulder bag and tried her best. This wasn't her first lock, but it was stubborn. She swore under her breath as the tool jerked back again. A crash from the fire made her drop the screwdriver entirely, and she cursed under her breath, dropping to her knees to search in the dark. That's when she noticed the three-inch gap at the bottom of the door. She pulled out her phone and pushed her hand through the opening, taking photos from as many different angles as she could. The flash made her cringe every time, but she worked fast. In less than a minute, she was scurrying away from the shed back to the creek.

Merritt knew she should wait to look at the images but opened them anyway. The first few shots were blurry, but her hand stopped shaking at some point. There was nothing on the floor, but every wall had shelves lined with what looked like aquariums. Not exactly valuable. Not exactly worth locking up. She zoomed in on one, not exactly shocked to see eyes staring at her, bright white from the flash. Little halos in the dark. Merritt didn't know anything about snakes, but this wasn't the one that had almost bitten her the last time she'd swanned into Vintera. This one was much, much bigger.

'I can introduce you, if you'd like.'

Merritt screamed, and something splashed behind her. She'd read somewhere that you could drown in as little as two inches of water.

Granieri looked bigger, too, as he blocked her view of the fire and anybody who might help her. She'd been stupid not to look for her screwdriver.

'Kind of you to offer, but I'll pass this time.' She summoned a smile. It had no effect on the preacher.

'You sure? You seem so eager to meet my friends.' Granieri's smile was as fake as her own.

'Not that eager to meet my maker though.'

They stood in the dark, testing each other.

'Best let me walk you somewhere safe then.'

Merritt half-expected Granieri to pull her into the water, a deadly baptism, but he gestured for her to lead, and she stumbled back toward the firefighters, police officers and spectators. Relief made her dizzy, but it was followed by embarrassment. The man seemed determined to get the best of her. And Merritt Callahan liked to win.

FIVE

Righteous fury wouldn't drive her home. And Essa was as scared as she was angry anyway. If the cops had arrested her brother on one man's word, that man's word must be powerful. Not a scrap of evidence, though she admitted there was motive. New Hope Pentecostal Church had taken both their parents.

She stood in the parking lot of the Thorngold County Police Department, wondering how to get home. She'd been brought there in a patrol car and had no intention of leaving that way. She remembered dropping her keys in the lab parking lot and worried somebody might take them, but it was a small worry considering her night, like a mosquito bite on her ankle while trying to stanch a head wound. The only person she would ever call in such a situation would be her brother. She scrolled through her phone anyway, counting on inspiration. Her finger paused over Dr Kester's name, but it was late. Her boss was probably fast asleep beside his wife and dog. The road didn't get much traffic, and there was a decent-sized shoulder. She could walk.

The gravel crunched under her feet, and she appreciated the noise. It didn't take long for the stretch to feel desolate and dangerous. There were woods on either side, and Essa tried not to think about what might be lurking within. She could name all the predators native to the area, and while she didn't expect to see a black bear rumble out in front of her, coyotes scared her. Alone, they weren't that intimidating, but as a pack? As a pack, they could be vicious. She didn't like their cry either – the wail of a baby coming from something with such sharp teeth. Like goblin children. She shuddered and stuffed her hands into her pockets. They'd turned red from the chill in the air.

She was so lost in thought that she didn't notice the car coming around a curve. The light spooked her, and she froze in place, throwing her hands up as if she could make it stop. Wheels squealed, tossing gravel, and Essa tried to scream, but the sound got stuck in her throat as the car swerved toward her. She closed her eyes against the impact, but the wheels squealed again, and the car sped past, close enough to blow her hair back. By the time her brain registered what happened, she was already shaking, her legs barely able to hold her upright. She stumbled to her left and leaned against a tree, gasping for air.

Essa could have stayed there all night except somebody spotted her and stopped. The sound of her name made her head jerk up. She saw a flash of pink in her periphery, but when she swiveled her head, no color remained.

'Essa Montgomery, honey. That you?' A dog barked from inside a pickup truck, and the driver turned toward it. 'Hush up now, Tilly. Don't you see we've got ourselves a situation?'

The woman slid out and walked toward the woods. Essa dusted off her skirt out of habit. Her teeth chattered when she tried to respond, and the woman clucked. Essa didn't recognize her at first in her bulky hunting jacket and black knit cap, but slowly she realized it was the owner of Charlene's, a bar not too far away. They'd never met before, but Essa wasn't surprised the woman knew her name. Everybody knew her name around there. And that made them think they knew everything about her too.

'You hurt? I need to call someone?' Charlene held out a hand, and Essa ignored it. She found her voice though.

'Thank you, ma'am. I'm all right, I think. Near got hit is all.'

'Walking at night along this road? No wonder, honey. Come on then. Don't mind Tilly none. She licks a little. She'd lick a bird, I think, instead of kill it.'

Essa took Charlene's hand then leaned against her shoulder as she made her way to the truck. Essa had always been a small thing, so it was awkward to clamber inside. Tilly nuzzled Essa on the cheek then greeted her owner when the woman climbed back inside. Essa didn't have a natural affinity with animals like her father. He could charm honey out of bees.

'You headed home?'

Essa nodded then said yes in case Charlene couldn't see her. She started to give directions, but Charlene did a three-point turn and headed the right way.

'Sorry to make you go out of your way and all.' Essa shifted, the feeling returning to her limbs.

'Ain't nothing. What I got waiting for me? A bunch of drunks.'

Essa didn't say anything, but those drunks kept Charlene's lights on. It was the only watering hole this side of town. It wasn't that

far to Rosetta though, with the chain places. That's where the folks
who lived river-side went on the weekends. But Charlene's place
was decidedly creek-side. If the beers cost more than a few bucks,
nobody was coming.

'You lookin' after yourself?' Charlene asked, cranking the heat.

'I've never known what that meant, to be honest with you.'

Charlene laughed, which made Tilly bark. 'Fair enough, Essa.
Fair enough. Ain't my place anyway.'

Essa stuck her hands close to the heater vents and started to thaw.
She didn't like being obligated to a stranger, a bar owner at that.
Not that she thought drinking was a sin exactly, what with Jesus
turning the water to wine. But she'd never seen it lead to anything
good and stayed away herself. When you're left on your own at
eighteen, you make your own sort of code of conduct. She'd never
written it down or anything, but she stuck by certain principles.
They kept her afloat.

Essa watched the dark trees outside the passenger window. How
could she have been so dumb? Walking home on such a night.

Essa's agitation increased when they got close to her house, and
she saw a crowd assembled. There were at least two dozen uniformed
officers plus firefighters and a sizable group of spectators. The
thought of walking past everybody made Essa feel faint.

'Holy shit,' Charlene whispered. 'Sorry, honey. I'd heard there
was a fire but didn't think it was nothing like this.'

Charlene tried to park her truck in Essa's driveway, but emergency
vehicles cluttered the space. She pulled on to the grass, and the
women climbed outside. Tilly barked to be let out too, but Charlene
shushed her. New Hope was gone. Sure, a few boards remained,
maybe some pews, but the building was unrecognizable as a church.

Essa had fantasized about New Hope exploding or crumbling to the
ground in neglect. That had seemed likely in the year after her father
died. With only a sleepy, old interim pastor, quite a few families
stopped coming. Then Pastor Micah appeared, a sort of mist in the
morning, and the congregation had doubled – then tripled. A whisper
network said there was something special about this one's services.
Something electric. Standing room only. The *Herald-Dispatch* had
even done a feature on his new program for opioid addiction treatment. Folks who'd never heard of Vintera, West Virginia came to
see what all the fuss was about. And Essa stayed in her kitchen,

watching the cars pull up from behind her curtain and hoping for the whole operation to shut down, wondering if that was self-serving, blasphemous or both.

Essa's face flushed from guilt, and she was glad Charlene couldn't see her well in the dark. She noticed a couple of families from the old days, crying and holding each other. It would be neighborly to comfort them, tell them everything would be all right. They'd dropped off food after her mother died and again after her father. But she stayed put. Pastor Micah led a small prayer circle. Essa didn't know what he was saying, but she could guess. 'God's will' and 'strength in faith' and 'tested by the Lord'. Amen and amen and amen.

She couldn't talk to him tonight. That was a blessing at least. There was no way she could approach him like this, plead for her brother's life in front of everybody. Instead, Essa thanked Charlene for the ride, braced herself then rushed toward her front door, assuming nobody would notice her. A policeman grabbed her arm though, making her jump.

'Apologies, Miss Montgomery, but you can't go inside yet. Not safe.'

Essa thought she recognized the cop. There'd been a brief investigation after her mother had been bitten. Social services had come too. But it had all been glossed over. New Hope followed the letter of the law. Her father made sure that children remained at the back of the church during services, that nobody was forced to drink the poison or handle the serpents. Always 'serpents', never snakes. Because snakes were only animals, but serpents? Serpents were tricksters, little demons come to earth to tempt and sway. They meant something, and that something was bad news.

Essa sank on to her front porch to join the vigil. A hymn rose into the night, the preacher lifting his voice in song. His deep baritone carried, and Essa admitted that the words provided comfort. Others joined during the second verse, even people who'd never attended New Hope. 'The little hills lift up their voice,' they sang. 'And shout that death is dead.' It was out of tune, only the preacher's voice a pleasing sound, but the intention felt right.

The spectators grew quiet and calm as if a spell had been cast over them. Essa found that she was crying. It'd been a long day, she told herself. She resented the church, but her great-grandfather had preached there, then her grandfather, then her father. Her brother hadn't refused exactly, but nobody had asked him. And women weren't allowed. Not that Essa could stand to go inside ever again. And now she wouldn't have to cross the threshold. Not even for a wedding or a funeral. God had heard her pleas. God had heard her pleas, but at what cost?

She wiped her face with the back of her sleeve and noticed Pastor Micah looking at her from across the parking lot. Her gut tightened. But he couldn't know that her tears weren't for him or for New Hope but for herself. The place should have burned to the ground before she was born. She could have had a real childhood.

Essa stood and unlocked her front door, ignoring the protests she received. It was her home, at least until somebody told her otherwise. She wasn't about to blubber in public if she could help it.

The curtains over the oddly high living-room windows blocked most of the light and prevented anyone from seeing inside as she pulled off her dirty skirt and threw it in a hamper. She stepped into a pair of her brother's old high-school sweatpants, sank on to the couch and dragged a quilt to her lap, rubbing her hands over the embroidery her mother had completed. It wasn't pretty, the flowers more like weeds, and the vines like dental floss. Momma Montgomery had been kind and cheerful but not exactly an artist. Essa loved it anyway. She'd never blamed her mother for what had happened. Only her father. He was their leader, and he should have done a better job of keeping them safe.

Her heart ached for Sara Beth Booth, and Essa prayed that the girl would be the church's last victim. New Hope had a way of eating people alive, no matter what the new preacher promised. But the church hadn't ignited itself, and that preacher thought her brother was to blame? Was he?

As soon as Essa had the thought, she pushed it away. She thought about how much he looked like her gentle mother. He'd inherited a little of her temperament too, although it had been changed by the world. He could be neglectful and moody, but violent?

Essa closed her eyes to pray, to ask God what to do, hoping He would hear her pleas again. Hoping this time He wouldn't demand a human sacrifice.

SIX

The practice had all but died out. The South had once claimed hundreds of so-called 'signs-following' Pentecostal churches, congregations that took the Gospel of Mark literally and praised Jesus while dancing with cottonmouths or drinking strychnine. Now only a handful remained. West Virginia was the holdout, the last state to legally allow the practice. And yet New Hope thrived. New Hope promised a future for serpent handling, reimagined for a new congregation. Folks who'd been swindled by pharmaceutical companies into believing pills could solve their problems turned toward prophecy. They'd been stripped for parts, but Pastor Micah could reassemble them, or so he promised on the morning news.

Essa watched him on her television, but she could also see him outside, surrounded by cameras. Every news crew wanted a turn, and she marveled at the reaction. Donations had poured into the rebuilding campaign overnight. Phrases like 'domestic terrorism' were dropped liberally with 'ongoing investigation' and 'suspect in custody' thrown in for good measure.

Essa thought the high windows of her house made it resemble a horse trailer. The interior stayed dark except for an hour or so a day when the light slanted to the floor, making rectangles. Only the kitchen had a regular window, and Essa took her time doing the dishes each morning, opening the screen sometimes to see more clearly when the mosquitoes weren't bad. Over the years, she'd trained herself to ignore New Hope and study the trees lining the little creek that edged her yard. The creek flooded on occasion, but there hadn't been rain or snow for months. Wasn't that always the story? Too much or too little of something, making life harder on people who didn't need another challenge.

The knock at her door didn't startle her. Reporters had been knocking all morning, and she'd been ignoring them for the same amount of time. She'd showered and dressed and planned to spend her day with the kitchen curtains shut, maybe working a puzzle. She knew she should turn off the television, but her curiosity outweighed her unease about the operation. Her damp hair lay against her back, and she took her time plaiting the whole length. It would take until the afternoon to dry, but she wasn't going anywhere. There was still no way to speak with Pastor Micah privately. She would wait, hope something changed so that she didn't have to speak with him at all. A new discovery in the ashes. A clue exonerating her brother. A girl could dream. The knock at her door didn't startle her, but when someone said her name, she froze, recognizing the voice.

'Essa, it's important. I wouldn't be here if it weren't important.'

Essa had known the Lincoln twins since birth and had nursed a crush on Washington Lincoln throughout middle and high school. Her brother's best friend had tolerated her presence. She'd been quiet even as a child. Not much trouble. But she hadn't spoken to Wash in a year or so, and now he was knocking at her door, his voice deeper than she remembered, but somehow like a lake lapping a sandy shore. He'd married a girl who worked at the hospital with him. They were raising a family.

Essa peeked out to make sure that it was him, that the shocks of the previous night hadn't addled her brain. He waved at her then gestured at her car in the driveway, his brother Harrison sitting in an idling pickup truck. Harry didn't go out in public much, not since the mining accident took his left ear and part of his jaw. Essa tried not to be nervous around him but found herself ducking behind cereal boxes if they happened to be in the grocery store at the same time.

Essa opened the door because she had to open the door. They'd done her a favor, and she couldn't rightly refuse to acknowledge them.

'Spotted it at the lab, keys on the ground for all the world to take,' Wash said before she could greet him. He pushed his long wavy hair behind his ears. 'Figured you could use a little help today.'

'Thanks, Wash. I owe you one.'

Essa didn't know what else to say. Wash lingered though, so Essa tried her best. 'How's your momma doing these days?'

Wash was tired, his eyes rimmed with red as if he hadn't slept in a while. She knew he worked night shifts sometimes, was probably coming home from one when he saw her car abandoned. She was grateful but also embarrassed that he'd gone to the trouble. She didn't like owing anybody.

'Oh, she gets around. You all right?'

Essa nodded, aware of the reporters glancing in her direction like vultures. There was a woman in a red shift dress and matching blazer that seemed impervious to the chill. Essa could guess her intentions. A few sentences from the church's neighbor as human interest, make New Hope seem quainter. She'd been used as a prop before. Or, worse, maybe her brother's name had been leaked to the press.

'Listen, I hate to ask. I know this is hard on you,' Wash said, interrupting her thoughts, 'but you best check on Juliet today. She's losing her mind, and I got another shift.'

Essa knew that Wash and her brother hung out. They had the kind of friendship that would last until they were regulars at the senior center – if they lived that long. But she'd never thought about Wash spending time with her brother's girlfriend too. Essa's reaction felt a little like jealousy.

Essa had never met Juliet, though she'd seen her around. She had small black tattoos on both arms – occult symbols that made a lot of locals uncomfortable – and wore a jet-black wig most of the time. Bodice dresses and heavy makeup completed the costume, and Essa supposed that it worked. Anytime she drove by Juliet's trailer, there were a few customers parked out front, waiting to have their fortunes told, waiting for somebody to assure them that their luck would change. Essa thought she seemed more like a reaction than a love interest for her brother, but what did she know about relationships. She'd never so much as held hands with anybody.

'I reckon she'd rather see somebody else.'

For years, nobody except for Dr Kester had asked anything of her, and now she couldn't seem to escape responsibilities.

Wash coughed and glanced back at his brother as if to make sure Harry didn't mind waiting. But neither twin was the impatient sort. They could wait all day for the right buck to walk into their sights. They could even go home empty-handed and not make a fuss about it. *Good boys,* their parents and teachers had called them. Essa couldn't disagree, and she waved at Harry, thanking him from afar.

'I'm afraid she might do something,' Wash said.

'Do something?'

Wash turned toward the front porch railing and stretched against it, hanging his head. He looked at his brother again as if together they might come up with a reply. Essa realized that he still wasn't impatient with her, only ready to be done with this errand. Ready to be done with her. She tried not to take it personally. Her closest friend was a stuffed hawk for a reason.

'I ain't gonna tell you how to live your life, but if I was you, I'd check on Juliet. That's all I'm saying about it.'

Wash paused for a moment and held out an arm as if he might hug her. Then he changed his mind and walked back to Harry's pickup, his boots crunching the gravel. The two pulled out of the driveway, and Essa looked around, feeling as lost as she'd felt in a while. Her half acre of land was a wreck. Deep ruts from the emergency vehicles surrounded the place. The water hoses had made a muddy mess out of everything. Thin layers of ice covered the puddles. Charred wood and ash smoldered, making the scene look like hell as far as Essa was concerned. Where else did you get ice and fire and no relief? It would take months to clean up, but that didn't worry her too much. Her brother though. His fate gnawed at her bones.

The Lincoln family had left the church when she and Clyde did and for the same reason. One day the mirage had lifted, and they'd seen the place for what it was. It was like having the lights turned on in a Halloween haunted house. What would Essa have found if she ever returned to New Hope? Pity at best. More likely hollow exhortations to trust in the Lord's will. Maybe even judgement that it had taken her so long to find her faith again. 'For by grace you have been saved through faith. Ephesians 2:8.' Essa had faith though – that had never been the problem. She didn't trust humans much was all.

The reporter in red broke away from the pack and headed toward her. Essa realized that she'd been staring off into space, a deer in headlights. The reporter beckoned one of the cameramen to follow her, and Essa ducked inside, locking the door behind her. When the pair knocked, Essa mumbled, 'No comment please,' then repeated it louder. In response, a business card slid under her door: Merritt Callahan, WTGX-Roanoke. Essa didn't touch it, instead going to get her parka and purse. If she waited, she would lose her nerve.

Merritt loitered on her porch when Essa left, trying to get some sort of reaction out of her.

'I saw you the last time I was in town,' she said. Essa pushed past her, saying something about not remembering her. 'I wouldn't expect you to remember me, but I was here all the same. Interviewing the pastor?'

Essa paused and acknowledged the woman. Merritt gestured for her cameraman to step back a few feet, and he complied, moving the camera off his shoulder and shutting it off. He looked young for the job with a smattering of acne on his chin. Even though he wasn't recording, he stayed close enough to hear their conversation.

'I don't know him,' Essa said.

'You live right here by the church and don't know the pastor?' The reporter squinted at her, making creases appear around her precisely lined eyes. 'He's something.'

Essa tried to read her tone. Was it admiration or disapproval?

'I'm sorry I can't help you,' Essa said after the silence stretched to an uncomfortable minute.

The woman cocked her head to the side, and Essa resisted the urge to smooth her hair. If she stayed outside any longer, it would start to freeze. She hated when that happened, the tightening at her scalp from the extra weight.

'You've got my card, if you need me.'

Essa glanced back at her own front door. She'd left the business card on the rug where it had landed, but she nodded at the reporter, who seemed satisfied by the response.

The dash to her Honda was less eventful than Essa expected. Nobody else pushed a microphone in her face, though a few watched her curiously. Even better, her car started on the first try. That wasn't always a foregone conclusion. A full tank of gas. She owed the Lincoln twins.

She slid the car into reverse and pulled on to Little Pine, driving without thinking about driving, the way you can on certain familiar stretches.

Juliet's tidy white trailer served as both her home and business, with a parking lot in front and a patch of dirt in the back. Essa could see the 'Open' letters even though they weren't lit up. A blue sign with an eye framed by a triangle stood by the road. It always seemed to peer back at Essa and gave her the heebie-jeebies. They'd never been allowed so much as a Magic 8 Ball when she was little, not even for play.

Juliet offered basic readings for only ten dollars, but her regular customers spent a lot more than that. For the most part, Essa minded her own business, but she'd read the online reviews, all gushing about how Juliet was the 'real deal' and 'worth every penny'. Essa tried not to judge her future sister-in-law for making a living, even if most citizens of Vintera lived paycheck to paycheck. Essa walked around to the back, not wanting to be mistaken for a customer.

Juliet opened the door before Essa knocked, as if she'd been waiting for someone. She took one look at Essa and covered her belly with both arms. Essa followed the gesture and tried to hide her surprise at the obvious pregnancy.

'Guess you were bound to find out soon or later,' Juliet said. 'Might as well come in.'

SEVEN

'And so pretty.'

Sara Beth Booth's family lived in a subdivision near the high school, and Mrs Booth told Merritt how she'd always been scared to let her daughter walk by herself. 'It was only half a mile away, but you know what it's like out there. For pretty girls like my Sara Beth.'

Merritt nodded, not wanting to interrupt. She'd learned to let interviewees talk, forget they were being filmed. She hadn't called P.J. either, sensing tripods for a camera and lights would make the woman clam up. Before she'd arrived at the Booths' home, she'd looked at the daughter's Facebook page. And her TikTok. And her Instagram. And her secret Instagram. Sara Beth was very much online, making up for lost time perhaps with selfie after selfie showing a perfectly made-up face and low-cut tops. There were a few with the boyfriend, Carter Hoyston, and he never looked as comfortable. Sara Beth had probably twisted his arm, flirting with him until he cracked, the gap between his front teeth making him look sweeter than a starting linebacker wanted to look.

'They were gonna get married. Least that's what they said. You know how kids are. You got kids?'

Merritt shook her head. When it seemed like Mrs Booth didn't have anything else to say, Merritt added, 'But I would want a daughter like Sara Beth. What a bright light.'

'A bright light. Yes, that's it. And so pretty.'

Merritt told herself not to get irritated with a grieving mother, but did the woman have anything to say about her daughter's classes, career plans, extracurricular activities? She could have asked a follow-up question, but, instead, she looked around the clean living room. The carpet had been vacuumed that morning, if Merritt had to guess. The potpourri on the table smelled faintly of lavender but also medicinal. Merritt would have thrown it in the garbage. The mantel was cluttered with photographs of three children. Sara Beth had a brother and sister – that much had been easy to google. In the early photographs, the children wore long-sleeved, old-fashioned clothes. Paisley prints with opal buttons. Snapshots, not professional. They stood in stark contrast to the new ones of the girls in cheerleading outfits, the boy with a soccer ball. There was a recent one of the whole family on a beach. The father wasn't home now, Merritt noted. His daughter had been killed, and he wasn't there to comfort his wife or other children.

Merritt had been the first to interview the Booths, though she knew another reporter from a rival station had tried to contact the Hoystons. They'd told her as much when she called. They'd used what might generously be characterized as colorful language. Merritt had heard worse and thought piranhas were misunderstood anyway. But the Booths were the real get, their daughter, yes, so pretty, her senior photo custom-made for national coverage. It could be on the cover of *People*. It could flash up on the *Nightly News*. And with any luck, clips of Merritt's interviews would go viral.

'Cheerleading?'

'Oh yes,' said Mrs Booth. 'She never missed a practice.'

'Well, she missed one.'

Merritt hadn't noticed the younger sister sneak into the room. The girl wore sweatpants that said 'Salty' down one leg and 'Sweet' down the other. She looked a lot like her sister with curled, light brown hair and a thin frame. But there was still something of a child in her, especially when she crossed her arms, giving herself a hug. Her blue nails were bitten to the quick.

'Hush up, honey,' said Mrs Booth, but her tone was gentle. Mrs Booth didn't wear any makeup, but her hair had been cut recently, the ends fresh. Still, she had her flowered blouse buttoned to the top. Merritt guessed that the kids had adjusted to life outside of New Hope faster than the mother. And the father?

'One practice don't matter,' said Mrs Booth to her daughter.

Amy June balanced on one leg like a flamingo. 'It could have—'

'Sssshhh. Enough. I don't want to hear anything more about it.'

Mrs Booth gave Merritt an apologetic look, and Merritt held her tongue. She wanted to know about that missed practice. Instead, she asked about Sara Beth's volunteer work, watching the sister in her periphery. She'd been crying – that was easy to see. So had the mother. Their grief was genuine. Not that Merritt had expected anything different, but it was Journalism 101 to keep an open mind. The police had decided on a suspect, but you never knew when something else might be uncovered, might get the story back in the news cycle. If nobody else planned to investigate, she would gladly step into that gap. For now, Merritt would be satisfied with some human-interest footage. Her producer would run the interview even if he hadn't approved it. Merritt didn't plan on going anywhere for a few days, her dislike of Vintera a footnote at this point. The other reporters could give up, if they wanted to be quitters.

The one question she kept posing to herself was why this teenager – a girl who'd embraced life outside the church with relish – was at the church at all. If she'd wanted a place to hook up with her boyfriend, there were plenty of secluded parking places. A small rural town like this? Kids knew the spots for booze and sex. Merritt had, that's for sure.

She wanted to shudder at the thought of her own Virginia home-town, determined to never go back there. It served as a reminder of why she was in the Booths' living room. To 'let America know about a bright light gone to a better place' – she was mentally writing her lede – but also for the story. Merritt was opportunistic, sure, but she also wanted to know how every story ended. There was nothing more frustrating to her than a loose end. The fact that 40 percent of murders in the US went unsolved? Well, that stuck in her craw.

Pepsi. That's what Merritt noticed when Amy June opened the refrigerator. There were a few pans of leftovers, a gallon of milk and at least two dozen cans of Pepsi.

Amy June took one out and opened it, the sound making her mother jump. The house felt on edge, as if waiting to wake up from a bad dream. Merritt's house growing up had kept sodas in stock too, but Merritt never touched them now.

That was it. What had been bothering her. She'd thought that the Booths would seem strange, belonging to something like a cult for so long. But they reminded her of hometown neighbors. 'The girl next door has gone to the Pearly Gates—' No. That was reaching, but Merritt did have an unorthodox question, one that might be construed as insensitive. She asked anyway.

'What church do you attend now, Mrs Booth?'

The woman shook her head back and forth as if trying to shake free of her answer. 'No, none around here seem like a good fit, you know? Rock 'n' roll music, Christmas pageants and who knows what else. I don't know what I'm saying. I'm sure they're nice enough.'

'I'm sure they are.' Merritt clicked off her small camera and leaned closer to Mrs Booth, going so far as to squeeze the woman's hand. 'I was only asking about support. If you have anybody.'

Mrs Booth's eyes filled with tears. 'You can't throw a rock without hitting a Booth around here. And my family's over a ways in Rosetta.'

'Good, good. I'm glad to hear that.' Merritt rose to her feet, slipping her small, portable camera into her shoulder bag. 'Any reason Sara Beth would have been at New Hope so early in the morning?'

Merritt tried to make the question sound natural, but Mrs Booth was too lost in her own thoughts to think about appropriate and inappropriate topics.

'That new preacher's been checking on her. He visits the high school sometimes, talks about the dangers of drugs. Started a little club of some sort. He says the doors are always open.' Mrs Booth paused and looked at Merritt, perhaps finally weighing if she should have agreed to this conversation. It was too late now though. 'He's a good man,' she added.

'I'm sure he is,' said Merritt, not so sure at all.

EIGHT

Juliet looked like she could give birth any day. She padded around her kitchen in bare feet, incapable of sitting still while Essa perched on the edge of a chair. The place smelled like her brother. She hadn't been expecting that. And she hadn't known until that moment that he even had a particular scent beyond his shampoo and deodorant. But there it was. Earthy and sharp.

She sat in his new home feeling homesick. Would he even want her there? Was she invading his privacy? In the first few months after Clyde left, he'd stopped by from time to time but eventually got tired of her reluctance to change. He resented her maybe, a living reminder of his painful past. Couldn't she have cut her hair at least? Or bought a pair of jeans? The thought of either made her stomach churn as if those simple acts would mean she'd abandoned her mother. Wearing her braid long, slipping into her mother's things were Essa's way of grieving. Nobody had taught her any other way.

Essa thought it must mean something that Clyde hadn't told her about the pregnancy. A text message would have been easy enough. He could have told her at the police station even, though she could understand not wanting to share that detail with the detectives. They were bound to find out though. Already knew, most likely.

'Have you picked out a name yet?'

Juliet wiped the kitchen counter without turning around. Essa couldn't see anything that needed cleaning, but Juliet continued to scrub. She didn't have her wig on, and her short brown hair stuck flat to her head. Essa could make out the words 'Some by virtue fall' in pretty cursive amidst the markings on her arms. When Juliet noticed Essa staring, she took her sweater from a kitchen chair and pulled it on; started cleaning again.

'We were waitin' to find out if it's a girl or boy until the big day. The big day. Huh. Thought it would be fun. Now I don't know. You project different futures. Don't mean to, but you do.'

'You'll be good parents either way.'

Juliet laughed, but the sound was hollow. Essa knew immediately that she'd said the wrong thing. How would she know what kind of parents they would make? But her brother had done the best he could with a teenage little sister, and he could have left her to fend for herself. She knew that much at least.

'Arson can be fifteen years. I searched it. And involuntary manslaughter?' Juliet sprayed more bleach on to the stove. Her lips looked anemic, pale and chapped. Her eyebrows were dark for her complexion, as if they'd been swiped on with a marker. 'A whole lifetime. More. He'll die in there.'

'They don't know it was him. They don't know it was anybody.'

'Don't have to. That preacher says it's him; they say it's him.'

Essa started to respond, but Juliet cut her off. 'The two of them got into it a few months back.'

'Got into what?'

'Oh, it was stupid. We'd had a couple of drinks up at Charlene's, and that asshole was in the parking lot when we was trying to leave. Had the nerve to invite Clyde to Sunday services. You can imagine how that went over.'

Juliet stopped moving for a second without turning around, then pulled out a rag from under the sink and started attacking the faucet. Essa stood and took the cloth from her. An electric shock passed between them. There was something about the property that felt different. Energized maybe. Essa didn't like it.

'Let me do that. Least I can do,' she said.

Juliet narrowed her eyes at Essa then sat at the kitchen table, almost collapsing into the chair. She glanced at the unopened mail, going so far as to pick up a few envelopes before putting them back. She rubbed her belly at the top of her ribcage, wincing a little.

'They think he's God's gift.'

It was true that the local police department treated Pastor Micah like a hero. A few months before he arrived from who knows where, they'd had a shortage of naloxone, the antidote for an opioid over-dose. Too many needed in too short a time. Cops and EMTs alike were overworked and underpaid. No amount of complaining to the state would magically make extra resources appear. A fair number of responders quit. The governor suggested more thoughts and prayers. Pastor Micah arrived, as if he'd heard them, and addicts started to call themselves 'saved'. Never 'cured' but 'saved'.

Essa remembered when he'd rolled into town, or at least when he'd first come to the church. One night, as Essa and her brother tried to stay interested in something on television, a light from the church had caught her eye. It had been dark at night for months. Then someone had pulled the thin cord to the bare bulb in the foyer. Let there be light. Pastor Micah's slick new electric car never left the parking lot until morning. It wouldn't be the last time, and Essa wondered what he did there in the darkest hours of the night. But it had never been any of her business. Was it her business now? Maybe if she'd gotten to know Pastor Micah, at least a little, he'd have been slower to point his finger at her family. What had Clyde said to him?

'You know anyone else might have wanted the place gone?' Essa asked.

'You mean besides you?' Juliet asked, making Essa stop, rag hovering over the microwave.

As she struggled to respond, Juliet kept talking. 'We ain't had anything to do with that place. Clyde don't even like to drive past it, no offense. We were building a new life together until all this shit. I don't know what I'm gonna do.'

Essa was supposed to say that she'd help out, that whenever Juliet needed her, she'd be there. But she couldn't force the words out of her mouth. She didn't know if that offer would be welcome. Not to mention that Essa didn't want to stay in Vintera. It wasn't as if she'd woken up one morning and announced to her empty house that she intended to leave. All the same, she'd been looking for an exit. When she started saving money, when she started taking classes, when she looked at sample résumés online, putting her name in bold font at the top of her own: Essa Montgomery. Even when she nursed unrequited crushes, she never let herself daydream about a life in Vintera. No, she'd seen her gentle mother give her very life for love. She wanted none of that, and she wasn't about to give up on her plan because her brother had knocked somebody up.

Essa flushed, ashamed by such an ugly thought, and opened the microwave to clean inside. When she closed it, a flash outside the window drew her attention.

She could have sworn she saw a familiar woman in hot-pink pants walking toward the trees, but Essa shook herself. Juliet's pregnancy had thrown her. She kept thinking about family, including her favorite relative, Great Aunt Cecelia. CeeCee made her living as a backup singer for some of the biggest acts of the seventies and eighties. Fleetwood Mac, Styx, The Byrds. Van Morrison on a few of his American tours. She was a tiny woman, not quite five feet, and wore platform heels to make up for what she called her 'doll-like frame'. Confident and brassy. Everything that Essa would never imagine for herself, but maybe her great-great-niece or nephew would have some of that spunk.

'You got any family nearby?' Essa asked.

'My mom's around. Not that wild about me shacking up. But she bought me a crib. Can help on her days off some. She works two jobs though. You know how it goes.'

Essa finished polishing the sink then searched for anything else that might need attention to avoid having to sit with Juliet. But the whole place was cleaner than her own home had been in years.

She opened the refrigerator then worried it would seem like she was snooping. The sight of packaged sausage made her heart clench. She remembered when Clyde learned to grill, cooking dinner for the two of them on a secondhand Weber most afternoons, even if it was cold or rainy. They'd split the other household duties, but Clyde always put food on the table. Cereal and canned soup at first, but later meals were more substantial. He'd never complained either, though all that responsibility couldn't have been easy for him. Essa thought again that he'd be a good parent and believed it more this time. They'd grown distant, but that didn't change the three years he'd taken care of her.

'You gonna take any time off?' she asked, and Juliet made a frustrated noise. 'I could make you a sandwich.' Essa felt as awkward as she'd ever felt in her life, a kid again. This place didn't feel right to her, though she couldn't have explained the sensation. Like a deer might know a mountain lion from the wind.

'A week or two,' Juliet said before she started crying.

Essa didn't notice right away because the woman was silent, letting the tears run down her face. When Essa did notice, she flapped her hands in the air then sat at the kitchen table and reached out. Juliet ignored the gesture, tucking her sweater more tightly around herself.

'I don't need food. No offense, but I don't need you neither. I need your brother.'

Essa watched as the woman cried. She'd known that kind of grief, the kind that feels as if your lungs are being pulled out through your chest. As if there's so much sadness inside you that there's no room for your organs. But Clyde wasn't dead, and maybe Essa could help.

'Clyde wants me to go see the preacher. Talk some sense into him or something.'

'Would you lie? Say you saw somebody else sniffing around?'

Essa's ears started to ring, and she knew that was a bridge too far for her.

'Thought not.'

Essa hated to admit that was true. But she hated to admit that she wouldn't try either.

'He might help anyway. His word would go a long way. He doesn't have any proof that it was Clyde besides some argument,' Essa said.

Juliet wiped her face, her skin pink and swollen. Any bluster she'd had when Essa walked through the door had evaporated.

'I mean, I'm not promising anything, but he's a man of God. He'll hear me out at least.'

The hope in Juliet's face blinked off.

Essa didn't understand the warning, but she felt uneasy all the same. People had a way of letting her down, but Clyde had been there when she needed him. She'd try not to let him down now he needed her.

NINE

Yellow police tape surrounded the perimeter, and a forensics team walked the property, their standard-issue jackets making them look like an army of scientists. Essa watched them from inside her car for a while. She'd been on-site with Dr Kester occasionally when an endangered species had been found killed or an illegal trading outfit had been raided, taking notes and sometimes photographs, but those days had looked nothing like this. A man with slate-gray hair seemed to be in charge, directing his soldiers as they put stakes in the ground and filled evidence bag after evidence bag.

As if the property needed more commotion, a group of New Hope volunteers congregated in the field beside Tyson's Creek. What would become a large, white plastic tent flattened the grass. A few men worked on nailing poles into the ground, and a metallic ringing echoed into the afternoon. Their wives and daughters circled nearby with thermoses.

Despite all the hubbub, there was only one patrol car in sight, and it was pulled up to her house, lights on but no sirens. Essa turned off her ignition and took a few deep inhales and exhales. They didn't help, but she couldn't stay in her car forever. She shut the door behind her but, in her nervousness, caught her skirt. When she tried to tug it loose, the fabric ripped, and she stumbled a few feet before regaining her balance.

'Happens to me all the time,' said Lieutenant Barnes as he climbed out of his own car. Essa couldn't see his eyes because of the mirrored sunglasses. 'You remember Sergeant Sallis. We hope to steal another moment of your time.'

They'd taken more than a moment of her time. They'd taken hours. Essa could see her own breath as she smoothed her skirt, wondering if she should invite them inside. Smoke lingered in the air, pulling the oxygen out. It made Essa uncomfortable, but no visitors had set foot in her place since the day Clyde had left.

When she didn't respond, the detective stepped closer to her, holding out his hand. 'You're in a unique position over here, so close to the church.'

Essa didn't like the way he said 'close to the church'. She looked at his hand, outstretched as if approaching a wild animal, letting her sniff before deciding what to do. She knew 'unique' was another word for 'odd'. If the detective had been hoping for a fresh start, this wasn't the way to proceed. She didn't much care for Lieutenant Barnes. She didn't like his unfamiliar accent or his casual tone. Essa didn't want to cause any more trouble for Clyde though, so she shook his hand briefly, managing not to wipe her palm after, then gestured for them to follow her.

'Best get on out of the cold then.' How long had they been waiting for her? She'd stayed with Juliet for a while, sometimes talking but more often sitting in silence. Juliet seemed to think that Clyde being charged was a foregone conclusion, and that Essa was naive to hope for anything else. Essa felt for her brother's fiancée; she really did. And she was surprised by how much she wanted to meet her niece or nephew. She'd never thought much about children before, one way or the other. 'Mind your step there.'

Essa's front porch had collected ash and debris during the night, and she'd have to clean that up. It was empty besides the swing, but a few boards needed attention. She cringed at the possibility of the lieutenant or sergeant crashing through. She didn't pay for home insurance, much less a liability policy. She glanced back at the pair of officers. Lieutenant Barnes smiled at her, but Sergeant Sallis remained stone-faced. At least she wasn't wearing sunglasses. It must be hard being a woman cop, especially around here where every boy got a shotgun on his thirteenth birthday and thought he was tough shit. Girls got makeup and lectures about wearing tank tops that made the boys think about sex. Well, not Essa. Essa got a *Precious Moments Bible* with her name engraved on the cover.

'We appreciate your time, Miss Montgomery,' Lieutenant Barnes said.

Essa wasn't great at reading tones. It seemed like he was courting her favor today, and she couldn't think of a single reason why.

She unlocked her front door and flipped on the lights, picking up the reporter's business card and throwing it into her purse along with her keys. She saw how the place must look to the visitors. She'd never given the living room much thought besides keeping it tidy. But she'd left it as her parents had left it. Faded paisley couch with her mother's quilt slung over one arm. Padding showed through the worn carpet. The small coffee table had teeth marks where she'd gnawed on it as a toddler from some sort of vitamin deficiency. The decor consisted of pieces her mother had picked out or inherited. Pink lampshades and porcelain figurines. She liked the dolphins best because she'd never seen one in person. The only possessions she'd bought herself were the books she kept along the baseboards. A bookcase had never occurred to her until that moment.

'Something to drink?' Essa asked to cover her embarrassment. 'Water? Or I could make some coffee or something.'

'Water sounds great.'

Lieutenant Barnes picked up a family photo, and Essa watched him, possessive. It had been a long day – a long couple of days – and she was exhausted. When she turned on the tap in the kitchen, her hands shook. Outside her window, she could see the competing agendas, one group crawling over the rubble, the other making a tent appear in the sky corner by corner. It would take weeks to clean the fire damage. Months maybe. And longer to rebuild no matter how much money was raised. Hopefully she would be gone by then, wouldn't have to hear the hammers and saws every morning. She'd saved enough to rent a place in Roanoke, to start over. But she needed a job too, and thus far nobody wanted her.

Essa filled two glasses and brought them back into the living room, slipping coasters underneath even though the table already had rings on the surface. More habit than anything else. She sat on the only chair and let her guests perch on the couch. She was aware that nobody could see them inside, and it made her nervous. They wouldn't hurt her, would they? She examined the sergeant, noting that she'd pulled her hair back in a tight bun and wore foundation that had sunk into her wrinkles. The lipstick had bled outside her mouth, making her look like she'd eaten a plate of spaghetti. She kept her hands near her hips, drawing attention to the holstered Glock. Sergeant Sallis seemed tense, ready for any little sign of trouble, and made Essa even more anxious. Essa didn't think much about guns, but she didn't like them either.

'We know this has been a trying time for you, but we need to ask you a few more questions about what you saw the morning of the fire,' said Lieutenant Barnes.

It wasn't the opening she'd expected. Before, they hadn't asked her any questions about the morning of the fire. They'd told her Clyde had set the church on fire, case closed except for the bow.

Were they really investigating now? Essa faced Lieutenant Barnes, a sliver of hope straightening her spine.

The detective leaned forward, arms resting on his knees and hands clasped, head tilted slightly to the side. His red hair was cut short, but a few curls stuck up a little. He'd taken off the sunglasses, and he had big expressive brown eyes. A little like a fawn, she thought, noticing he was young to have the lieutenant rank. Thirty tops. Then again, the local force had a high turnover, troopers getting tired of the same overdoses and heroin busts.

Barnes's posture looked posed, as if the position had been suggested in a handbook on questioning witnesses. Interested but casual. His sports jacket fit close to his chest, and his pants were ironed, the pleat sharp as a knife. The lieutenant didn't move as Essa looked him over, and again she got the feeling he was treating her like a stray, letting her decide to trust him.

'I'm not feral,' she said, which made his partner chuckle.

'Told you.' Sergeant Sallis relaxed a little then looked directly at Essa. 'I told him we just act different around here.'

Lieutenant Barnes laughed, too, but wasn't chagrined. If anything, he seemed pleased with himself. He tugged once at his jacket sleeves, making sure they covered the cuffs of his shirt.

'She likes to torment me. I'm from Pennsylvania, not another planet.'

'Might as well be some days,' Sergeant Sallis said.

Essa couldn't tell if they liked each other. The sergeant must have been about fifty and could have resented the younger man outranking her. Essa let them have their little joke, though, and didn't say anything. What had she seen the morning of the fire? Truthfully, nothing she could remember.

'You belonged to New Hope?' Lieutenant Barnes said, making it a question.

'Not for a few years now.'

'But you grew up in that environment?'

Essa felt piqued again by the way the detective said 'environment', like he'd snapped a rubber band against her wrist. When she was little, she hadn't realized there was anything strange about passing around cottonmouths or drinking watered-down strychnine. Heck, she didn't even know what strychnine was, only that the blue bottles were pretty and that her father kept them behind a trick back in their end table and then – after she discovered the hiding spot

– above the kitchen counters, out of reach for her even with a chair. She'd thrown away all the bottles, but she kept her Bible and emergency cash in the end table. The snakes had never been kept inside. New Hope had a designated shed that her father secured with a heavy deadbolt. Not that she or Clyde – or any nosy neighbors – had ever been tempted to break into the place. A rattler is better than a guard dog.

'I know you know about my momma and daddy. Everybody knows. That's the way it is.'

'You were too young to lose your parents.'

Essa nodded but didn't respond. It was Sergeant Sallis's turn to squirm. She was probably accustomed to telling people their relatives had died of overdoses, but snakebites were a different can of worms. Especially with Pastor Micah's growing popularity. He made the practice seem hip, an answer to the town's prayers. Maybe even the whole state. And nobody had been so much as nipped since he'd taken over. His congregation thought he must be divine. Essa thought he must be starving the snakes, making them lethargic. On the brink of death, they wouldn't hurt a soul. Her father, for all his flaws, would never have treated an animal like that. He kept a careful feeding schedule taped to the refrigerator, had a rewards card for the pet store over in river-side. The frozen mice in the freezer were part of the deal. No matter the species, animals seemed drawn to her father's gentle nature. Other signs-following preachers weren't true believers, and the snakes suffered all manner of abuse. Having their fangs yanked out or their mouths sewn shut. You'd think parishioners would notice, but they hardly looked at the deadly beasts they held aloft, fueled by faith or fear. And from a distance, the mutilation didn't show. But Pastor Montgomery? Daddy Montgomery? There walked a true believer.

'Sure enough, but I survived all the same.' Essa didn't like thinking about her father, especially not the good parts. She blamed him for making her an orphan. He *had* made her an orphan.

'Survived. You see, Sallis. It's like I told you. They're basically children.'

The insult hit home. Essa noticed the lieutenant and sergeant didn't touch their water glasses. She wasn't sure if that meant anything though. Maybe they thought she might poison them. Maybe they thought the glasses were dirty. Maybe they weren't thirsty.

'Not feral and not a child,' said Essa, but it came out petulant. Like a child.

'Of course not, but we wouldn't blame you, you know. If you're protecting your brother, that's all we mean. Why wouldn't you? I've got family too.'

No, Essa wasn't great at reading people, but she knew when she was being manipulated. The officers wanted her to believe they were on her side, but they weren't. She trod as carefully as she knew how to tread.

'He's not a violent man.' Essa made herself meet the detectives' gaze.

'I know this is difficult, but we need you to be straight with us. Did you see your brother the morning of the fire?' Sergeant Sallis asked.

Essa didn't like the implication that she would lie. The morning after her father's funeral, Essa had gone to the New Hope shed. The last thing she'd wanted to do was venture inside, but the snakes hadn't done anything wrong. It had been at least a week since they'd been fed. She'd shaken with the lock in her left hand, willing herself to do the right thing. More than willing, praying. Telling God she didn't have as much faith as Job, but she had a little left, and couldn't he sprinkle her with some courage? Maybe she'd wanted to be bitten, to be done with the world. When her brother had taken the key from her, she hadn't been surprised. He'd turned her back toward their house, and she'd let him and Wash and Harry deal with the animals. She'd never asked if they'd let them go or killed them. She didn't want to know.

'I haven't seen him in a few months,' she said. 'We filled up at the Gas 'n' Stop at the same time a while back. September maybe? He bought me a Coke.'

Sergeant Sallis looked skeptical, but Lieutenant Barnes only nodded.

'I see. Did he ever talk about New Hope?'

Essa knew what they wanted her to say. That her brother hated the place, that he blamed the church for their parents' deaths. But if Clyde was angry, he was angry at their dad, same as she was. And there wasn't much that could be done about that rage. Some people might say Clyde had abandoned her, but she disagreed. He'd been a kid himself when granted informal custody, though legally an adult. And he hadn't let her starve or go to school without washing her hair or brushing her teeth.

When she'd graduated high school with a decent GPA, Clyde had encouraged her to get her associate's degree, even tried to help her with the loan paperwork, though eventually she'd asked Dr Kester when they'd both failed to make sense of all the questions. Dr Kester had filled everything out for her, and now she got a bill in the mail every month for her student loan. They'd grown up somehow or another. Tumbled into it, you might say. Essa hadn't thought about leaving until Clyde moved in with Juliet. Now, she dreamed about it, even if those dreams were muted. She could hardly picture what life would be like outside of Vintera.

'He never talked about the church or our folks around me. For a while there, we pretended like they never existed. Easier that way, I reckon.'

Without meaning to, Essa glanced at the framed family photo Barnes had picked up. Essa must have been four or five at the time and half-hid her face in her mother's skirt. She flushed when she realized it was the same skirt she was wearing now, the one she'd ripped in her car door. It was at least fifteen years old, probably older. Practically an antique.

'That must have been hard to do, living here with all the reminders.'

Essa couldn't tell if the detective believed her, but it was too hard to explain to outsiders. When her mom had died, she'd tried her best to absorb what everyone had told her, that she'd gone straight to paradise, that they'd all meet again. There would be joyous celebrations. But then her dad had been killed soon after, and she'd slept with her Bible, reading and rereading Mark 16:18 and finally deciding humans were a whole lot of stupid to put so much weight on a single word: 'shall'. They *shall* take up serpents.

Her faith in people had cracked, turned into a canyon, and there was no way to repair that kind of rift. It was elemental, something inside her that couldn't be found on an anatomy chart. She looked for her mother in every storm and in every shadow caught in her periphery. She craved ghosts, even spoke to them some nights after she'd shut off the television and closed her eyes. Essa could pretend she was surrounded, that she could talk directly to her loved ones or at least send them messages. Once, she'd left a candle burning in the window, hoping to tempt them back.

'Gettin' up in the morning was hard. Everything else? We managed,' she said before she let herself get lost.

'Have you noticed anything happening at the church? Anybody lurking around?'

It would have been useful to have another suspect to offer, but Essa answered truthfully. There'd been a crowd the previous Friday night, as always, when the support group met and played music until late. And Sunday morning for the regular service. She may have seen the preacher a few other times, but she couldn't say for sure which days. A cleaning lady came on Mondays, sometimes with a helper. Locals, not an official company of any sort. She didn't know their names.

'So you haven't noticed anything unusual?' Barnes glanced at his notes and frowned. 'I mean, out of the ordinary?'

'I don't keep tabs on the place, but it's hard to miss right outside the door. It was an old building. Who knows when the electrical was updated. Maybe never.'

It was as close as Essa was willing to get to a fib. The fire could have been an accident.

The detective closed his notebook, shaking his head. He exchanged a glance with Sallis, and Essa shivered. They were keeping something from her again. The pair stood, and Barnes held out his card. Essa had never received a business card before today, and now she had two.

'If you think of anything later, give me a call. No detail too small.' He smiled, and it looked so genuine that Essa smiled back. 'We'd hate to charge you as an accessory.'

It felt as if she'd been sucker-punched. They left without saying anything else, and Essa watched them drive away, mad at herself for trusting them, even for a second.

She went to her kitchen sink to splash water on her face then peered out, hoping for inspiration. Without the church, she could better see the trees that lined the little creek at the edge of her property. Their branches swayed in the wind, like tired sentinels. Snow would be a relief, she thought. Something to show for all the cold. But it wouldn't snow. It would only grow colder and colder until something broke.

TEN

P astor Micah watched the girl sweep her front porch and held up each vice as if it were a pane of stained glass, trying to see which one fit her aura. Not vanity, to be sure. Essa kept herself clean, but if she'd ever so much as curled her hair, the preacher would be surprised. Not gluttony either with her small, birdlike frame. It bothered him that Essa Montgomery refused to sort herself. He'd watched her since she was a teenager, at first with her brother then by herself. Puttering out in that old car of hers. Hauling in groceries after working all day. The little light in her kitchen window made his heart clench in a way he hardly recognized, switching on and reaching toward his church like a beacon. She was alone and determined. Not sloth. He'd understand if it were envy or wrath, but he'd never seen signs of them. Yes, he'd watched her for years, dreamed about her even as if she were some sort of divine creature come to warn or comfort him. He held something like affection for this girl he'd never met.

Pastor Micah glanced around to make sure he hadn't lost his touch. He saw Mrs Campbell with her manicured hands and bleached-blonde hair. Vanity. *Too easy,* he thought. You didn't need a special gift to see that one.

Her husband offered more of a challenge. The man set out folding chairs, making sure they lined up evenly. But it was wrath. Bottled up and rarely released, but there all the same.

Pastor Micah paused to thank the Lord for his blessings. Outdoor services would draw even bigger crowds than usual on Fridays and Sundays until he could rebuild. And what couldn't he do with pity? A humble service out of the ashes of a hate crime. The donation baskets would overflow, even in January, always a difficult month financially for the congregation. His own failing was pride, he knew, but couldn't a man be proud of good work? God more than forgave him. God understood him.

The morning brought dueling chaos disguised as efficiency. In his white tent, Pastor Micah reigned, commanding his followers to set up audio equipment, including speakers. He'd need to reach the ones who crept into the back, pulled by desperation or curiosity. He could use either motivation. You worked with what the Lord provided. Snakes. He'd never seen them coming. They got the job done though – no sense denying their power. There was something about fear that made folks stronger. A test of mettle. Or maybe adrenaline flushed the drugs right out of their systems.

The other scene unfolded to his left. Forensic specialists combed through the remains of New Hope. A church fire got extra attention. A church fire got the governor's attention; made for a compelling news conference. He got to seem like a leader in touch with the people and their needs. Greed of course. The reporter had returned, her pride too great to resist, though she'd been scared of him. More than scared. Still, she'd spin the story in his favor. There was no other choice now lest she be seen as attacking a survivor, a holy one at that. He played the stoic victim – blessed, so blessed – with precision.

'You want we turn the heaters on?'

Pastor Micah turned toward the teenager in front of him then clapped him on his shoulder. 'A good thought, Bobby. For the volunteers.'

The youth ambled off, pleased with himself. Pastor Micah didn't feel the cold, only the rush of anticipation, all those eyes on him, trusting him not to lead them astray. And he never would, so God help him. He'd been given great responsibility, and he knew you didn't have to strike the rod against the stone. A touch was all you needed. A caress. Miracles without force.

A movement at the rectory caught his attention, and he watched the girl go back inside. A few moments later he could sense her peering out, at his tent or the crime scene. He couldn't be certain which one. They were both spectacles for Vintera. He would understand if retirees parked their cars to watch.

He considered the girl again. Lust was the only choice left. She never had callers that he'd noticed. No midnight visitors. Not even a pimply date holding out weeds he'd plucked from his front yard. Pastor Micah squinted in her direction as if he could see her fresh from a shower, skin warm and soft. Untouched before. An imaginary hand as erotic as any real one. A little push in the right direction. Could it be that simple? She was the right age for it. And had to be lonely. Lust, yes. He could work with lust.

ELEVEN

'The spirit of New Hope cannot be extinguished by fire alone. This evening, members and volunteers from the community have come together to set up a place for tomorrow's worship service. We spoke earlier with Pastor Micah Granieri about his experience,' Merritt said, staring into the camera light without blinking. When she'd learned that women blink almost twice as often as men, Merritt had trained herself to keep her own lids open longer.

Her cameraman gave a thumbs up to indicate they'd cut to pre-recorded footage, and Merritt jumped up and down to keep herself warm. The studio wouldn't object if she wore a coat, but she knew viewers didn't like it. They let her know in message-board comments that ranged from mildly sexist to downright threatening. She'd grown used to people feeling like they were entitled to her appearance though. Even in elementary school, adults would tease her about being 'a flirt' and ruffle her blonde curls. In high school, there was basketball and homecoming. It took her a while to even notice she was smart too. Nobody ever bothered to compliment her on grades. But in college, she'd taken an English Lit course because her boyfriend was enrolled, and her TA had scrawled at the top of an essay 'Come see me during office hours'. She'd expected a lecture about her non-participation, but instead, the young grad student had peered out from unflattering glasses and said, 'Merritt, this is an exceptionally smart analysis, especially for a freshman. Have you thought about your major yet?' She'd liked the way the woman had said 'exceptionally'. She'd liked that a lot.

'Ten seconds,' P.J. said, and Merritt ran her tongue over her teeth to make sure they stayed lipstick free. She stretched her mouth as wide as it would go before snapping a close-lipped smile into place.

'Inspiring,' she said when the recording light blinked on. 'Services begin tomorrow at 10 a.m., and a large crowd is expected. This is Merritt Callahan, reporting live from Vintera, West Virginia in Thorngold County.'

She stared into the camera until P.J. gave another thumbs up. She knew better than to relax too soon. You never knew when there would be a problem with the feed, or the anchor might ask her a follow-up question if he needed to fill time.

'And we're clear,' P.J. said.

Merritt still wasn't his biggest fan, but his Vintera footage had been decent so far. She wouldn't say *exceptional,* but decent. And he worked for college credits from Washington & Lee, which was all WTGX cared about. Their budget shrank a little each quarter as their steadfast viewers died off. The younger generations got their news from social media or watched YouTube clips the next day. That's what she needed. Something to go viral or at least get picked up nationally. Cable news had more stability at least.

'Let's get a few more shots of the forensics team then call it a day.'

When Merritt had arrived at the scene, several news vans had been in place for their morning broadcasts. She was the only one who'd stuck around for the six o'clock news though, getting another interview with the preacher because of her previous interest in his work. That interest had been tainted with dread, but she'd take the breaks she got.

When they moved too close to the police tape, an officer asked them to keep their distance, and P.J. shot back like he'd been stung.

'It's all right, P.J. Film from there. See if you can zoom in though.'

She thanked the officer for letting them know the boundary, smiling as sweetly as she could. Maybe somebody from the assembled crew would talk to her, at least off the record. After interviewing Mrs Booth, she'd gathered some good quotes during lunch at a fast-food place not too far away. A few people were spooked by what they called town 'witchcraft'. The local bat population seeming to swell. Unsightly symbols spray-painted on to bridges. It sounded like graffiti to Merritt, but she listened to anybody who wanted to talk, tell her their theories. A few interviewees used the term 'domestic terrorism', and she felt vindicated by her influence. On the other hand, the police officers had been tight-lipped. She still needed an in with the department. Could she bake cookies? That might be outside her skillset.

P.J. fiddled with switches, turned the bright light toward the crime scene, which was already illuminated by two large cranes. A church fire was a big-enough story, but with a double homicide – Merritt shivered from anticipation. What if she could find some crucial piece of evidence, something the local yahoos had missed? Podcasters did it all the time. Why couldn't she?

Merritt didn't sense the preacher coming up behind her, but she didn't scream either when he grabbed her arm. Not painfully but with enough force to show he could cause pain if given half a chance.

'Still on the clock?' he asked.

'The news never sleeps.'

Pastor Micah looked over the rumble of New Hope, waving at a few of the investigators there who nodded or waved back, familiar with him.

'Do you know the story of Jericho?' Pastor Micah asked, his voice loud enough to make P.J. turn and gape.

'That's the one with the seven loops around the city then poof – everything destroyed,' Merritt said. She didn't remember much from Sunday School, but the trumpets were hard to forget.

'Yes, that's the one. "Joshua said to the two men who had spied out the land, 'Go into the prostitute's house and bring her out and all who belong to her, in accordance with your oath to her.'" You remember that part?'

Merritt bristled at the word 'prostitute'.

'Listen, Granieri, I don't give a rat's ass about your little Podunk operation here. You think you're powerful because what? A few congressmen owe you favors? A few dozen drunks think you're a sign from God? I deal with bigger dickheads than you every day.'

P.J. slid the camera from his shoulder, forgetting to turn off the camera in his shock. His mouth opened like a fish, and Merritt turned to him briefly. 'Don't repeat that.'

P.J. shook his head, and she knew she'd have to give him a lecture on the way back about professionalism versus the real world. She'd have to make sure he erased the footage too. That's not the kind of viral she wanted to be.

Pastor Micah laughed, which made Merritt angrier.

'You misunderstand, my child.' There was a pause between 'misunderstand' and 'my child' too big to miss. 'Rahab was the heroine of that story. She and her brethren were spared for their good work. I wish you all the best.'

She saw what he was doing too late, that her little speech had attracted more than P.J.'s attention. The cops on-site had all turned to stare at her, disgusted by her language, by how she'd talked to a man of God. They'd never cooperate with her now.

'Peace be with you,' Pastor Micah said, calling louder to his audience. 'And all of you. May God bless and keep you safe.'

Son of a bitch.

TWELVE

K udzu claimed the house's exterior, growing up the left side then across until it devoured even the windows. In summer, the place might come across as magical, a home that seemed to leap from the earth itself. In January, the place looked dead, eaten by the tangled, leafless vines. An abandoned home or a witch's lair. *Appropriate*, thought Juliet, though her stomach dropped at the sight all the same. She doubted whether Madame Clarita even lived there anymore, but there were a few letters in the mailbox, and she'd come a long way to turn back. Juliet took a step toward the front stoop, her legs heavy. She pulled her coat as far as it would go around her belly and trudged on, her hand hovering over the knocker when the door creaked open.

'I'd all but given up on you.'

Juliet cringed away from the smell, sour and strong, like takeout left too long on the counter. She could barely see Madame Clarita's face, but her substantial body swayed as she took a few steps back into the darkness, beckoning Juliet inside. While not one to hesitate, Juliet glanced around. How long would it take to notice she was gone if something happened to her? Clyde was still in custody, and her mother was working double shifts for the week, unlikely to check on her. But Madame Clarita was eccentric not dangerous, she told herself, holding out the candy bars she'd bought from the gas station and hurrying out of the cold.

'My favorite,' Madame Clarita said. 'You remembered.'

'Couldn't rightly forget, could I? You had me fetching them every afternoon for months.'

The chuckle turned into a cough, and Juliet peered closer at her old mentor, surprised to see her face hadn't changed, the same pale and watery expanse. She'd always seemed weak to teenage Juliet, but everybody had seemed weak to willful, sullen teenage Juliet. Now she felt weak herself, her body bruised from her failed ritual the night before and now her heart nearly broken at the thought of losing Clyde to a prison sentence. Embarrassed by her frailty in front of Essa, she'd come here instead of staying at home and cleaning something else.

Madame Clarita's books remained scattered about the floor, although she had space for them on her shelves. Sometimes Juliet had tried to organize everything only to find her efforts thwarted by the time she arrived again the next afternoon. At first, Juliet had looked forward to the lessons, Madame Clarita monologuing about her time with a traveling carnival, how she'd found a lover in every city, how her train car never emptied of bouquets. But after a while, Juliet had grown weary of the repetition, how the woman never paused to ask if she'd heard this one before, and Juliet had always heard this one before.

'You've been expecting me?'

'You could say so. Sit.'

Juliet cleared off a chair at the kitchen table, putting the magazines and socks on the floor. The place was warm, she would give it that, as if the vines tucked them in. For one panicked moment, Juliet felt the branches wrapping tightly around and blocking the entrance, trapping them inside until they both starved to death. But she shook her head to clear the image.

'You always were more talented than me.'

Madame Clarita waved off the compliment, which Juliet hadn't meant anyway, and the woman knew. Even though she never left the house, Madame Clarita was dressed in a loose black dress covered with an old but beautiful velvet shawl. Perhaps she still had a few clients, though Juliet doubted very much even the most desperately lost souls were pounding down her door.

'I get the local gossip. I was sorry to hear about your boy. Truly.'

The 'truly' made something catch in Juliet's throat. It was a loaded word, covering all the ways Juliet had mistreated Madame Clarita, taking advantage of her books and advice then abandoning her. For a while, all of her clients had been former Madame Clarita clients, though Juliet was proud of her current, robust business. Hers alone.

'Still,' Juliet said, not sure what she meant.

'Let's have at it then.'

Juliet watched Madame Clarita put the kettle on, hoping the cup would be clean at least. The woman sprinkled leaves in a porcelain mug, humming to herself all the while. Juliet remembered the song,

a Brahms sonata. The medium had played piano in her youth,
abandoning the instrument when she realized she had her grandmother's second sight. It was hazy, to be sure, and sometimes wrong,
but Juliet was jealous all the same. On a whim, she reached out to
Madame Clarita, trying to read her emotions, but as always, something blocked her. Madame Clarita herself, Juliet suspected. The
woman knew how to throw up a wall between them.

'Here now.' Madame Clarita turned away from the stove to put
the lukewarm cup in front of her guest. Tasseography had never
been Juliet's favorite avenue of fortune telling, mostly because she
didn't care for tea. Tea was for river-side folks, she figured. Creek-
side, they drank Cokes and beer. And yet she gulped the liquid,
eager for what might be revealed. She'd come for answers. 'What
do you see?'

'Don't got much talent for this, you may remember,' Juliet said.
She swirled the remaining liquid three times then turned the cup
over on a saucer. When she righted it, a few leaves stuck around
the sides and bottom.

'Meditate on your question then.'

Juliet did have questions, and she summoned them to her mind.
Why had the ritual failed? Why couldn't she see what was coming?
Madame Clarita clucked as if she could read Juliet's thoughts but
said nothing. Juliet tried to remember the basics as she hunted for
a pattern in the dregs. She focused on a thick line close to the
handle.

'Outside forces more than inside ones. This cup's saying it's my
fault, huh?'

'You know I was fond of you. And I don't blame you none for
not coming to see me before. It's a dark, depressing bugaboo in
here. I know. But safer than what's out there, and I don't have the
energy for what's out there no more.'

'You could try.'

'Pft. It's too late for me. You don't want to see what's coming,
not really, and that's the problem right there. You know what can
happen if you're given too much of the future. No good can come
from that.'

Was Madame Clarita right? No, that couldn't be. Juliet had done
the rituals, hadn't she? One every January for years now. A wave
of regret washed over her so powerful, she almost vomited. Her

eyes began to water, and she pushed back from the table, clutching her stomach.

'Stop, please,' she said to Madame Clarita.

But Madame Clarita let the full force of her emotions take hold of Juliet. Regret and anger – a lifetime's worth.

'Don't go looking for what you can't handle, child. You've got burdens enough.'

Wave after crashing wave of emotion pushed Juliet to her feet, stumbling out of the kitchen. As quickly as the pain came, it subsided.

'You can't see the future, Juliet Usher. But you've got sense enough to shape it. Now—'

Juliet took a deep breath, steadying herself and trying to respond.

Madame Clarita straightened her shawl, picked up the teacup and dropped it into the sink as if nothing had happened. 'Now,' she said again. 'Get out of my house.'

THIRTEEN

As soon as Essa parked outside the preacher's house, she doubted her plans and her intentions. She'd changed into a dress her mother saved for funerals, the nicest one in her closet, but the dark color did little to disguise the cheap fabric. It had long sleeves and fell to Essa's ankles. She'd looped a belt around the middle, so it didn't sag, but she could have been a nun all the same.

Staring at the brick colonial home in front of her, she left the car engine running. How could she possibly knock on the door? Go inside a place like that? It looked like a president's home, something that might go with an estate. She should have waited for him after his meeting at the makeshift New Hope, but she worried someone might see her. That alone should have been a warning. If she wasn't doing anything wrong, why did she worry about getting caught? The hour was late too, nearly eleven.

Essa switched off her headlights, so they wouldn't shine into his windows. She put her hand on the gearshift to put it in reverse but hesitated. She'd promised Juliet she'd do something to help her brother. And Essa tried to keep her promises.

She shut off her car and stepped on to the newly paved driveway. Before she lost her nerve, she hurried to the front door and rang the doorbell. She could hear the chimes inside, followed by footsteps.

When Pastor Micah opened the door, Essa's unease increased. They'd never exchanged so much as a 'Hello' despite having seen each other at least once a week for years. Up close, Pastor Micah was even more attractive. His black curls were wet, as if he'd not long come out of the shower, and he smelled like mint. Her stomach flipped, and her cheeks flushed. The preacher must have been used to that reaction – people feeling a jolt of electricity at the sight of him – but Essa didn't recognize herself. Despite the hour, he wore a pair of slacks and an untucked, buttoned shirt. Essa let him pull her parka off, his hand accidentally touching her neck, and she shivered. If Pastor Micah noticed, he didn't react.

'I'd say I'm surprised to see you, but that would be a lie.' Pastor

Micah gestured toward an ornate sitting room with a blaze in the fireplace. The warm space had dark wooden floors partially covered by a crimson rug, and when Essa sat on one of the couches, she noticed the row of buck heads staring at her. She should have been used to that sort of thing considering her job, but they felt forlorn up there, had no purpose other than bragging rights.

Essa started fidgeting when the preacher didn't say anything to her, only stared. He took his time settling into an armchair, picking up his glass. Essa had never so much as touched a drop of alcohol and didn't know anything about liquors, but it was chestnut-colored, a bit like maple syrup. She watched the liquid rather than meet the preacher's eyes, but she could feel him assessing her. When he lifted the glass to his lips, she couldn't help but watch those too, feel something stir inside. After a while, the silence got to her, and she thanked him for letting her come inside, apologized about the time.

'You know better than anyone I don't sleep much. You must see the lights on at New Hope late into the night.'

Essa had always assumed the new preacher hailed from West Virginia, but she couldn't place his accent. His voice was deep and almost gentle, as if it could lull someone to sleep. She wondered about his sermons, how he held an audience's attention for hours. He probably put on an act. Her father had developed a sort of act as well, though it was more an exaggeration of his everyday personality. Earnest. A true believer. Did Pastor Micah fit that description?

'I mind my own business, best I can,' Essa said.

'And I admire that. And yet here you are, to plead for your brother.'

Essa swallowed the panic that rose into her throat and nodded, trying to think what she should say. She kicked herself for not preparing something, a little speech maybe about false witness or mercy. She'd hoped for inspiration, thought God might help her even. Her heart was in the right place at least, wasn't it?

'My brother's not like that. He wouldn't burn down a church.'

'I wish that were true. For your sake, Essa.'

Her name came out like a caress in his mouth, drawn out.

'I know that building better than anybody, and it's old as Methuselah.'

Pastor Micah let out one bark of laughter. His expression softened, then he rose and went to a sideboard. It seemed like an heirloom with brass handles and ornate carvings. Essa thought it belonged in a movie. The feeling of unreality increased when Pastor Micah pulled two crystal wine glasses down and filled them from an already opened bottle.

'I'm not old enough,' Essa said, her face burning again.

'You don't have to finish it,' he said, handing her the glass.

She didn't like the smell, like one of the fluids at the lab. He inhaled deeply though, pausing before letting out his breath again. He watched her, so she took a small sip. It didn't burn as much as she'd expected, but she wished she could put the glass down somewhere. Instead, she placed it awkwardly on her lap, struggling to turn the conversation back to her brother.

'I only mean, the wiring's old. The wood's old. A cold night like last night? Somebody could have left a space heater on is all I'm saying.'

Had the fire only happened yesterday? Essa felt bone tired. She felt spent and a little resentful, to tell the truth, that her Saturday routine had been disturbed. It seemed like she was taking three steps backward, getting pulled down by her family again. That wasn't fair though. Her brother wasn't to blame for her father's bad choices. She took another drink of wine, and it didn't burn at all this time.

'I've been wanting to meet you for a long time,' Pastor Micah said. 'I hate it's under these circumstances.'

'Nothing much works out like you think it will.'

'Truer words. You're not what I expected.'

Essa knew she was supposed to ask 'How so?' or something like that, but she didn't want to hear what the preacher thought about her.

'It gets lonely in this town, wouldn't you agree?'

Essa didn't like self-pity, and she wasn't about to feel sorry for this man with his fancy house and newfound fame. He could talk to her about loneliness when he went days without speaking to anyone. When your co-workers didn't notice you'd walked into a room and all that remained of your family was in jail. She took another drink of wine, feeling her cheeks flush with something besides embarrassment.

'You've got all those worshippers. You've got a whole town on your side. What do I have? I'll tell you. I've got a brother, and he's a good man. He did right by me.'

'He abandoned you.'

'He raised me.'

Pastor Micah sat down his wine glass and kneeled beside Essa on the rug, humbling himself at her side. Whatever temper she'd been nursing slipped out of her body, replaced by surprise. He took her glass and sat it on the floor beside his own; clasped both her hands.

'I don't want to anger you. Like I said, I've been wanting to meet you, to try to make things right. New Hope isn't the same place as when your father led things. I won't speak ill of the dead. I don't want— I don't want to hurt you. I'll only say this. I know your mother asked for a doctor, and I know one wasn't called for her.'

Essa's eyes tightened, tears threatening to spill over. She hadn't cried about that in years, and one touch from the preacher threatened to release something in her. She tried to pull away, didn't like the intimacy, but he held on tighter.

'I would have called an ambulance. She didn't have to die.'

Essa stood, ripping her hands from Pastor Micah and retreating across the room. She'd waited to hear those words, that help should have been called. That God worked through humans sometimes too. It felt like a blister bursting, a painful sort of relief. But she didn't like that Pastor Micah had known what was in her heart. It struck her as uncanny. She walked into the hallway to get her coat, wiping at her cheeks.

'I didn't mean to upset you,' Pastor Micah called, standing. She peered back at him, tall in front of the fireplace, imposing.

'My brother didn't burn down New Hope, and you can tell the police that. He didn't kill those people, on purpose or by accident.'

Pastor Micah stared at her, on the verge of speaking, then turned away. He rubbed his face with his hands before turning back.

'I saw Clyde, you know, a few months back.' The preacher's voice dropped. 'He was wild, Essa. Unhinged. Ranting about how what I was doing was wrong, that if I didn't shut down the church . . . that it broke families. I tried to explain, but he wouldn't listen.'

Essa knew she was only hearing one side of the story and wasn't impressed. 'Go on then.'

'Ask him yourself. He threatened me, Essa.'

Essa wanted to tell him to stop saying her name, that every time he said it, claws dug into her back. But she stopped when the preacher began unbuttoning his shirt. She tried to turn away but felt stuck. After the third button, he pulled back the fabric, revealing a tan chest and a red, three-inch scar.

'He had a knife,' Pastor Micah said. 'I think he wanted to kill me, and that's what I told the police. That's all I told them. The truth. That Clyde Montgomery wanted me dead.'

Essa shook her head. Juliet had said they 'got into it'. That meant an argument, right? Not this. Essa needed the preacher's words to be lies, needed the whole story to be some kind of sick fabrication. But how well did she know her brother these days? And she had rage inside her too. Oh, she hid it all right, but it was there, waiting to be stirred up.

'He's all I have left.' Essa's voice broke.

As Pastor Micah buttoned his shirt, he lowered his gaze to the floor. 'It's late. Maybe it's not appropriate you're here.'

Essa took a step toward him, but Pastor Micah held up a hand. 'Let me pray on this. Come to the service tomorrow, and we can speak after.'

Her body turned cold at the thought of entering New Hope again. But New Hope was gone, and a pile of rubble couldn't hurt her.

'I'll try.'

The preacher helped her into her coat. He didn't touch her exposed skin this time.

Essa walked back into the night, looking around. Pastor Micah's house was tucked into a neat subdivision with new but historic-looking lampposts and sidewalks for all the families. There was nobody out at that hour though, and the effect was eerie, as if reminding her bad things happened to girls who broke their curfews. She glanced around, making sure nobody was around, and her eye caught a car parked across the street, the only vehicle besides hers not tucked safely into a garage. Had it been there when she arrived?

When someone moved inside it, she stifled a gasp and thought about running back to Pastor Micah, but what would he think of her? Would he think she'd made it up? An excuse to stay with him? Instead, she got her keys and jumped into her own car, locking the doors behind her.

'Come on,' she said to nobody, relieved when the car started. Her hands shook as she buckled her seatbelt and reversed down the driveway. When her headlights illuminated the other car, she could see the silhouette of a driver. She turned on to the main road and drove with extra care, making sure to follow the speed limit and not cross any lines. She didn't feel drunk, but what if she got pulled over and was beyond the legal limit? The whole day had been too much, and her head started to pound.

When she finally pulled up to her house, her knuckles were white from gripping the steering wheel. She released them, and the blood returned, prick by painful prick.

FOURTEEN

H is house felt emptier without her, that's what the preacher noticed first. It was as if somebody had removed the furniture, and he could hear his voice – his thoughts – echo in the newly cavernous space. What had gone wrong? The opportunity had presented itself, this girl showing up on his doorstep like a stray. Her wide, scared eyes. Hair tangled from such a long day. Had she even looked at herself in a mirror before marching into her foolhardy mission? His heart clenched at the sight of her, and when he called the emotion pity, Lucifer laughed at him. He could hear the mean caw in his skull.

Oh, Pastor Micah went through the motions of his plan to target her. For years, he'd wanted to bring her back into the church's fold. He wanted her brother to return as well. It was an idle wish though, a sort of feather in his cap.

New Hope had called to him. He'd heard about the Montgomery family on the news, how the mother had been killed by a snakebite then the father. At the time, he'd grown bored with his manicured congregation in Charlotte, their perfumes and shiny shoes. They might as well have worn signs around their necks, bragging about their failings: greed, wrath, lust, envy, pride, sloth and gluttony in equal measure. His followers presented no challenge, and he wanted a challenge. He'd called the Pentecostal headquarters and asked to be relocated. They'd objected at first, scoffing at the New Hope traditions they didn't endorse but more worried their coffers would suffer from the move. Pastor Micah assured them that his old church would flourish without him, and he could make the new one profitable as well. He'd delivered on that promise – more than delivered – and still something was missing.

Now he understood. Essa was missing.

Was he the first to notice how lovely she might be outside of those old-fashioned ensembles? She felt like a secret. She felt like his secret. He thought perhaps after she'd left, he'd see sense again, but no, her scent lingered.

He crossed to where she'd been sitting and thrust his face into the upholstery, inhaling dirt and sweat and maybe cedar. There was a hint of something chemical, seeped into her skin from work at the lab. Oh God. But no, this was anything but divine. He'd tested her, he told himself, rocking back to sit on the rug like a schoolboy asking for a story. Nothing more or less. He was disoriented because she'd passed, and the sheep so rarely passed. He'd shown her riches. He'd shown her his body, and she'd not been swayed. They were always swayed by something, but not this one. That was it, he told himself. He couldn't remember a time when anybody had surprised him. But he could break her. She'd come back to him after all, wouldn't she?

The doubt made his pulse wild, and he stood, reaching for his glass of wine. Another man would have poured the liquid down his throat, but Micah – Pastor Micah, he reminded himself – needed something stronger than drink. He rinsed the wine down his kitchen sink – such a nice kitchen, such a nice sink – and paused, looking out over his deck. The never-used patio furniture and state-of-the-art grill, frost on the cover. He couldn't descend like this. The girl had infected him, but he ruled himself.

Outside, the trees swept their branches in a conjuring spell. They jerked rather than danced, and Micah didn't flinch when one snapped in two and crashed to the ground. He'd been warned.

When his heart stilled, he unlocked the small door beside his stove and walked into the darkness. The rattles started immediately. They could sense him – knew on nights like tonight, he demanded sacrifice. Obedience. And they would give him venom or blood. They would give him whatever he asked.

FIFTEEN

Merritt didn't like to think of her cameraman as protection. She didn't like to think of him at all, the scrawny kid with aspirations of being the next Quentin Tarantino. His student films were violent and nonsensical, with dialogue that sounded like it was written by some sort of computer algorithm. He called her 'ma'am' and stared at her breasts when he thought she wouldn't notice. She always noticed. Men liked to look at her, and she knew that was at least partly why she'd got the job at WTGX. Merritt also knew her looks wouldn't last forever, and if she wanted to move out of the local demographic, she had to strike fast and be bold. The thought of a major network job in DC or New York had brought her back to New Hope, even though her stomach churned uneasily. She hadn't forgotten the preacher's little tricks.

She'd done some research on the species he'd held when they'd first met. Coral snakes weren't native to West Virginia. More worrisome, there was a coral snake antivenin shortage in the US. She doubted the local hospital near Vintera kept the precious liquid in stock. But maybe with a church famous for serpent handling, they stayed prepared. And Merritt had to admit the church was famous in its own way. She wasn't the only reporter to have come sniffing around for a story before the fire, drawn by the strange practices and track record for success in curbing addiction. It was a feel-good story. If you didn't mind the occasional pit viper. Merritt wouldn't hold her breath for West Virginia changing its laws anytime soon. The powers that be seemed serious about not interfering with religious practice, however dangerous.

'Do they really drink poison?' P.J. asked, and Merritt turned to watch the kid clean the camera lens with a microfiber cloth. He was starting to gain some muscle in his shoulders from carting around equipment all day but still resembled a coat rack.

'I guess we'll see. Can you get some footage of people coming in?'

The tent began to fill even though the service wouldn't start for another half hour. A few volunteers set out extra rows of folding chairs. The audience would come from all over the county and beyond. She glanced at the assembled faces to see who might make a good interview subject. She considered who might be a little cynical, a little skeptical of the proceedings. She no longer had any desire to make Granieri into the hero of her story. If she could expose him, that would be a get too. Hell, maybe he destroyed his own church. He'd sure made a lot of money from the tragedy. That story had national coverage potential. People liked a victim, but a fraud? Blood in the water.

'Credentials please.'

A man in pressed khaki pants and a fitted wool coat stood next to her, showing his badge. The man resembled a sitcom version of a small-town cop. Clean shaven, freckled nose, bright red hair cut short but growing out.

'Of course,' she replied, pulling the plastic case from the pocket in her blazer.

'You're required to wear that somewhere visible.'

Merritt saw P.J. shift and decided the kid had definitely never talked to a police officer before. He liked violent movies he could watch from the safety of his dorm room. She nearly rolled her eyes. Nobody was putting them in handcuffs for not bringing their lanyards.

'Not while filming surely. It would mess with the lines of my dress.'

Merritt put a hand on her hip as if to illustrate the point. She was well aware that it was the most expensive item of clothing in the tent, but tailoring made the real difference. The officer didn't take the bait but handed back her ID with a nod.

'You'd get a better view from the third row.' He gestured toward a small empty space that could accommodate Merritt and P.J. without blocking many views.

'I'd like to get some crowd reactions too.'

'You know best.'

Merritt had noticed the empty spot but she didn't want to get too close after her run-ins with Granieri. She stared at the third row while the officer stared at her. He seemed to be analyzing her, not checking her out.

'I'd love to get a sit-down with you, as well, Officer . . .?'

'Otis Barnes. B-A-R-N-E-S. I'm not allowed to discuss an ongoing case, but I can refer you to our PR liaison.'

'Of course – I understand. But an exchange of information never hurt anyone.'

'If you know anything that could help, you're required by law to share that information.'

Merritt stopped herself from grinning at the officious cop. She liked a challenge, especially a cute one.

'Oh, nothing definite. A few whispers here and there. Gossip, most likely, not the sort of thing you'd concern yourself with.'

'Lieutenant,' someone called from a few yards away, and Otis turned toward the man, holding up a finger to tell him that he needed a minute.

'Oh, *Lieutenant* Barnes, is it? Well, that changes things.'

The tips of the lieutenant's ears turned red, but otherwise, he didn't react.

'Gossip can be useful.'

Merritt paused to consider whether she should share her findings. The Thorngold County PD had someone in custody. She doubted they were even investigating at this point. What she knew wasn't enough to break a case wide open anyway. Not to mention that she could use an ally. She hadn't exactly made a lot of friends in the area.

'Well, let me tell you then. Rumor has it Granieri was married, left his wife and kid somewhere.' Otis absorbed the information, his brow furrowing. 'Might not mean anything, but the word "hero" gets thrown around so casually these days, don't you think?'

Merritt could see that comment hit a nerve, but she kept her expression concerned rather than triumphant. Oh, she did like a challenge. She excused herself and beckoned P.J. to follow. In his excitement, the kid almost dropped the camera, ruining the effect of their retreat. But the lieutenant was right. She'd get a better shot from the third row.

SIXTEEN

E ssa dreamed about them again. Her neighbors might have told her the old wives' tale, that dreaming about snakes means you're coming into money. But she never dreamed about snakes – she dreamed about serpents, and there was a difference. A snake hid in brush piles and ate rodents. It lived in the wild and rarely bothered humans. A danger to cattle sometimes, depending on the species or the time of year. Depending on if there'd been enough rain or if hay bales had arrived from other states. A serpent spoke in honeyed words and led you straight to hell. He was exquisite, with scales that shimmered in the sun, hypnotizing. And wily. Boy was he wily. Smarter than you could ever hope to be. And only God could keep him from striking, caressing your skin with his slender tongue then sinking his fangs into the most vulnerable parts of your soul.

Essa dreaded the service, but she thought Pastor Micah might help her after all. He hadn't refused at least.

She ate a piece of toast over the kitchen sink, watching men put out additional folding chairs. Rows and rows of them as if they expected a crowd. And then the crowd started to show. She recognized a few faces from when they'd belonged to her father's church. The Culvers arrived and also the Garrells and the Danes. Mrs Dane was a widow now, but her two sons flanked her, accompanied by their families, including a boy who couldn't be more than five. Her people – what used to be her people – were outnumbered by a different sort. Scraggly beards and visible tattoos on their hands or necks. They could have been a traveling circus crew, not the newly converted. A few didn't even have coats, but they joked around with each other all the same. They didn't seem bothered that their church had burned to the ground. They seemed happy to be alive, and Essa tried to be pleased for them.

Before she could lose her nerve, she grabbed her own parka and headed outside.

As soon as she stepped off the porch, a cold wind blew against her face and skirt, almost pushing her back, but she zipped her coat all the way up and kept moving, weaving through the charred wood that had landed in her yard.

'Oh, Essa! If you aren't a sight for sore eyes. You come over here, little one.'

Essa turned toward the voice and saw Mrs Laurie moving toward her and leaning heavily on a walker. It had been three years since she'd seen her mother's friend. Mrs Laurie had dropped off casseroles a few times during the first year, but after a while, when Essa and Clyde seemed to be all right, she'd stopped coming by. Essa didn't blame her. Everyone had their own burdens to carry. Parkinson's had aged Mrs Laurie. Her voice was strong though, and Essa squeezed her shoulder when she got close enough.

'Well, isn't this a fine mess,' Essa said.

'Isn't it though? I heard about your brother, but don't concern yourself about that. Nobody blames you, and that's the truth.'

Blame her? Essa hadn't even considered the congregation might not want her. She'd been so wrapped up in her own fear that she'd never considered she might be a snake in the grass herself. That people would stare. She stopped moving, and Mrs Laurie clucked her tongue.

'No time for cowardice now. Trust in the Lord, etcetera.'

She pinched Essa's cheek hard, and Essa cringed a little before following behind her. A couple of children handed out programs by the tent entrance, and Essa took one for something to look at while everyone looked at her. She tried to mitigate the situation by sitting in the back, but she could hear the whispers when people spotted her. Some shot scowls in her direction, and a few who'd joined the church under Pastor Micah seemed confused. They turned to stare too though. Maybe the whole crowd wanted her gone, and she was about to make their wishes come true when Pastor Micah arrived and walked straight to her, holding out his hand. Essa felt awash in gratitude, and it must have shown in her face. He pulled her hand toward him and kissed her knuckles as if daring anyone to say she was unwelcome. She flushed, ready to believe she'd misjudged him. Ready to believe he would help her, be her savior even.

Then he was gone, shaking someone else's hand and walking toward the front of the audience. She watched to see if he greeted anyone else the way he'd greeted her, but nobody got so much as a hug. The handshakes were enthusiastic though, often double-handed. After he passed, the congregants closed their eyes and held their arms to the sky, swaying slightly. A few 'hallelujahs' could be heard above the shuffling. She saw a mother push her daughter in front of him as if offering her up on a plate. The preacher was an eligible bachelor, and the mothers of Vintera weren't above a setup.

The makeshift room electrified, ready to be comforted and reborn. Ready to rejoice beside the ashes. Essa read the program again, the words swimming before her. She told herself to take deep breaths and tried to do so without calling attention to herself. Nearly everybody else was standing, but she didn't trust her legs. She calmed a little when somebody started to strum a guitar, and she could concentrate on singing along. It was the same hymn they'd sung the night of the fire, and Essa knew the words without having to check.

When Pastor Micah stood to read from Isaiah, Essa better understood the spell he'd cast over Vintera. His voice – with a slight twang Essa still couldn't place – caressed the crowd. When he whispered, everyone else leaned forward, and when he boomed, it felt like being baptized in warm lake water. She listened to his sermon on making peace with our circumstances, surprised to find herself nodding along, forgetting to be anxious.

'Those who walk uprightly enter into peace,' Pastor Micah concluded. 'They find rest as they lie in death.'

Amens cascaded through the rows, and Essa gripped the sides of her plastic chair. It was the Isaiah verse that had been read at her mother's funeral then at her father's. She'd been so worried about her brother that she'd hardly sympathized with the grieving families, the pain they must be feeling. She knew that blinding pain. Were they there? She looked around but couldn't spot the Booths. She didn't know what the Hoystons looked like.

When Essa brought her attention back to the service, she thought Pastor Micah might be staring at her, but she couldn't be sure. And when he pulled out a familiar velvet bag, she stopped caring, her focus shifting to what might be inside.

Soon the mottled triangle of a cottonmouth emerged, peering out at his captive audience. He had a couple of companions, but Essa kept her eyes trained on him. The first. The leader. She tried to calculate the distance between herself and the animal. A hundred feet perhaps. *A safe distance,* she told herself. *And you don't have to go any closer. You don't have to do anything you don't want to do.*

Pastor Micah picked up the serpent and let it curl around his arm, slither right to the worn old Bible in his hand. It seemed to rest its head on the leather, defiant or perhaps chilled. It was too cold for snakes to be out in the wild. She wanted to cover her eyes but couldn't seem to move at all.

"'In my name shall they cast out devils,'" Pastor Micah began to another chorus of amens. "'They shall speak with new tongues. They shall take up serpents; and if they drink any deadly thing, it shall not hurt them; they shall lay hands on the sick, and they shall recover. Mark 16:18.'" The two other snakes lay at his feet, awake but lethargic. They didn't hiss and draw attention to themselves but were there all the same. The cottonmouth settled, moving its tail from time to time but otherwise motionless. 'You know these verses, but have you thought on what it means to cast out devils?'

Pastor Micah's drawl became a little more pronounced. Essa had only been fourteen when her mother had been bitten during a service. Her mom had held two snakes at the time, dancing with her eyes raised to the ceiling and calling out to God. It had been a brutal August morning, already sweltering at 10 a.m., and New Hope's window units could hardly compete. She remembered sweat dripping down her mother's face and soaking her yellow dress. Essa had thrown that garment away. It was too painful to see in her closet, and the small bloodstains would never come out anyway.

Experts would be quick to tell you cottonmouths are venomous not poisonous, and Essa supposed there was a difference. But it didn't much matter when the face of someone you loved turned purple and began to swell. When she foamed at the mouth and fell to the floor. When the adults in the room prayed and placed their hands on her, but not one of them reached for their phone. An ambulance could have arrived in twenty minutes. Such a small number to make the difference between life and death. *I would have called an ambulance. She didn't have to die.* Pastor Micah's words from the night before echoed in her head as loud as the ones he spoke in front of her.

'If anyone feels so called, I hope you'll join me.' Pastor Micah stepped over the snakes at his feet and spread his arms wide. The cottonmouth raised its head and seemed to peer out as well, daring anyone to come for him.

The whole audience stood as if on cue, and a man began to play the guitar again. Someone from the middle of the room jangled a tambourine. A song of praise replaced the mournful music from before.

A young man with jaundiced skin jumped forward, practically running to the front. He jerked one of the floor snakes into the air and began to gyrate, his face full of joy. He was soon joined by a few other members of the congregation, though none from her father's New Hope, Essa noticed. Mrs Laurie leaned on her walker with one hand and held the other up.

When the strangers started shouting 'hallelujah', Essa's unease turned to terror. Her skin grew hot, and she could hear her heartbeat as if blood pulsed out of her ears. She felt feverish despite the weather and tried to peel off her parka. It got stuck on her wrists though, and she yanked at it blindly.

She collapsed back into her chair, putting her head between her knees. Her vision swam red then black as she tried to remember how to breathe. A woman nearby asked if she was all right, but she could hardly hear her, the words like a ripple in a pond. She knew she had to get outside and forced herself up, stumbling toward the tent opening. Essa clawed at the plastic, trying to find the Velcro before somebody stepped forward and opened it for her. Then she tumbled into the arctic air, her knees slamming into the ground. She let the rest of her body follow, unresisting.

SEVENTEEN

Merritt decided she had enough footage, thank you very much, and headed for a slit in the tent's side. The audience was too consumed by the onstage spectacle to notice her, but she could sense the preacher's eyes on her back. When sleet whipped across her face, she welcomed the chill, not even worrying about her mascara. She didn't plan to be on camera again for the rest of the day. The church fire and deaths had consumed the media cycle, but now there was a celebrity divorce and a politician using the F-word at a charity event. The next forty-eight hours would be taken up by handwringing over lost American values. But Merritt wasn't done with Vintera. She'd hardly slept the night before, Granieri getting under her skin like venom spreading at an injection site.

'You want me to splice the service with your interviews?'

P.J. looked a lot less pleased than her about the weather. He'd tied his coat around his face again, leaving a little circle in the middle for his nose. His edit made sense though.

'Good idea,' she said, and P.J. beamed. What did it feel like to need so much approval? *Good boy,* she almost said, but she wanted the kid on her side. She might need him. 'Can you do it from your laptop?'

'I'll send you the file after I drop the van off at the station.'

P.J. marched off, not bothering to ask about her plans. It probably never occurred to him she might do anything besides report the news. But Merritt tried not to miss an opportunity.

The tent had been erected only a foot from the creek's edge, and she maneuvered over the frozen ground like a tightrope walker, one heeled foot in front of the other, not willing to touch the fabric for balance. Somebody could see her hands from inside. Instead, she concentrated, not exactly an athlete anymore, but she hit the gym twice a week. It was a long stretch, and a cheer from the service made her tense, almost lose her balance. She chided herself for being afraid. The creek was only a few inches deep. But it looked cold. Dangerously cold.

She pushed forward, refusing to rush. When the shed came into view, she checked to make sure nobody could see her from the parking lot then sprinted to the locked door. When her fingers touched the wood, she let out the breath she'd been holding.

Merritt dropped to the ground, peering into the gap underneath the structure. She hoped to spot her screwdriver, but it was too dark.

After a moment's hesitation, she swept her hand into the black, almost shrieking when something crawled across her wrist. She slammed her hand into the floor planks then pulled her hand out, shaking off the bug and the pain. She flexed her fingers, worried she might get a bruise then tried again. This time, her fingers touched something hard that rolled away from her. *There,* she thought, getting on to her belly for a better reach. Her fingers closed around the screwdriver, and she felt a jolt of pleasure.

'Ms Callahan, I'm going to have to ask you to stand up.'

Merritt scrambled backward, flipping around to confront Granieri. But it wasn't Granieri. It was the red-headed lieutenant trying to look stern but only managing petulant. When she smiled, it was genuine. She could handle Lieutenant Otis Barnes.

'I dropped my screwdriver.' She held out the offending tool. 'Now all I need is a screw.'

The lieutenant blushed and forgot to look important. Instead, he focused on his shoes for a second then looked around as if checking the perimeter. Merritt could have given him a few seconds to get himself together, but she didn't.

'You know a good place for breakfast around here? I'm famished.' Merritt dusted off her dress and wiped under her eyes. She'd retouch her makeup in the car.

When Otis didn't respond right away, Merritt thought she'd misjudged him. Maybe she was losing her touch. Then she watched him shrug off his coat, flashing his Glock unintentionally. He held the coat out to her, and she paused long enough for Otis to pull it back toward him. Then she reached out, unsurprised by the look of gratitude that passed over his face. She wasn't refusing his help after all.

'Finally, a knight in shining wool.'

Merritt slipped her arms into the sleeves, knowing the size would make her look smaller, more vulnerable. A wolf in a sheep's peacoat. The shed could wait.

EIGHTEEN

When Essa experienced her first panic attack, she'd felt swallowed whole, death coming for her. Later, she'd understood that if she waited long enough – if she pried open the jaws of the beast – she could climb out. This time, she made it home, collapsing in a tired heap on her couch. She couldn't say for sure how long she stayed there, but the knock on her door came from above her, and she swam to the surface, gasping but alive. When she pushed to her feet, she was light-headed, and the sight of Pastor Micah didn't help.

'I wanted to make sure you were all right,' he said when she opened the door. He looked stricken, and Essa softened toward him a little. 'I didn't think through my invitation to the service. Of course you're not ready yet.'

Essa caught the 'yet', and the panic rose again. He wanted her to rejoin the congregation, and she'd never be ready for that. When she glanced down, she realized that she'd pulled off her sweater at some point and stood in her muddy skirt and a thin camisole, not what she'd call decent for company. She rubbed her hands along her bare arms, and Pastor Micah's eyes followed.

'Give me a second please.' Essa tried to close the door to gather her thoughts, but Pastor Micah stuck his hand in the way.

'Of course. Take your time.' He stepped into her home, looking around as if the place were a kitschy roadside attraction. The Museum of Bad Luck Artifacts or some such.

Essa didn't want to turn her back on him. She couldn't very well have a serious conversation dressed like that though, so she scurried to her bedroom, shutting the door and – after a second's hesitation – turning the lock. She tried to collect her thoughts while she pulled on a different floor-length skirt and sweater. She quickly braided her hair where it had come undone and wrapped it around her head, pinning the weight into place. Her scalp would hurt if she left it that way for long, but she thought the occasion called for a more formal appearance. If she were being honest with herself, she also thought it looked nice. She took a few more deep breaths and headed back into the living room, apologizing for keeping the preacher waiting so long.

'You never have to apologize to me,' Pastor Micah said, patting the couch beside him. He was more casually dressed than he had been at home, in faded jeans and a waffle shirt. A sort of costume, chosen to make him look humbler than he was. He was playing at being a man of the people, and Essa didn't want to fall for it. Yet there was something appealing about his interest in her. That he would single her out. Never mind that he held her happiness in his hands, could crush her in a second.

'Can I get you something? I could put on coffee.'

'Don't trouble yourself. I can only stay for a moment.'

Essa sat across from the preacher, tucking her hands underneath her skirt. It was cold in her house, but not as bad as it had been inside the tent.

'I've been thinking over what you said about Clyde. About the knife, I mean. And I've never seen him like that,' Essa said.

'And yet, he cut me pretty good.'

Pastor Micah smiled, but it didn't reach his eyes. They remained hard and fixed on Essa's face. A curl came loose from the coil she'd made, and she tried to stab it back into place with a bobby pin, only for it to fall forward again. Pastor Micah reached out as if he might touch her then pulled back. Essa pretended not to notice.

'The thing is, he must be worried sick about Juliet and the baby. For him to act that way, I mean,' she said.

Pastor Micah sank into the worn fabric, crossing one leg over the other and draping his arm across the back of the couch. He seemed comfortable there, Essa would give him that. He hadn't recoiled at the stuffing coming loose from the fabric.

'Essa, you know I want to help you. Before Clyde attacked me, I wanted to help him too. It wasn't right what happened to your parents.'

Essa nodded, her spirits buoyed until he continued. 'But two people were trapped inside. I can't very well let that go.'

Essa felt sick again. She understood. She did. She couldn't imagine much worse than being burned alive. But had it really been Clyde? Why weren't the police looking at anyone else?

'You don't know for sure it was my brother. It could have been anyone. It could have been an accident.'

Essa clung to that explanation because she liked it the best.

'Essa, Essa, Essa.'

'Stop it. Please. I'm not some sort of starving dog,' she said, her anger returning too late to warn her.

'But you're a little wild, aren't you? Out here all by yourself. Nobody to look after you.'

Essa pulled the sleeves of the sweater over her hands and tried to keep her thoughts straight when he ordered her: 'Come here.'

Essa couldn't say why she obeyed, but she got up and sat next to the preacher, keeping space between them. He closed it, pressing his muscled thigh against hers. Then he grabbed one of her hands and kissed it again, looking stricken.

'I've never acted this way before. What have you done to me?'

'I haven't done anything.' Essa cringed when her voice shook, overwhelmed by his flattery.

'Oh, but you have. After all this time, looking at me but never seeing me. Do you know what that does to a man? To be ignored?'

'I don't know what you're talking about.'

Essa jerked her hand out of his, and the preacher covered his face.

'You're not a wild animal. You're a witch.'

She stood, but Pastor Micah grabbed her arm and yanked her back down – hard. The room shrank. She glanced toward her high windows, but nobody could see her from outside. If she screamed, would anybody hear her?

'Essa, look at me. I would never hurt you. Don't be scared.'

'I don't know what you want from me.'

'Don't you though?'

Pastor Micah let go of her arm and leaned back on the couch again. Essa stood, stumbling toward her front door and opening it.

'You best be getting on home. Maybe I shouldn't be talking to you anyway.'

'Says who?'

Essa didn't like the dark expression that passed over his face, and she didn't respond.

'Are you protecting someone? Well, let me be clear. I can protect you, if you let me.'

For a moment, hope flickered again in Essa's too trusting heart. 'Tell them you don't think it was my brother. Tell them that you were confused is all.'

A gust of wind whipped into the room from outside, and Essa

shivered. Pastor Micah untangled his legs and crossed toward her, rubbing his hands along her sweater. Then he stooped to kiss her. Essa jerked her face away, and his lips connected with her cheek. He turned her head back to him and kissed her anyway, his tongue forcing itself past her teeth. When he released her, she stumbled outside, wiping her mouth. Her first kiss, stolen.

'I can tell them whatever you want, Essa. I can tell them Clyde Montgomery's an upstanding member of society who made a mistake, but I don't think he burned down my church. That I won't testify against him. I can tell them . . . what's that you want me to say? That I think it was an *accident*. Somebody left a cigarette burning maybe. God rest the souls who perished.'

Essa didn't like the name of God in his mouth, and she stepped away from him, feeling forced from her own home. How had she let him kiss her? She'd rather spit at him. She'd rather claw his eyes out. Except, hadn't she wanted it somehow? Her cheeks burned. She'd asked for this. The attention of such a handsome man was its own kind of drug.

He moved past her and down the steps, whistling as if he hadn't upended her life.

'Do that then. Tell them all that.'

Pastor Micah swirled back toward her, tucking his hands in his pockets and seeming to glide, graceful as a dancer, graceful as a serpent. 'Oh, I will. I can. I only need one favor in return. Do you know what that is?'

Essa shook her head and looked away. Because she was young but not that young. She knew what he was talking about, and it made her sick to her stomach.

'Don't take too long to decide. See you soon, Essa.'

NINETEEN

Juliet stared at the dregs of her tea then stared at her copy of *Reading Tea Leaves*. Was that a frog or a harp? Perhaps a boat? In a better mood, Juliet would have chuckled at herself, so ill-equipped for this type of divination. To be perfectly frank, when she looked at the tea leaves, she saw tea leaves. Bland, caffeine-free tea leaves that would clog her kitchen drain if she didn't get enough of them into the trash. It felt funny anyway, hoping to see the future from a book more than a hundred years old. Not Juliet's edition of course, a library copy she'd never returned.

Definitely a duck. She referenced the book, liking the interpretation – 'an influx of wealth by trade'. It was all she'd wanted before the starfish came along. Now she wanted everything for her child, including a father at home.

Juliet pushed the cup away and shook out her favorite tarot deck instead. The cards acted like a balm in their familiarity. She ran a finger along the gold-leaf edge of the Four of Wands.

Wind chimes broke her concentration, and Juliet looked to see a well-heeled woman stride into her reading room. Her customers rarely strode. They stumbled and creeped, tiptoed and occasionally charged. But never strode confidently through the door. This one examined her surroundings as if the place were a new exhibition at the Huntington Museum. Juliet didn't greet the woman, whose emotions were a neutral orange, like an underripe apricot. No agitation or anxiety. Whoever she was, she thought she had every right and reason to be there. Every right and reason to be anywhere.

'Merritt Callahan, WTGX-Roanoke. I'd love to ask you a few questions, if you have the time. I was sorry to hear about your fiancé. This must be hard for you.'

Merritt's face showed classic signs of concern, but Juliet felt no concern beneath them. How had she unearthed Clyde's name? The police department had so far kept it quiet and out of the news. The woman was such a blank that hard-to-impress Juliet was impressed. Impressed and wary. Merritt wasn't an apricot, ripening or otherwise; she was a salmon swimming into the currents while singing a show tune.

Juliet pushed the cup toward Merritt, who stepped closer and peered inside. 'What do you see?' Juliet asked, genuinely wanting to know.

Merritt picked up the cup, still serene. 'By the handle?'

'Sure, if you'd like.'

'Looks like a little cart to me. For produce and such.'

Juliet looked again. She could see a cart – why not? Maybe wheels? She checked her book. Fluctuations in fortune? That didn't sound as promising. Juliet shut the book and scooted it to the edge of the table. She would have liked to push it underneath her chair but didn't think she could bend that far.

'It's twenty for a reading,' she said. She still hadn't risen and didn't plan to. Instead, she put the cup to one side as well, trying to push thoughts of divination away at the same time. Juliet had always wanted to see the future, but lately, it seemed imperative. It seemed like the only way she would survive.

Merritt reached into her shoulder bag and took out her wallet. 'Do you take Visa?'

Juliet most certainly did. She gestured at the chair across from her, which the reporter took, tucking her feet underneath like a schoolgirl about to receive a lesson on algebra.

Juliet shuffled her deck, letting her fingers dance among them as they stirred. She closed her eyes, feeling The Queen as it slipped into her palm and out again. She could have been a magician, dazzling audiences with tricks. She knew all seventy-eight cards by touch, The Queen the most worn but The Well a close second. The Moon had a little tear along the top. Reluctantly, Juliet opened her eyes, and for a second – only a second – she felt frustration radiate off Merritt before it was tamped back down.

'What's your question then?' Juliet asked.

'Does Mr Montgomery often hike the Alleghenies before work? Seems like quite an expedition for such an hour.'

'No, what's your question for yourself?'

Unperturbed, Merritt reached for the deck, which she cut three times then handed back. Not her first reading then. 'For myself? I don't have any.'

'Everybody has a question,' Juliet said. 'Everybody seeks an answer that'll make their journey easier. No boulders or scorpions. No fallen limbs or scorching heat. Only a path to walk.'

'In these shoes? I'm not much of a hiker myself. But Mr Montgomery—'

'That's a question for somebody else.'

'Forgive me, but it's a question for you.'

Juliet considered why the woman wanted to know about Clyde's whereabouts the morning of the murders.

As if sensing an opening, Merritt plowed into it. 'Because far be it for me to infer the Thorngold County Police Department has an agenda, but I don't like a foregone conclusion either. Do you?'

Juliet flipped a card, opening it like a book, weighing her options. She didn't trust the woman – she didn't trust anybody who didn't feel at least a little melancholy. The world was a hard place, and if you avoided that hardness, good for you, but stay away from her front door. Still, if Merritt Callahan, WTGX-Roanoke, could help . . .

'If you don't want to talk about Clyde, tell me about the Mercury Order. What's with the bats?' Merritt asked.

Juliet felt the heat rise to her cheeks; wanted to defend herself and her friends. They were hardly an institution, though they had given themselves the name Mercury Order. It was meant playfully. And it's true that a few members from time to time got out of hand. There wasn't much to do around here that didn't involve booze or pills, so sometimes they'd howl at the moon, spray overpasses with gaudy colors and call it performance art. Mostly they talked about astrology with each other, compared tarot decks or their objects for throwing bones. When the group got together they knew their ideas would be met with nods of understanding rather than snickers of disapproval. And they damn well didn't kill any bats.

'We'll do a basic three-card spread. I know what you're asking anyway,' Juliet said, avoiding the subject of her friends and their proclivities.

'What am I asking?'

A sliver of curiosity accompanied Merritt's words. Good. A place to start.

'You're asking if you'll succeed.'

'Works for me.' The curiosity grew a little despite the casual response.

'In this story. In your investigation. But that's not enough, is it?'

Merritt shrugged, unbothered by being seen so clearly. 'I don't think there's any reason to hide my ambition, do you? You're a self-made woman, working for yourself, answering to nobody.'

Was that true? Juliet didn't appreciate the reporter analyzing her rather than the other way around.

'Maybe you like not having a man around even.'

Juliet hissed at her in response. She flipped two more cards, so that she had a trio: Eight of Pentacles, Eight of Swords (reversal), King of Swords (reversal). Two eights and two swords. Juliet saw the patterns shift into place like tiles into a floor. No surprise there. The reporter was ruled by reason, forgetting she even possessed a heart sometimes.

Juliet tapped the Pentacles with a fingernail. 'You don't have the skills you need yet, but you're getting there.'

'Mmm-hmm. Do you meet regularly with the other practitioners? Or do you prefer to be called witches?'

'You're sure enough tenacious though. Yeah, we meet every few weeks or so at a diner river-side. No blood sacrifices or any such thing like that. What would I want with some smelly old bats? And we don't call ourselves anything, thank you very much.'

'I see. And what does the pretty woman with the blindfold mean?'

Juliet looked at the Swords card, jarred by the change in subject. 'Something is holding you back from true success. What could that be, do you think?'

'You order hamburgers and grouse about the stars?'

It must have been some sort of interview technique, flipping back and forth between topics. The police had tried to pin everything from vandalism to cyberattacks on Juliet and her friends, nothing sticking because there was nothing to stick.

'Something like that. Listen, a lot of people hated that place. New Hope. What a stupid name. Nothing more ancient than hope. Nothing more tricksy either. You think the owners of these shuttered pain clinics are happy about the church's little experiment?' Juliet asked.

'Using snakes as a non-chemical means of addressing addiction? I would imagine not.'

'You would imagine not. Geez. Listen, you're not from around here, and I wish you all the best. Truly. Nobody wants you to succeed more than me, but I'll look after myself, thank you very much.'

'Got it. And this guy?' Merritt pointed to the King of Swords.

'He's a nasty sort, standing in your way. Get past him, and you're golden, honey.'

'That sounds about right to me.'

Juliet held out her hand, and Merritt deposited her credit card and business card. Without knowing how to explain herself, Juliet gripped Merritt's hand in hers and pulled. The woman looked surprised and felt if not exactly afraid at least cautious. 'The past doesn't matter. It's what's ahead. That's the ticket.'

Merritt shook herself free, studying Juliet as she ran her credit card, perhaps wondering if she was about to be the victim of fraud.

'I used to believe that too,' Merritt said, a little less confident than before. 'It didn't matter where I came from or what I'd done there. But that's the whole story, isn't it? You figure out the past, you figure out the present.'

'I already know the present.'

'Maybe. But that's what everybody thinks. And I'm thinking, if Mr Montgomery was out hiking the morning of the fire, he wasn't setting the fire, was he? And that picture gets erased, so that another can be drawn.'

Juliet handed back the Visa. The woman was right, and she resented her for being right. Still, Juliet wasn't a fool.

'He hikes a few mornings a week. Regular.'

Merritt beamed, and genuine delight radiated into the room. When she left, the room felt colder, her own thoughts bringing her low. Could that obnoxious woman be right? Was Juliet being stubborn, wanting to know the future when there was plenty to uncover in the present?

With some effort, she heaved herself out of the chair, feeling the starfish move, too, kick their legs. Juliet pulled back the curtain, letting the streetlight flood the room. Merritt opened her door and waved. Juliet resisted the urge to move away from the window. No, she wasn't going anywhere. Let the reporter see that somebody was always watching.

TWENTY

'You got a Santa fetish or something?'

Merritt zipped the back of her dress and put on her small, gold earrings. She was aware of Otis watching her, so she took her time, made the act of dressing its own kind of performance. The night before hadn't left much time for observation, but now she examined the elf floor lamp with some concern. The Christmas tree air fresheners and tinsel above the doorways. Angel figurines. Otis's small efficiency apartment looked like a fire sale for a holiday bric-a-brac store.

'Oh yeah,' he said. 'Nothing turns me on like candy canes and yule logs.'

'Rudolph?'

'All the reindeers. Blitzen, Prancer, Teddy.'

Merritt slipped into her heels then put her hands on her hips, impatient for a real explanation.

'Pre-furnished. But I might keep it, ya know? It seems to bring me good luck.'

Merritt crawled on to the bed, and Otis reached for her as she hiked up her hem and straddled him over the blanket. When she bent, her hair dropped to his chest, and he met her mouth with his. He tasted like cigarettes, but Merritt had never seen him light up. He must have snuck outside while she was sleeping. Merritt slept like the dead. Merritt slept like she had nothing to worry about.

'We've both got to work.'

Merritt hadn't seduced the lieutenant for information. He'd given her everything she needed over their breakfast date. Oh, he thought he was being coy, not using names and avoiding forensics talk. Merritt could read between the lines though. She'd done her own research, and he'd spilled everything when she'd presented him with her findings. No, Merritt had seduced Otis Barnes because he was cute. And when he'd stopped pretending to be tough, kind of sweet.

'Turning over every rock,' he said.

Merritt almost felt protective of him. It had taken all of ten minutes to determine the lieutenant had arrested Clyde Montgomery because he'd been told to arrest Clyde Montgomery by the senior brass. Even better for Merritt, he felt guilty about it. And if she'd pressed on that guilt like it was a bruise, made him think about checking out some other angles? Well, Merritt figured you still got credit for doing the right thing for the wrong reasons.

'You best watch yourself around here. A lot of creepy-crawlies like to hide under those rocks.'

Merritt checked herself in the mirror, wiping some residual mascara from her cheeks, then pulled open the door. Icy air shot through the room in an instant. 'This place is a dump,' she said, letting herself out.

Merritt navigated the metal stairs, holding on to the rail in case of black ice. She was glad to see her Volvo unscratched. This seemed like the kind of apartment complex where rims got stolen and doors got keyed. As if on cue, a woman started shouting at her boyfriend to let her back inside, calling him a name so creative that Merritt deemed her a poet. The woman banged on the door until it finally opened, as if it couldn't take any more abuse.

Lieutenant Otis Barnes was cute, but Merritt couldn't see herself returning anytime soon. Maybe he would drive over to Roanoke. She liked the cop enough to want to see him again. Interesting. She'd worry about that later. Time and place to be determined.

The general feeling of the precinct was that Otis and his partner were wasting their time – wasting everybody's time – when they pointed out some discrepancies in the case against Clyde Montgomery. For starters, he'd signed the Cavern Trail guestbook the morning of the fire. More than a formality, those logs helped rescuers if anybody went missing in the mountains. Otis sensed the sister was hiding something, but he couldn't say for sure if that related to the case or not. Witnesses hid things for all sorts of reasons, and the girl was a secretive sort to begin with. Merritt disagreed with that assessment but didn't correct the lieutenant. In the two minutes she'd spoken to Essa Montgomery, she'd seen equal parts fear and frustration. A little bit of anger at this mortal coil. She'd liked the little mouse all the better for it. You could do a lot with rage. You could burn shit down.

Otis thought he'd be stripped of the case in a couple of days if he didn't charge Clyde. But you could do a lot with a couple of days, couldn't you? *Especially someone like you,* Merritt had said.

Merritt was lost in self-congratulation when she clicked her car fob and slid into the driver's seat, adjusting the rearview mirror in time to see a bright streak slide off the back seat. She screamed before her body could react then fumbled for the door handle, cursing when her hand slipped off the first time. She fell out of the car, slamming both bare knees into the ground, then twisted round, still screaming as she shut the door with an outstretched foot. That's how Otis found her, back on the dirty concrete, panting, both hands on her stomach.

'Did he get me?'

'Did who get you?' Otis reached for his gun, perhaps realizing too late he'd dashed outside in his bare feet and underwear, unarmed.

'Did that stupid snake bite me?'

Otis lifted her legs and arms, turning them over and grunting. She liked that he didn't ask any other questions for a while. She liked that he helped her without knowing what he was up against. She liked that he didn't seem embarrassed to be in his skivvies.

'All clear.'

Merritt sat, yanking her skirt down and reaching for her shoes. Otis held them out one at a time, and she leaned on him as she slipped them back on. She leaned on him for longer than necessary, then she brushed herself off.

'*Micrurus fulvius*. From the Elapidae family,' Merritt said.

'From the what now?'

'Eastern coral snake. Small little fuckers, but their venom packs a punch. Paralysis then respiratory failure.' Merritt let herself imagine her own excruciating death. The way her body might become frozen as the venom hunted for her heart. The way her lungs might burn as she tried and failed to breathe, drowning in the open air. She let the fear then the rage fill her body. Oh yes. You could do a lot with rage.

She locked eyes with Otis, made sure he was paying attention before she spoke. 'That preacher's a sociopath. I'd ask you not to forget it.'

TWENTY-ONE

T he lab looked foreboding early in the morning, the animals casting long shadows on the back wall. The heat hadn't been running over the weekend, so Essa could see her breath when she stepped inside and flipped on the lights. They buzzed, dull orange at first as if they were waking up like the rest of Thorngold County. Except Essa had been up since four, replaying the conversation she'd had with Pastor Micah. Could she ignore the bargain she'd been offered? Her brother hadn't been officially charged with anything, and the police had finally released him when the forty-eight-hour holding period expired. Essa tried to picture different outcomes. She'd learned that trick from her guidance counselor after she'd sat through five sessions without speaking a word. Picture the worst case then picture the best. The truth will probably land somewhere in between. Except Essa knew sometimes the worst-case scenario was something you'd never dream up in your wildest nightmares. Except even in the best-case scenario, somebody was dead. Two somebodies.

Essa had watched a news report, recognizing the reporter and her pink lipstick as she'd lowered her voice solemnly to share the teenagers' names with the public: Carter Hoyston and Sara Beth Booth. Their photos had flashed on the screen, young and hopeful. High-school sweethearts who'd snuck into the place for a tryst. Merritt Callahan called them 'star-crossed lovers', but Essa didn't think that was the right term. Unlucky seemed more accurate.

Another thought made her pause, a jolt of possibility running through her body. Maybe *they* had started the fire.

Essa turned on the central heat but didn't take her coat off. She went to the supply closet to get more paper towels and syringes. You could never be too prepared before the other staff members arrived. There would be Monday morning gossip while everyone had coffee and reviewed their orders. Dr Kester would assign tasks, and Essa would observe everything.

Despite feeling like an outsider, she liked the weekly meetings. She liked hearing about who was throwing a baby shower and which schools were closed because of a flu outbreak. Gloriana had an uncanny knack for remembering funny details. On a good day, she could even make Karl laugh, his sour mood lightened for a few minutes. Sometimes Essa felt like an anthropologist doing fieldwork on West Virginia communities. But that was fine by her. She'd always liked science. It was the rest of the week that dragged sometimes. Nobody really acknowledging her, assuming she'd be the one to stay late and arrive early. She'd clean the spills that had been neglected until they'd dried on to the floors. She'd run to the grocery store for more coffee grounds and toilet paper. She'd order the formaldehyde and phenol when they ran low.

'Good morning, Essa.'

Essa screamed, her hand slamming into her chest in shock. She whirled around, but Dr Kester didn't seem to notice her reaction. She'd been staring so long at the supply-closet shelves that she'd forgotten what she needed.

'Good morning. You startled me.'

'Did I?' Dr Kester looked up from his clipboard and seemed to see her for once. 'Oh, Essa. You look dreadful.'

She knew that was true, but she cringed at the words.

'I haven't been sleeping much.'

'More iron, I say. Will set you right up. I may have some around here.'

Dr Kester patted his pockets as if the vitamins would materialize because he'd thought of them. When he didn't find anything except pens, he went back to his clipboard. Sometime before they'd met, Dr Kester's hairline had receded then stopped halfway back on his skull. The visible skin was mottled and sunburned during the warmer months. He let what was left of his hair grow long, as if he couldn't be bothered with such pedestrian matters as a barbershop.

'We've got a busy day ahead of us, I'm afraid. I'd be glad to start early if you are.'

Essa nodded, closing the closet door and figuring she could fetch whatever they needed when the time came. She felt sluggish, as if she could hardly string two coherent words together.

The shock of seeing the burned snakes made her pause at the dissection-room entrance. For a moment, she confused them with the live ones she'd seen the day before at the worship service. But then she realized they were from the fire. Four in total: two rattle-snakes, a copperhead and one burned so badly that its species was too hard to identify at a glance. Their bodies had shriveled, but Dr Kester stretched them out to their full lengths, the longest about five feet. Essa tried to ignore the buzzing that started in her ears. She could barely hear Dr Kester as he outlined their work for the day. He didn't seem to notice she had a hard time moving, and she was glad for once to be an afterthought. She walked into the room, wiping her sweaty palms against her skirt and shrugging off her coat. *Dead,* she told herself. *They couldn't hurt anybody.*

'These from New Hope then?' Essa asked, her voice weak.

Dr Kester seemed confused she'd spoken but didn't seem to mind the question. 'Damn waste of time. They'll learn more from the human autopsies. You know how they like to make us jump from time to time though. Remind us who's in charge around here.'

Dr Kester seemed to consider something then looked at Essa, seeing her again for a few seconds. 'Will that be a problem for you?'

'Not for me, no, but is it right? They think my brother—'

Essa couldn't bring herself to finish the sentence. They thought her brother what? That he'd killed two people. He could be locked away for life, and Juliet would be forced to raise their baby alone.

'I see,' Dr Kester said, looking at his clipboard then back at Essa. 'I know you've been applying for other jobs.'

The change in topic surprised her, and Essa looked at her boots. It felt a bit like a betrayal. Dr Kester had given her a job, no questions asked, and helped her get a degree. He'd set her on something like a path, and it was more than she could have hoped for. He wasn't exactly a mentor, perhaps too old to take on such a role. Or maybe too absorbed in his cases. But he'd helped her, and she should be loyal to him. She even liked the work. She'd never make it in a job where she had to converse with strangers all day.

'It's not that I'm ungrateful.'

'Gratitude and a quarter will get you some gum. No, I don't need it. These dissections are a formality. Nobody's getting charged for killing snakes. They should be, mind you, but they're not. What's that saying? Dotting Is and crossing Ts? Nonsensical. Like a children's nursery rhyme.'

Dr Kester put on his magnifying glasses and hovered over the snakes, the discussion closed as far as he was concerned. Essa handed him a pair of latex gloves, and he snapped them on without looking at her again. Then he lifted one of the rattlesnakes, turning it from side to side, clucking softly to himself. His professionalism always inspired Essa, but in the right mood he could rail against humans as the most dangerous animals until his voice grew hoarse.

Essa arranged the scissors, probes and forceps on the stainless-steel rolling table. Given the state of the bodies, she doubted many paper towels for fluid would be needed, but she reached for them anyway, remembering they were nearly out. That's what she'd meant to get from the supply closet. She walked out of the room, knowing Dr Kester wouldn't notice. Once he started his work, he was gone – might as well have been on a different planet.

As she walked back through the specimen room, she considered the cases they'd worked on since she'd arrived. Well, she hadn't worked on the cases in the beginning of course, but eventually she'd been given more responsibilities. Her official title was now 'Lab Technician', which she thought sounded nice, a little fancy even. Her first dissection, a salt marsh harvest mouse, had made her queasy, but she'd mostly grown used to the sights and smells. The larger animals sometimes challenged her. A months-long case the year before had meant two or three gray wolves at a time had to be examined. Dr Kester had been tasked to determine if they'd been killed by humans and, if so, if the killings fit into the livestock danger exemption. Motive in those sorts of investigations was often elusive, but they'd eventually charged a group of young men for illegal hunting practices.

If Essa's job were located anywhere else, she wouldn't move. Some days were monotonous, but often, she'd learn something, be exposed to new ideas. The notion of always being the serpent orphan was bleak though. She wanted a fresh start. She'd dropped off her résumé at nearly every veterinarian office in Roanoke. A pharmaceutical company had reached out to her but didn't like that she only had an associate's degree. They'd said to get in touch if she ever went back to school.

She saw Karl walk through the front door, hunched over a thermos. He muttered a bit, shaking himself off like a dog who'd come in out of the rain, though it was dry as a bone outside. He spent his spare time camping or rock climbing in nearby state parks, but Essa had stopped asking about his weekends years before.

'Good morning, Karl,' she said, not wanting to be rude.

'Is it though?'

He'd be unhappy stuck inside all day, and Essa ducked a little as she headed back toward the dissection room. She fit paper towels into the holder and watched Dr Kester make purple markings on the rattlesnake's remaining scales. After fifty years of experience, he hardly needed guiding marks, but the doctor was nothing if not meticulous. Essa hated to interrupt his concentration, but she had to ask again about the ethics of her assisting.

'I can ask someone else,' she said as quietly as possible. 'Karl's here.'

Dr Kester paused, removing his magnifying glasses. He stared at her long enough to become uncomfortable. 'Has your brother been charged with anything?'

'No, he was released yesterday.'

'Well, I don't see a problem. And even if he were, I don't see how your assistance would matter one way or the other. I file the reports, and I'd hardly be biased, even for a colleague. We'll be thorough and precise, as always. Then we'll move on to something that actually makes a difference.'

Essa cringed, though she knew what he meant. It was unlikely any evidence they recovered would be presented in court. The human autopsies would take precedence and provide more information. There had most likely been other critters in the fire – a few mice at least – but they hadn't left enough behind for examination.

Dr Kester snapped the glasses back down and turned his attention to the markings. He pulled out a few pieces of detritus that had melted into the scales. Essa handed him a scalpel and watched him make an incision in the abdomen. He used a small pair of scissors to finish the slit. It reminded Essa of cutting wrapping paper, though the skin gave more resistance.

Essa watched him remove the single lung, black from smoke inhalation, and place it on a tray. The kidneys and intestines followed. The stomach looked empty from the outside, and sure enough, the rattlesnake hadn't eaten recently. There were a few undigested bits of particles though, and Dr Kester took them out with tweezers along with three thin pieces of clear plastic the snake had picked up somewhere. Essa took notes and soon lost her anxious feelings. Work made that possible for her. Frankly, she'd rather be at the lab today than waiting for bad news at home.

The second necropsy passed in a similar manner, and Dr Kester dictated information about the burn patterns. He speculated about their defensive positions after they'd realized they couldn't escape or perhaps were too exhausted to keep trying. Dr Kester spoke in a level, uninflected voice, but Essa felt sorry for them. They'd dissected other burn victims, most notably a small black bear that had proved useful in determining where a brutal forest fire had started one August. They hadn't been allowed to keep that specimen, but Essa had named him anyway. Hank Williams, may he rest in peace.

'As I expected,' Dr Kester said, and Essa jumped. She'd let her mind wander again. 'Smoke inhalation. I doubt we'll find anything different about the others, but we'll tackle them after a break.'

Essa glanced at the clock to see that a couple of hours had passed. Dr Kester peeled off his plastic gloves and tossed them in the hazardous waste container. He rubbed his knuckles, and Essa wondered how much longer he could run the lab. Who would take over? She hoped it wasn't Karl, his bad attitude permeating the place like the smell of a dead rat in the walls.

'Have the humans been autopsied already?' Essa asked, and Dr Kester focused on her.

'I suspect so, though we're not much involved in those investigations, as you know. We stay in our lane over here.'

'More like the shoulder,' Essa said, and Dr Kester surprised her by chuckling.

'Right you are. But it's important, you know. What we do. People like to believe they're the boss of everything, and we see those horrors here from time to time, don't we? But the truth of the matter is that nature doesn't need us. We need nature. Without the trees and the rivers, what would we do? Perish. You can't get water from a stone.' Dr Kester paused before continuing, even going so far as to clear his throat. 'I know you've been looking for a different job, Essa.'

'Yes, sir. You said before.'

'I'm not losing my mind. I don't know quite how to say what I need to say.'

Essa waited, not sure she wanted to hear anything that was difficult for Dr Kester to communicate. He was a straightforward sort of person. His hesitation couldn't mean anything good.

'Well, I might as well come out and say it. Essa, you'll need some new clothes. And I don't know if you're keeping your hair that way for some sort of religious reason—'

'I'm not,' Essa said too quickly.

'Good. I'd be happy to have you here if you wore clown costumes and bright-green wigs, but nobody knows you outside of Vintera.'

'I understand,' Essa said, her face burning. She forced herself not to glance at the skirt and blouse she'd picked out for the day.

Dr Kester nodded once then asked for a pair of gloves, forgetting he'd wanted to take a break. Essa didn't need one anyway. She wiped the scalpels with alcohol and handed one over before she was asked.

TWENTY-TWO

The smell of a high-school gymnasium made Merritt feel at home. That specific combination of bleachers and sweat. She'd been a star forward her senior year, outgoing and popular. She would have preferred being captain of the cheerleading squad but had been told in no uncertain terms that she was too tall. Merritt could hear the squeaks of sneakers as soon as she opened the door and stepped into the lobby, where two heavily rouged mothers sat behind a folding table, guarding a metal cashbox with their lives.

'All we got left is Snickers bars, but it's for a good cause,' said the one with her hair in a long braid, pointing at the sign that indicated all snack proceeds went to team travel expenses.

Merritt smiled at her, digging in her purse for cash. 'I'll take two. You never know when you'll need a little sugar boost.' She hadn't touched sugar in three years, not since she'd lost out on a job at CNN for not having enough on-camera experience. 'Coach Perisin is expecting me. To talk about Sara Beth?'

Merritt had used her gentlest tone, but one mother burst into tears.

'I know this is an emotional time for you all. Were you close with Sara Beth?'

The non-crying mother nodded.

'Oh, surely we was. My Claribel sits at the table next to hers every lunch. And Martha's boy—' The woman stopped to give her friend a sideways hug. 'Martha's boy had a history class with her last term.'

'This is a lot for everyone,' Merritt said, giving the women time to settle.

She'd eventually spoken with Carter Hoyston's grieving parents, but they hadn't offered much in the way of suspects. They thought the church was the target, not their baby, and the father had some pretty unchristian words for New Hope, 'fucking freak show' being the nicest. Carter played football and drank a little bit 'like kids do' his older brother had said, looking to Merritt for affirmation.

Maybe forgiveness. If they'd only kept a closer eye on him, maybe Carter wouldn't have been messing around with his girlfriend where he shouldn't have been messing around. And why had Carter taken Sara Beth there anyway? Merritt suspected it was the girl's idea, but gut instinct would only get you so far.

After taking her money and handing over candy bars, the mothers pointed Merritt toward the basketball court, where a group of girls had made a pyramid with their bodies.

'Sara Beth's sister is the one at the top. Sweet girl.'

Merritt thanked them for their time and offered her condolences. She stepped into the gym in time to see Amy June waving both arms in triumph. She calculated the girl was at least fifteen feet in the air, and there were no mats underneath her.

When she wobbled, Merritt caught her breath, imagining the teen's skull cracked open like a cantaloupe on the scratched wooden court. But somehow Amy June righted herself and folded into the arms of the girls below her. With a jaunty hop, she landed back on the ground, clapping as her teammates cheered and got into a military-worthy formulation, not a toe out of place.

When Merritt clapped, the girls looked startled, though, and huddled around each other for support. If their performance had been intimidating, their faces now reminded her of abandoned kittens. She was shocked at how young they looked, nothing like the teenagers portrayed on television. They were children, no question. Sara Beth's sister couldn't have weighed more than ninety pounds, her scrawny knees streaked with self-tanner. For a moment, the girl's face seemed to turn into her sister's, and Merritt felt sick.

'Get it together, Callahan,' she whispered to herself. She must have been more affected by her morning death scare than she'd realized. Still, a plan was a plan.

Merritt scanned the area for their coach and found the woman already walking toward her. She wore a baby-blue velour sweatsuit with matching wristbands, and her short-cropped hair stood up in places where she'd pushed it off her forehead from frustration or heat. The furnace was roaring at Thorngold High, and sweat formed in Merritt's armpits. She'd changed into a silk blouse and slacks to cover her scraped knees. The kids seemed oblivious to the heat, but they weren't oblivious to her presence. They whispered behind their hands, and Merritt doubted she would hear those secrets. She was good with interviewees but never underestimated the loyalty of a teenage girl.

'The students call me Mama P.' The coach held out her hand for a firm shake. 'You're late. Girls, stop tittering please.'

'And I apologize for that.' Merritt bristled only a little and resisted the urge to share her tale of woe. 'And I'm only here to talk. Nothing frightening.'

The coach shook her head. 'Nothing scary about the death of their teammate? You have daughters, Ms Callahan? Never mind. I know already. We can chat at the far end. Girls, can you check your uniforms for tears or stains please?'

A chorus of 'yes, ma'ams' followed, and a girl with curly black hair hugged Amy June before slinging her bag on to a bleacher. Merritt wished she could talk to all the teammates, not only the sister, but she'd need permission from the parents, which would be a headache to say the least.

When they sat, the coach took her charge's tiny hand into her own, squeezing encouragement. Merritt sat too and put on her most sympathetic face then tried to pry information out of the girl.

'Thanks for chatting with me again, Amy June. I heard there's a big tournament coming up.'

Amy June looked at her coach, who nodded her permission to answer.

'Next week. Mom said I should come to practice even with everything going on.'

Merritt leaned closer to hear the soft-spoken words. 'You were pretty impressive up there.'

'It's Sara Beth's position at the top. I'm not as flexible as her.'

'You look talented to me.'

Amy June shrugged in response, and her coach interjected.

'Talent is for lazy girls. Mine work hard. Third in the state last year.'

Merritt knew. The Thorngold cheerleading squads – junior and senior – were more than decoration at football games. They took their sport seriously.

'Tell me about your sister. What was she like?'

'There's not much to tell.'

'She volunteered at the nursing home.'

Amy June frowned before responding. 'Sometimes? I mean, with the tournament around the corner, we're both busy AF.'

'Language,' the coach said. 'Sorry about that.'

'Sara Beth is Sara Beth, you know? Head either in the clouds or up her own ass. Sorry, Mama P, but you know it's true.'

Merritt noted that she was still using the present tense.

'We were supposed to go to the movies Friday night. It's her own fault, you know. Carter's a moron.'

'Why's it her fault?'

'She's always sneaking around with him. Ugh. He's not even that hot, you know? She even missed practice once to make out or whatever.'

'That's enough,' the coach said. 'I don't think this is a good idea.'

'Only a few more questions,' Merritt said.

'No, we're done here. Girls, back in formation please. Remember we're doing spikes at the top of minute two now.'

Merritt didn't leave right away. She could tell that her presence was unwanted, but the coach hadn't kicked her out yet. She thought about how Pastor Micah told teenagers that his church had an 'open door policy'. Sara Beth must have seen that as an opportunity, maybe even relished the thrill of a rendezvous in her old church.

'Does the pastor from New Hope ever stop by?'

Merritt knew he did. She'd found a photo of him leading a pre-basketball-game prayer for all the players and cheerleaders.

'Half the girls think they're in love with him.' Coming from somebody else, the statement would have been accompanied by a rueful grin, a little nostalgia for first crushes. Coach Perisin looked annoyed.

Merritt took a guess on the reason. 'Quite the distraction.'

'You said it, not me. The parents like the wholesomeness. Think a preacher praying means something. I think if your god hurts children who don't pray the right way, you should find yourself a better god.'

'Can I quote you on that?'

'No, you may not.'

The coach strode into the middle of the court, the girls circling her like ducklings. Merritt didn't stay to watch the routine again, but when she got to the door, she turned back to see Amy June being tossed into the air and caught above the cold, hard gym floor. One misstep away from another tragedy.

TWENTY-THREE

A clown costume. Essa didn't think it was possible to be more humiliated. All she wanted was to wash off the stench of dead animal that had seeped into her pores then forget the day had ever happened. Instead, she needed to see her brother.

She kept a bottle of saline solution in her purse, but she hated to blow her nose in the car. It seemed unsanitary. She tried to focus on the roads. The temperature hovered around thirty degrees outside, and black ice could form, especially over the bridges.

When she made it home, she threw the necropsy notes on to her kitchen table, hoping she'd have time to type them before morning. Dr Kester had sent her home early after Karl had insisted on taking over during the final dissection, his restless footsteps distracting everyone.

Essa didn't normally leave early or take work home. *I don't normally get called a clown at work either,* she thought before scrubbing off the day's germs from her hands and heading back into the night. She stopped and picked up a pizza from the gas station, not knowing what else to bring and not having a lot of options this side of town. Charlene's served potato skins, but they would be cold by the time she arrived.

Essa saw the 'Open' sign illuminated, so she pulled around back, not wanting to take any parking spaces from Juliet's paying customers. She ran a hand over her long braid. Maybe she could hack it off herself, take a knife to the base of her skull. She'd never bothered much with her hair before, but she knew the length wasn't in style. Had it ever been? *A clown costume.*

After she knocked, her brother opened the door carrying a beer. His eyes were dark, and he squinted at her from inside. For a moment, she worried he might be high. But her brother didn't touch drugs, and she didn't believe he could have changed that much since they'd lived together. Of course, he'd never drunk much either. For a moment, his face lit up with hope, but something in Essa's expression must have told him that she'd failed him.

'All right,' he said. 'You tried, I guess.'

'I tried,' she said.

Clyde didn't say anything, and for a terrible minute, Essa thought he might not let her in. Then he walked away, and Essa followed, hurrying to close the door behind her and keep the heat inside.

'I say anybody bringin' food is welcome.'

Essa turned toward Wash, who had his boots up on Juliet's clean kitchen table.

'Hey, Wash. Harry.'

The twins nodded in response, and Essa looked around the previously spotless kitchen. The counters were littered with cans and bottles, and it smelled rank, as if nobody there had showered in days. If this was a celebration, it was a sad one.

'I didn't mean to interrupt.'

'You ain't interrupting. We're taking all your brother's money is all. He ain't gonna need it.'

Wash winked at her, but it was forced. He put down his cards and counted the chips in front of him. Her brother popped him on the back of his head, hard enough to make him flinch, but not so hard as to hurt.

'Juliet working tonight?' Essa asked.

'Couldn't talk her out of it.'

Wash snorted. 'Crazy as a loon. The baby's blood connects her to the universe or some shit. Wasn't she saying?'

'You tryin' to start something with me?' Clyde looked menacing, but Wash ignored him, swallowing the last of his drink and crossing to the pizza. Essa realized she should have brought two. They would eat everything before Juliet finished for the night. Juliet's clients tended to stumble into the place until midnight or so, when the self-doubts started to eat you alive. Essa knew those nights, when the voices in your head listed everything you'd ever screwed up. When you wanted a little comfort from scripture or stars. Anything with a promise.

'Could I talk to you for a sec?'

Essa glanced around the small space, considering where it might be a little more private. Clyde hesitated then grabbed his coat. He gestured back outside, and Essa turned around. It wasn't the kind of evening you wanted to linger in, and her brother might have taken her outside on purpose. Whatever she had to say, she'd better make it quick.

Clyde pulled a pack of Marlboros from his back pocket and lit up, exhaling three perfect rings into the air. He never smoked inside when they lived together, and he wouldn't around Juliet either. Definitely not around the baby.

'Not bad,' Essa said.

'I've been practicing.'

When he grinned, he looked his age, twenty-four come April. He already had wrinkles on his forehead and around his eyes, but there was a softness to his jaw that would eventually drop away. More like their mother every day. Not somebody you'd notice in a crowd, but up close, you'd see his long lashes and deep-set eyes. A professional photographer could have done a lot with their expressiveness.

'You got work tomorrow?'

'Nah, but they ain't fired me yet. Suspension.'

'They paying you?'

Clyde shook his head and took another long drag on the cigarette, glancing behind him as if to make sure they weren't overheard. Did Juliet own or rent the trailer? Essa had never thought about it before. In another week or so, they wouldn't have any money coming in at all.

'I need to ask you something.'

'Out with it then.'

'Say you could help get somebody out of a jam, but you had to do something wrong.'

'Like tell-a-lie wrong or rob-a-bank wrong.'

Essa thought that over before replying. 'Well, not illegal if that's what you mean.'

'That's what I mean.'

Essa was glad for darkness, so Clyde couldn't see her. She wished the floodlight would switch off as well, even though it pointed in the other direction, at the small parking lot. She kept her head down anyway.

'I went to see the preacher like you asked.'

'You tried.'

'I tried.'

Clyde didn't go back inside, but she could almost sense his spirit turning away from her. As if something about the property made that possible.

'Pastor Micah came to see me too. After.'

'What did that asshole want?'

'He said you attacked him. With a knife.'

Clyde walked away from her, kicking a can somebody had dropped. It disappeared into the trees lining the property.

'So what if I did, huh? That don't mean I burned down a fucking church!'

Clyde was yelling but not at her. He was yelling at the trees, and Essa stayed put.

'I'm not saying you did—'

'You think I did?'

He turned to peer at her, his expression so broken that Essa's heart clenched.

'Of course not. You didn't kill those people. But listen. It looks bad is all I'm saying.'

'He's got it in for me. They're going to lock me up and throw away the key. Maybe fry me in a chair.'

'They don't have the death penalty in West Virginia.'

'I wish they did. I'd rather fry than get cancer or some shit behind bars.'

Essa took a deep breath, the air burning as it slipped into her lungs. She didn't have to say anything. She could pretend she hadn't been given an option, however loathsome it was to her. But she didn't want to make this decision alone, so she blurted it out.

'I think he offered to vouch for you if I slept with him.'

Clyde put his hands on his head and stared at the sky. Essa looked too, wondering what he saw up there. It was a clear night, and she could make out a few of the constellations she knew. She recalled Job, trying and failing not to compare herself to a man tortured by the devil to prove a point. She remembered God asking, 'Can you bind the chains of the Pleiades? Can you loosen Orion's belt?' Job 38:30. Essa wasn't much for talking back to God, but she'd never seen the constellations change, take on new shapes. Not even once.

Her brother swearing in the distance brought her back to earth. He'd walked to the edge of the trees and, for a moment, seemed like he was going to wander off. He bent down and picked up the can he'd kicked, crushing it with his hands and putting it in his back pocket. He'd throw it away in the trashcan, so as not to junk up the land.

'Son of a bitch,' he yelled, loud enough for the twins inside to hear. Essa glanced toward the trailer to see if anyone came out, but the door stayed shut. He turned back toward Essa and lowered his voice. 'I could kill him.'

'Don't think that will help none.'

Clyde returned to her, hovering a few inches away. Then he hugged her to his chest, and a knot inside Essa loosened. The slight headache she'd had for the whole day vanished, and she almost sighed in relief. It would be OK. There had to be another way. She wrapped her hands around his waist, noticing he'd filled out since they'd last stood like this, the pair of them against the world.

'You gotta do it, String Bean.'

Essa thought she'd misheard him. He couldn't be pimping out his sister and using her childhood nickname in the same sentence. She pulled back from him to get a better view of his face, but he moved away from her again, back into the darkness.

'The police. They're not even lookin' at anyone else. Me and me alone.'

'But they let you go.'

'For now. It's a sham. They want this all wrapped up and delivered with a bow to Micah Granieri.'

'But—'

'But what?'

Essa forgot what she was going to say. Her brother had always been right, but not this time. What if once wasn't enough? What if she had to sleep with Pastor Micah until he got tired of her? Until she got pregnant? Or what if he decided he wanted money instead?

'You know we can't trust that preacher, Clyde. I'm not doing it.'

As soon as she said the words aloud, she knew that had been her decision all along. She hadn't come to Clyde for advice. She'd come for forgiveness. Her head started to ache again.

'Why tell me at all then? Why give me a glimmer of hope I might get to see my baby grow up?'

'I'm sorry. I shouldn't have said anything. I thought—'

'You thought what? I can't protect you forever, Essa. You gotta grow up sometime, and now seems as good a time as any.'

Clyde stalked toward the parking lot, and in the light, his whole body glowed. He jerked open the door to his truck and climbed inside. Essa wanted to ask for the keys, tell him he was in no shape to drive, but he wouldn't listen to her. Instead, she watched his tires throw gravel as he pulled on to the road.

'You got to watch out for an Aries when Mars connects with Pluto, sugar.'

Essa yelped and swung toward the voice, seeing Juliet silhouetted in the doorframe. She seemed like an entirely different woman than the one she'd watched scrubbing her counters. Older or ageless. Her wig absorbed the porch light hovering overhead like a natural halo. Her dark eyes were framed in blue eyeliner that made triangles at the corner, and her lips dripped with shiny red lipstick. It should have looked like a costume, but there was something about her stance that made her look powerful instead, if a little otherworldly. A tight T-shirt stretched over her belly, and she covered that with a floor-length sweater.

'Come on in then. In such a temper? He'll be gone for a good spell.'

TWENTY-FOUR

The room hummed from the old lamp in the corner that Juliet had covered with a red chiffon scarf. She disapproved of the cheesy effect, but she'd let go of a need for authenticity after opening her practice. Most of her clients liked a little flair; didn't care about the years she'd spent studying birth charts, astral projections, electromagnetic energies. She'd read Helena Avelar and Luis Ribeiro, formed opinions about Sue Tompkins, had three copies of *Astrological Insights into Personality*. Self-taught of course. There were no schools in the vicinity that would offer such an education, and anyway, she'd never have been able to afford them. Instead, she'd apprenticed with Madame Clarita, who'd let her watch sessions in exchange for picking up her groceries and unpacking them in the pantry.

Her first few solo readings had been awkward, Juliet's study not preparing her for real interactions – real reactions – but eventually she'd found a rhythm. She'd ask for a specific question and use her tarot to create a structure for the conversation. Often, she didn't need the cards, but she liked them all the same. She told people her favorite deck had been passed down from a great-grandmother, but she'd bought them at a yard sale when she was a freshman in high school. Her mother had cashed the payment checks for her until she got her own account, and eventually she'd saved enough to rent the trailer. Self-taught and self-made. And pre-ordained, she believed. Juliet rubbed her belly and whispered encouragement to her starfish.

The little one's future had yet to be seen, and Juliet felt a pang at not being able to prepare. For years, she'd worried her abilities were defective, but now she wondered if perhaps nothing was set in stone. Had Madame Clarita avoided whatever it was she'd seen in her own future? Had staying inside for years on end been worth it? Juliet turned her thoughts away from the medium, refusing to feel sorry for her anymore. Juliet would fight hard to give her baby everything, and that meant negotiating with the young woman sitting across from her, blinking those big doe eyes so like her brother's, fiddling with the end of her long braid.

Ungrateful, oblivious, pigeon-livered brat. Essa had never been Juliet's favorite person. The girl should have checked on her brother more often, especially as her financial situation improved. From the outside, Clyde looked like he had his life together – or at least he had before the arrest. But he kept all his feelings bottled up until she'd find him chopping down a tree or rebuilding a motor out back. Most months, they did OK, had extra money for a meal out on the weekends. They liked to grab drinks at Charlene's with a few friends. But now? Their expenses were about to skyrocket. Juliet had begged Clyde to tell Essa he was paying her home-insurance bill. Clyde had insisted she'd had a hard childhood, and it was the least he could do. She didn't know why, but tonight, for once, he'd seemed awfully mad at his sister. Juliet tried to drum up some pity, but instead, she felt justified. A thousand dollars. She'd decided that was a fair ask. Well-deserved back payment. And it would go a long way toward diapers and onesies.

Juliet didn't bother asking for a question. She picked up the deck and shuffled, turning the top half three times clockwise before setting them in front of Essa, who looked more scared than skeptical. How the girl had remained faithful after her parents passed was a mystery beyond prophecy. But she knew without asking that Essa saw the way Juliet made her living as immoral and maybe even Satanic.

The pause stretched, and Juliet watched the girl, reaching out to her and finding her troubled. No surprise there. It was a focused kind of trouble though, involving Clyde but not circling around him. There was another man, and when Juliet saw his shadowy outline, she shuddered.

As if Essa had been waiting for such a sign, she cut the deck in two and handed them back to Juliet. A car passed outside, and Essa turned toward the noise. Juliet knew the sound of Clyde's truck though, and he wasn't back yet. She cut the deck again and turned a card. Juliet half-expected The Devil, but instead it was The Fool.

'Go figure,' Essa said, low but clear, shrinking into herself.

The ignorance irritated Juliet, and she shook her head, trying to be objective but failing.

'Don't mean what you think it means. It means you're on the cusp of learning something that matters about yourself.'

Juliet concentrated, not wanting to dwell on the shadowy man but knowing it was the key to something important. She reminded

herself the reading was a means to an end, and she shouldn't pick
at wounds, but she couldn't help herself. Partly, she wanted the girl
to feel a little pain, and partly she was curious. Who knew this
unassuming dishmop had a profane influence in her life?

'What about the dog?' Essa pointed at the white terrier leaping
by the side of the Fool.

'That's your sort of cheerleader. Somebody wanting what's best
for you.'

Juliet started to pull another card, but Essa's scoff made her
pause. The girl didn't believe anybody was looking out for her, at
least not here on earth. 'You got somebody. The cards never lie.
Not even when we want them to.'

Essa's brow wrinkled as if running through the possibilities. Juliet
knew the list would be short, but somebody was there all the same.

'Dr Kester maybe.'

Juliet bristled at the girl showing off her fancy connections. The
starfish kicked, and her hand darted to her belly. She forgot Essa
was even there for a moment. The baby hadn't been planned but
would be loved. And would be comfortable if she had anything to
say about it.

The reversed Hierophant appeared next, and Juliet knew that was
right. The girl had some sort of internal belief system as firm as
any doctrine. She flipped the next card, not bothering to explain
anything to Essa. The Hangman. It made Essa blanch, and Juliet
felt smug for a minute. Maybe that internal guide wasn't so strong
after all.

'You got some decision to make, sugar. And you're thinking about
making yourself into a little martyr.'

Essa's cheeks flushed, and in the red light, it was as if her whole
face changed. Essa looked at her hands, and Juliet looked with her,
not surprised by the neatly cut nails. Her own were painted dark
blue, almost sapphire, and had been filed into crescent curves.

'I want to do what's right.'

'To sacrifice or be sacrificed. Ain't that always the choice? Listen
though, and I tell you this because you're family now.' Juliet almost
said 'because I care' but knew the girl wouldn't trust her. She was
a little backward, but she wasn't dumb. 'There's no grand battle
between good and evil, no God and the Devil bartering for souls.
There's a path though, sure enough. You got to walk, that's all. One
step in front of the other.'

Juliet had given this advice before, and it was generally sound – a sort of catchall – but her mind flashed back to the shadow man.

'Who you got stalking you?' she asked, deciding a direct approach might work better.

'It's all right.'

Juliet dismissed the answer. 'I can't help you if you don't let me. And I want to help.'

Perhaps 'want' was too strong of a word, but it was close to the truth. The reasons were complicated, sure, and she'd rather Clyde had a different kind of kin, but she'd work with what she had.

A police car screamed by outside, its sirens on and lights flashing. Juliet and Essa both turned toward the sound then back to each other. But the car passed, hunting for somebody besides Clyde. Juliet tucked a strand of her sleek wig behind her ears, silver pieces jangling like a wind chime.

'What's the worst kind of customer you ever had?' Essa asked.

Juliet wanted a smoke. 'The worst? Oh, you'd think it'd be the drunks and such, but they're easy to handle. The worst is the ones who don't want to admit anything bad about themselves. Wanna be told they're heroes and such for kicking their teenage son out or spending their whole paycheck at the slots.'

'I can see that.'

'This one man came the second Monday of every month, wanted to be told it was all right he'd left his family. It was like he needed me to say the words, so he could keep going.'

'And did you?'

'Did I what?'

'Tell him what he wanted to hear?'

Another cop car flew by outside, and they both turned for a moment. It was as if the air suddenly turned colder. Not colder, icy, and Juliet didn't like what that meant. Specters presented themselves in all manner of ways, from sentient shadows to darting orbs of light. Sometimes they resembled posters, two-dimensional and glossy. But the cold stayed consistent. Juliet had even measured it once: twenty-nine degrees Fahrenheit. Temperature of the afterlife. She looked around the room, trying to pinpoint the source. She laid the cards down when she noticed their visitor.

'Somebody's here to see you. But I got to tell you, I don't like ghosts.'

Juliet had never been scared of visitations, but this one had interrupted her business.

Essa looked around the room, her eyes falling on the lamp, which flickered theatrically. 'And I don't like tricks.'

She stood. The pause told Juliet everything she needed to know. Essa wanted to be in Juliet's life. Or in the baby's life at least. Juliet had already won. Money could be discussed next time.

'Thank you for your reading,' Essa said formally.

'I told him what he wanted to hear,' Juliet said, keeping her eyes on the three small lights that had appeared on her window. 'You asked about my worst customer? I told him what he wanted. Sometimes that's all people will hear anyway, no matter what you say.'

Juliet listened to Essa go out through the back door. Wash and Harry laughed at something, but Juliet didn't think ghosts were funny and she said as much aloud to the lights.

'I don't trust you none either. Just cause you crossed don't make you better than me.'

The lights didn't materialize into a figure, but Juliet heard the words in her head and flipped the next card in the deck. The Tower. Something had to fall apart for Essa's new life to begin.

'Not Essa's. Yours.'

Aunt CeeCee showed her face to the woman carrying her great-great-niece or nephew. Juliet had seen photos of her, and she looked almost alive with her round face and bow mouth and close-cropped curly hair. Aunt CeeCee was famous, at least to the Montgomerys. Famous and famously wild.

Juliet thought it might be fun to be visited by dead celebrities or historical figures. But no, it was always nosy relatives. And this one wasn't even hers yet.

TWENTY-FIVE

At first, Essa thought she might be hallucinating again. She'd dreamed of fire so many times that the sight of flames leaping from her own roof didn't surprise her. In fact, she felt calm, as if trying to puzzle out a message from God. Was it a warning of some kind? She'd worried the whole way home that she'd severed her relationship with Clyde, so maybe the destruction of her house was more of a symbol. She'd burned everything down.

She sat in her car watching until reality caught up with her, then it pushed into her body painfully, like blood coming back to a foot that had fallen asleep. She made a noise somewhere between a sob and a howl as she climbed out of the car.

The whole house wasn't engulfed, but it would be soon. Her hands shook as she dialed 911, and she hung up when she heard sirens in the distance. Someone had already called. She wasn't sure she could speak anyway.

She took a step toward her front porch, her nose itching from the smoke. The only tree in her yard caught fire, and leftover leaves from the fall ignited and floated into the sky. The oak wouldn't survive.

Essa threw off her coat and ran back to her car to grab the saline solution. She tore off her sweater and coated one sleeve as best she could with the liquid then wrapped it across her mouth. Her alarm turned into resolution as she threaded her way up the steps and unlocked the front door, cringing at the hot metal.

Black smoke billowed out, and her eyes began to sting. She couldn't see any flames though, and she darted inside as a police car pulled up. She prayed firetrucks would follow soon.

She ducked, trying to get under the smoke and crawled toward the end table with the trick back. She got it open on the third try and tucked the envelope of cash into her Bible then stuffed them both underneath her shirt. She began to feel light-headed and should have turned away, but she reached to grab her mother's quilt from the sofa. It wasn't there though, and she remembered pulling it into her bedroom the night before.

Essa paused, knowing she should leave it behind. A crash from outside made her wince, and she coughed again, a painful hacking down in her ribs. She started to crawl toward her bedroom when she noticed the hallway carpet. The flames seemed almost to cascade toward her, a river of fire.

She felt herself being lifted off the floor and pulled backward. She screamed in protest, but Lieutenant Barnes didn't let go. He hauled her body on to his shoulders and walked out of the burning house. She squirmed, but he held tight. Barnes tried to lay her gently on the grass, but her weight was too much for him, and she tumbled down, landing on her hip.

Barnes crouched in front of her as she pulled herself into a seated position and tried to catch her breath, removing the Bible and its hidden contents. Painful coughs racked her body, and her eyes burned from the smoke. She wiped at them, but her hands were as dirty as her face and only made the situation worse.

'Wait here,' Barnes said as if Essa had the energy to go anywhere.

She watched a firetruck arrive, men tumbling out and hooking up a hose. A few minutes later, water tried to fight the flames. They looked like spirits in a battle. She leaned on the ground, trying to spit out whatever she'd swallowed. After a while, she felt empty. What did she have left? A paramedic approached with Barnes, slipping an oxygen mask over her face. She barely registered the change.

'Your hair's kinda burned but not too bad,' Barnes said.

Essa saw his worried expression and knew she should feel grateful. Grateful that he'd saved her and that he didn't seem angry with her. She'd been reckless enough. Instead, she felt wistful. He had a respectable job, probably friends and family. Maybe even a dog. A normal life.

'I know it's important to you.'

Everybody thought she was devout instead of confused about how to live in the world. The Bible by her side didn't help. She touched her braid to find about six inches singed and warm to the touch. Barnes squeezed her shoulder and told her something about needing to talk later. Essa nodded but wasn't paying attention. She watched the roof of her house collapse. She'd never paid much attention to her roof beyond cleaning the gutters in November, a task she'd watched her father then her brother tackle. When it rained, she put out a pot under the living-room leak then didn't worry about the problem again until the next storm. Her roof existed, and now it didn't.

When Barnes approached his partner, they both turned to stare at her, and Essa thought she might giggle. She held in the hysteria, though, and watched the pair talk about her. But surely this would mean her brother was off the hook. He'd been at Juliet's with Wash, Harry, and possibly even some customers to vouch for him. She barely had time to be relieved when she remembered their argument. How he'd stormed out into the night. Could Clyde have set fire to New Hope and then their home? The old Clyde would never leave her homeless, but had the prospect of becoming a father made him snap? If they lived somewhere else or had been a different kind of people, they'd both be in therapy. Instead, they pretended everything was fine. That they could solve all their own problems with pots and pans. And knives.

Essa wasn't sure how long she'd been watching her house burn when she felt a hand on her shoulder. She looked to see Charlene Jones shaking her head.

'You all right, honey? Wait, don't answer that stupid question. They give you any water?'

Essa shook her head, and Charlene handed her a bottle. Essa removed the oxygen mask and took a sip.

'I was drivin' by and noticed you here. Not the only one, I'm afraid.'

Essa looked behind her to see a handful of spectators. Not as many as there had been for New Hope. Maybe a home wasn't as much of a story as a church. But there were people there all the same.

'Great,' Essa said.

'Ignore 'em,' Charlene said. 'And forgive me if I don't get down there with you. I might not get up again.'

Essa dusted off her skirt as best she could and stood beside Charlene.

'You got that young lieutenant all worked up.'

Barnes didn't look particularly worked up. He and Sergeant Sallis were talking to one of the firemen, and Essa noticed neither of the cops wore uniforms. They must have been off duty, though she imagined the Hope murders took all their time, on the clock or off. That's what the papers had been calling them. 'Hope Murders Have Vintera on Edge' and 'Police Follow Lead in Hope Murders'. Tacky headlines. Like two people being burned to death was some sort of euthanasia. But she understood that sensational tragedy sold papers. Subscribers were tired of reading about overdoses.

'You got someplace to go?' Charlene asked, and Essa nodded. She could always sleep in the parking lot at work, she figured.

'Maybe best you get on there. No sense waitin' around to watch your things go up in smoke.'

Charlene had the kind of voice that made drunks stay in line. Low and forceful. Her bar had been open for longer than Essa had been alive, and the sound of Charlene telling her what to do made her relax. It was laced with pity, but not enough to make Essa uncomfortable.

'I'm not sure if I'm allowed.'

'You go ask that pretty young thing and see what he says.'

On a different night, Essa might have enjoyed hearing the lieutenant described in such a dismissive way, but she only heard the instructions.

When she approached the police officers and fireman, Barnes broke away from the group. He had on jeans and a Philadelphia Phillies sweatshirt. When he tugged his sleeves down, he looked younger than her brother. His hair was flat on one side of his head, and his face dotted with black specks.

'I'm hoping I don't have to stay for all this.' Essa gestured around, noticing the angry red scratches on her bare arms. She'd feel the full force of everything tomorrow.

'You should probably go to the hospital.'

Essa was already shaking her head before he finished the sentence. 'I'm fine, thanks to you. I don't know what I was doing.'

'I need to talk to you, but it can wait.'

Essa thought about that. 'I'll be at work tomorrow.'

'All right. I guess I wouldn't take a day off either.'

The comment confused Essa. She'd never missed a day and didn't plan to start now.

She turned back toward her car, aware of the neighbors who'd gathered to watch. She didn't look at them, though, and said a silent prayer of thanks when her key turned in the ignition without any problems. Charlene waved at her then got into her own truck and drove away.

When Essa pulled into the lab parking lot, she was grateful for the lamppost. She noticed the familiar details. Stucco exterior in need of power washing. Dead weeds growing out of the sidewalk cracks.

She unlocked the front door, walking quickly to disable the alarm. When she began to wash her hair out in the bathroom sink, her eyes stung from the acrid smell, and she was alarmed by how much fell in clumps on to the porcelain. She used the hand soap as shampoo, and soon the tile under her feet turned wet. When she wrung out her locks over the floor drain, a few more clumps fell out, and her throat tightened. She pushed through the feeling though, cleaning up the mess she'd made.

First, she put all the hair into a hazard bag, then she began to wipe the water. She was on her hands and knees when something popped in another room. Essa paused, rationalizing the noise as the heat kicking on. She'd turned down the temperature before she'd left earlier, but it might be cold enough for the emergency system to activate.

She went back to wiping, but her hands shook. She carried the towels to the laundry room and grabbed the trash bag, typing in the security code and locking the door behind her. She'd parked in the front and didn't have to walk through the dark lot. She slid inside, knowing she could never sleep there, wondering how she'd ever sleep again.

TWENTY-SIX

Pulling up to a two-story brick home with white columns made Merritt check the address again. She hadn't been expecting a catalogue-ready neighborhood. The 'For Sale' sign out front looked new, the agent's photoshopped face as genuine as an ambulance chaser. The mailbox was shaped like a dachshund and had the correct house number: 567.

She stepped from the car, pulling her sweatshirt away from her body. It had become sticky during the ride with her heater cranked up, and she was glad to have worn jeans and sneakers. They made her look more approachable, and she needed Kimberly Granieri to trust her. She guessed the woman would be an ally. Maybe together they could take the bastard down. And after the cheerleading practice, she wanted the preacher's head on a platter. What was he doing sniffing around those teenagers?

When Merritt rang the doorbell, barking greeted her, and she peered through the glass to see three little dogs stampeding. They were followed by a woman in her early thirties who opened the door without checking to see who was on the other side. Too trusting.

'Can I help you?' the woman asked, smiling uncertainly then shushing her pets, who sat beside her, wagging their tails.

Merritt wasn't an animal person, but she had to admit these were an improvement over a coral snake any day.

'Adorable critters! And I hope so.' Merritt noted that they had the same blonde, shoulder-length hair and could have been sisters. Or at least clients at the same salon. 'I'm a reporter with WTGX-Roanoke, and I'm trying to gather some background information about your ex-husband Micah Granieri.'

The woman's smile faltered, and tears filled her eyes. Merritt had been expecting emotions but would have put her money on anger not heartache. She recalibrated, adjusting her features into ones of sympathy. Her colleagues sometimes called her a robot, but she didn't mind. Robots kept going long after their humans needed sleep or food. A little maintenance from time to time, and robots were poised to outlast even the most determined person. She'd learned her lesson from the tall tale of John Henry.

'I hate to bring up something so painful,' Merritt said in a quieter tone as the woman coughed and tried not to cry.

'Not ex. Plain old husband. Come on inside then. Watch your step. They do stay underfoot.'

Merritt processed that new information – no formal divorce – trying not to register her delight, and followed Kimberly down a well-lit hallway. She wasn't exaggerating about the dogs. They pranced around Merritt's ankles, excited by the prospect of company. Their tags jingled, and their nails clicked on the hardwood floors.

'Your home is lovely,' Merritt said and meant it. Once in the living room, she could see windows overlooking a park. 'I've never been to Charlotte before.'

'We moved to this neighborhood for the school district. Zach started kindergarten this fall.'

Kimberly's voice broke, and Merritt decided to fume on her behalf. Not only an abandoned wife, but an abandoned child? Mr Granieri deserved to crawl on his belly for the rest of his days. Maybe she could help speed the process.

'Again I hate to bring up something so painful, but when did he leave?'

'Four years ago. He came home one day and said he was unful-filled and unappreciated. His church here was popular but not growing how he wanted it to grow. Nobody watched his sermons online. He wanted to be like one of those preachers down in Texas. A household name. Invited on talk shows. He packed a bag and disappeared. I thought he would come back, you know? At least call to check on Zach, but nothing.'

'You didn't track him down?'

'Oh, I tracked him down. He runs some new church up in West Virginia now. I've even seen him on the news— Oh. That must be why you're here. Another story about the savior of whatever it's called county.'

'Not exactly.' Merritt saw a flicker of pique in Kimberly's eyes. She could work with that.

'I'm months behind on mortgage payments for this house Micah picked out. Savings emptied.'

Merritt nodded sympathetically. A divorce would mean alimony and child support. The preacher knew what he was doing.

Kimberly swallowed back her next remark. 'I'm sorry, I didn't offer you anything. And after that drive? You want some sweet tea or water?'

'Water sounds great, thanks.'

The woman disappeared into their kitchen, dogs trailing, and Merritt stood, walking over to the fireplace mantel with a row of photographs. She picked up one of the Granieris, Micah's hair cut short but face hard to miss. They'd made a beautiful family. She glanced around to see 'late notice' bills poking out from underneath a stack of magazines. She wanted a closer peek but didn't dare disturb anything.

Kimberly reappeared with two glasses and cookies on a tray like something out of a sitcom. She set the presentation down on the coffee table, coloring a little when she saw the bills in sight. Merritt pretended to be absorbed by a sailboat painting on the wall, and when she turned back, the bills had disappeared.

'This is going to sound ridiculous to a career woman like you, but all I ever wanted was Micah and a family. We met right out of college, and he mesmerized me. Not because of how he looked but how he acted, you know? Nobody ever made me feel more, I don't know, appreciated.'

Any brief glimpse of anger she'd shown had been replaced with nostalgia, and Merritt resisted the urge to gag. God help her if she ever let anyone treat her so badly and she thought of him as anything other than a son of a bitch.

'I understand,' Merritt said. She squinted her eyes a little to make the lines around them more prominent.

'We had trouble conceiving. Well, not conceiving, but I lost a few pregnancies along the way. Then Zach made it. Tough from the beginning.'

'Kindergarten? Must be fun.' Merritt did a quick calculation – Micah had left when his son was one.

'He's started to act out a little. No father around.'

'Why sell now? Why not when he left?'

Kimberly looked directly at Merritt, even straightening her posture a bit. 'I thought he would come back. I thought we were good together.'

'Mrs Granieri. Kimberly.' Merritt leaned forward to close the space between them. 'Would you consider letting me interview you?'

'I don't want to get him into any kind of trouble,' Kimberly said, and Merritt nodded even though she didn't understand.

'People deserve to hear your side of the story. That's all I'm interested in. Stories.'

It would be a scandal, the hidden wife of a beloved preacher. It would make for great television. If she stayed long enough, maybe Zach would get dropped off from school. Merritt petted the dog that had jumped on to the couch beside her. Its fur was soft and its expression adoring. Merritt scrunched her nose at the thing as if completely smitten, as if her career didn't depend on a languishing wife.

'Who's the cutest boy? Are you the cutest? Yes you are.' Merritt spoke pet owner.

'OK,' Kimberly said at last. 'Maybe if he sees how much I love him.'

Merritt didn't respond right away, continuing to pet the dog, glad she'd packed a handheld camera. The footage wouldn't be as good without P.J., but she couldn't handle a road trip with the kid. Three hours there and three hours back? No, this would be better anyway. More authentic. Kimberly Granieri would open up without a young man around, especially one who would be checking her out. Merritt's thoughts bounced in anticipation as she shuffled through questions she could ask for the most emotional response. This was a real get.

'Maybe,' she said, smiling. 'You might be right.'

TWENTY-SEVEN

Juliet laid out pants and tops on her red comforter, talking to herself about textures and coordination, lost in the task. Essa tried to object, saying she only needed to borrow a couple of things, but Juliet waved off her concerns.

'It's almost time for spring cleaning anyhow,' she said.

Without her wig and heavy makeup, Juliet could be a high-school English teacher fresh from college, eager to start her career and a family. It was as if Juliet had two different personalities, one for day and one for night. Her hair stuck up in places, and Essa guessed she normally didn't get up this early with her late-night clientele. Essa hated that she had nowhere else to go. Thankfully Clyde had gone to the auto shop after his boss decided to let him work off the books. The kitchen looked like the site of an all-night rager, but Juliet's bedroom was quiet and clean. Almost a retreat. She had plastic star stickers on her ceiling and an outdated poster of the solar system. Her bookshelves were filled with titles like *The Psychic Way Forward* and *Beginner's Reiki*. Essa admitted she might have been wrong about Juliet. It had been easy to dismiss her business as a racket. Her interest, at least, seemed sincere enough.

'Try these on. They'll look good on you.'

Essa obeyed, taking the jeans and soft, long-sleeved T-shirt into the bathroom. It smelled like roses, and warm air pushed through the floor vent. The trailer was light years ahead of the rectory in terms of creature comforts. Juliet had made the place a home. On any other day, Essa would have felt better, but it was all too much for her.

She took off her skirt and blouse, knowing they both were ruined. The hem was singed, and the smoke would never come out. She should have thrown away her underwear and bra as well, but she didn't have any others. She'd drive over to the river-side Walmart when she got a chance.

She pulled on the dark blue denim, rolling the cuffs. Juliet had a few inches on her, but the pants zipped. After slipping the T-shirt over her head, she looked in the mirror. It wasn't a total transformation, but the clothes fit better than her mother's ever had. She seemed to be wearing them rather than the other way around.

Juliet knocked on the door then opened it, brandishing a pair of scissors. Essa wasn't excited about the possibility of an amateur haircut, but she didn't want to spend money on a real one either.

'I can't do this standing up.' Juliet pushed down the toilet-seat lid and dropped on top of it. She rubbed her belly. 'The starfish's eager to get out, get things going.'

'Can't blame the little one,' Essa said, sitting on the linoleum in front of Juliet and unknotting her hair. A few more pieces fell off the ends, and Essa picked them up.

'You want to keep some of this mane as a souvenir?'

'A souvenir of what?'

'From when you were—' Juliet stopped talking, and Essa could sense her considering what to say. 'You know, I've never liked you much. You probably shouldn't let me cut your hair.'

'Vidal Sassoon was all booked and such.'

'Maybe you best put it back up,' Juliet said after a pause.

Essa obeyed, wrestling her long strands into a low ponytail. Juliet made a satisfied murmur behind her.

'You know, you got to forgive Clyde. He's all twisted up right now.'

Essa's cheeks grew hot. She was angry at her brother but didn't want to lose him either. Maybe in his shoes, she would have done the same, grasped at any straws available, even broken ones. She knew deep down what Pastor Micah asked was wrong and not only because of some Bible verses her father might have recited.

'He always thinks he knows best, but not about this.'

Essa guessed Clyde had filled in his girlfriend on Pastor Micah's proposition.

'I'm with you, girl. That preacher ain't a preacher. He's an asshole. But your brother? He acts like he knows everything, but he's scared. It was hard on you when your parents died, but it was hard on him too, you know?'

Essa did know and made a strangled noise in response. She'd ruminated on the issue a lot, how she would react to being eighteen and left in charge of raising a fifteen-year-old. Anger and gratitude warred inside of her, and Juliet nodded as if she knew.

'We should have a word for that, but we don't. Conflicted, I guess, though that sounds like trying to decide between ice-cream flavors. I'm not telling you what to do—'

'It sounds like you're telling me what to do.'

Juliet laughed, and it ended with a hiccup. 'You're right. I'm telling you what to do. That's my way, I guess. But you'll want to make things right with Clyde eventually. You know you will. Might as well start now before it's too late.'

Juliet tugged the elastic in Essa's hair until it landed a little past her shoulders. She held tight with one hand and snipped with the other, the scissors making a rustling noise like a squirrel rooting around a shrub. Essa's head snapped forward as the ponytail came off. She tried to feel lighter. She couldn't muster the energy for a lofty emotion like hope, but at least Juliet believed her. It was something.

TWENTY-EIGHT

With both the church and rectory gone, the shed stood like a symbol of resilience – or stubbornness. But Merritt had decided long ago that stubbornness was a virtue. It wasn't enough to be determined. You had to dig your heels into the dirt from time to time. She'd opted for boots and a dark coat that blended into the night. It was pre-dawn, and Merritt parked her car, switching off her headlights and waiting. It was unlikely anybody would be around at such an ungodly time of day. Still, Merritt waited, letting her eyes adjust. It was the hour of dog and wolf, when a friendly neighborhood mutt might be mistaken for a deadly predator – or the other way around. Merritt didn't plan to pet any animals, canine or otherwise.

When ready, she made her way to Tyson's Creek, reaching the trees and walking toward her target. It loomed ahead, the wooden frame silhouetted against the sky, darker than the night. For a moment, it felt like she walked toward a portal, that instead of touching planks of pine, her hand would disappear into another realm, followed by the rest of her body. Merritt didn't appreciate such thoughts and resented Thorngold County for making her superstitious. There was something about this place, this land, that felt otherworldly, citizens communing with the beyond. Merritt hurried, glad when she reached her destination and found it to be a regular old storage container. Her happiness soured when she saw the deadbolt was gone.

She pushed open the door and stood back in case something slithered out. Nothing stirred at all though, and Merritt shone her flashlight on to empty shelves. No terrariums, no snakes, not even any dust. It smelled of lemon and bleach. The place had been scrubbed clean, scrubbed of any evidence she'd hoped to find. Micah Granieri had known that she'd return. He was one step ahead of her.

Frustrated, she stomped back toward her car, careless now. What did it matter if somebody found her trespassing? There was nothing to steal. Nothing to steal and nothing to find.

Of course, it was probably wishful thinking on her part that anything would be left in the shed. But Otis had told her in no uncertain terms that the fire and murder investigation being carried out by the Thorngold County Police Department was cursory at best. He and his partner Sheila were the only ones remotely interested in alternate theories. And they weren't winning any favors around the water cooler. At least, that's what he'd told her.

No matter. Merritt had other plans for the day.

The sun peeked over the horizon as she headed out of town. She flipped the visor down and her sunglasses on, humming along to the radio. She lost cell phone reception about ten miles outside of Vintera, which made her quiet. Oh sure, she knew how to read a paper map, and she kept an atlas in her glove compartment. But she didn't like the idea of being so far away from civilization, given her present predicament. Granieri seemed to have it out for her. But she'd decided that she had it out for him too.

Merritt couldn't stop flirting with a theory that Granieri targeting Clyde Montgomery was a way to punish his girlfriend. Her meeting with Juliet Usher had been more opaque than enlightening, but she understood how the woman might make somebody like Granieri uneasy. Merritt's footage with Granieri's wife was moving, but her producer had been unimpressed. The New Hope fires were old news, '*domestic terrorism* or not'. But if she could prove the preacher started the fire himself? Now that was award-worthy. That was make-Merritt-Callahan-a-household-name-worthy.

The Alleghenies stretched out before her as she drove, snow covering the peaks. She'd driven back to Roanoke for a night, needing clean clothes. Since she'd forgone her usual on-air armor, nobody gave her a second look when she stopped by the Cavern Trail entrance. Sure enough, Clyde Montgomery's name was scrawled on 19 January. He had a looping signature like a third grader who'd only recently learned cursive. Not that schools still taught cursive. One quick photo, and Merritt climbed back in her car, humming again. The signature didn't prove anything, but it was a loose end. Viewers liked loose ends, anything they could pull apart like coyotes on a fresh kill.

A car behind her honked, and Merritt waved before putting her car into gear. With a little luck, she wouldn't get murdered by a country bumpkin with a shotgun and road rage.

She felt a thrill of excitement as she drove toward the caverns where Dr Wick Kester, head of the Vintera Wildlife Investigation Laboratory, conducted fieldwork for an occult-related case. Otis had heard whispers about the project around the precinct but hadn't paid the rumors much attention. They'd seemed more like ghost stories than a worthwhile pursuit to him. Strange wooden structures in the woods. Butcher blood symbols drawn on overpasses. Teenagers acting out, Otis figured. He'd gotten into some trouble himself, though it involved cheap whiskey and fast cars. Nothing that would make his grandmother roll over in her grave, he'd told her. Merritt could hear his voice in her head, and she admitted it sounded nice. A touch of gravel in it at odds with his boyish appearance.

She passed a Citgo station opening for the day then searched for the road that would take her to the rock faces. A billboard advertised the publicly available caves and their accompanying camp, but the private road would take her closer to the lab's work-site. Finally, the 'No Trespassing' sign came into view, and she jerked toward it, noticing the fresh tire tracks. Five minutes later, a van came into view, and she pulled alongside, surprised by the high-tech equipment set up at the bottom of a cliff. Then again, Dr Kester was considered one of the best in his field. The department had to lure him to Thorngold County somehow.

The man himself was easy enough to recognize, his white hair blowing in the wind. He sported an enormous headset and didn't hear Merritt approach, but an ancient dog wagged his tail and struggled to his feet. The reporter didn't mind being unnoticed by Dr Kester. It gave her a chance to observe, though she wasn't sure what she observed. The man held some sort of giant remote control in his hand and stared at a bundle of ropes and pulleys that swayed slightly. Merritt followed his gaze, seeing a man's face appear out of a crag that looked too small for a human. It was hard to tell from such a distance though. The opening must have been a good hundred feet in the air.

The man shouted something, and Dr Kester took off his headset.

'He's trying to warn you,' Merritt said, making the doctor turn.

'Oh, I heard you. Welcome to my office. Careful now. Sander could take your head off in the right mood.'

Sander lumbered forward, his paws covered in mud but his shaggy white coat otherwise clean. Merritt suspected the giant was an indoor pet, though he looked like the kind farmers kept around to guard their livestock. A 150-pound beast.

'He does seem fierce.'

Sander gave her a few sniffs then collapsed again at his owner's feet. Dr Kester reached to scratch his ears, mumbling endearments before straightening and locking a neutral, professional expression back into place.

Up close, Merritt could see the deep wrinkles on the man's forehead and the loose jowls. Well past retirement age. But he seemed content enough in the middle of nowhere on a frigid cold morning.

'My name's Merritt Callahan, and I'm investigating the New Hope fire and wanted to ask you a few questions.'

'Oh, I know who you are, Ms Callahan. I saw your report on methadone and buprenorphine. Important work.'

'That was ages ago.'

'False modesty doesn't suit you, my dear.'

Merritt grinned. He was right. 'What can you tell me about the Mercury Order?'

'They have a name now? Progress, progress.' The doctor chuckled, waving at his colleague, who disappeared back into the cliff face.

'I'm not ruling anything out. A church burned to the ground? This could be a hate crime.' Merritt had mixed feelings about calling the crime 'domestic terrorism' now. It had gotten her story the attention she wanted, but donations continued to pour into New Hope and – Merritt suspected – right into Granieri's pocket.

'Could be, but I'll be frank with you. The police department's been on me about this supposed occult case for months now. So far, I see no evidence of tampering. I don't think anybody's catching bats, for nefarious purposes or for kicks.'

'What have you found out?'

'I'll send the public report over. You needn't have come all this way.'

'Oh, I like the fresh air.'

Dr Kester gave her a once-over, scanning Merritt as if she were a lab result. He wasn't uncomfortable with humans, but Merritt got the sense the doctor preferred four-legged creatures.

'Dead bats, that's what I've found. Dropping from the sky like some sort of omen, riling everybody up.'

Merritt remembered seeing a tabloid headline while waiting to check out at the grocery store. Something about 'End Times'. The usual. She even knew the writer. An opportunist kook who'd successfully pitched a show to the Discovery Channel.

'Does seem odd, birds falling from the heavens,' Merritt said.

'Not birds and not heavens. Mammals tumbling from trees because they're disoriented about the seasons. Twenty years ago? They'd be hibernating mid-September to mid-March. Now? With summer sometimes lasting through October? Anybody's guess.'

'Feels cold enough to me.'

Dr Kester pushed his glasses up his nose for an even better look at Merritt, and Merritt knew what he saw. With her hair pulled back and no makeup, she resembled a schoolgirl and that came in handy sometimes. You'd be surprised what people told you if they thought you wouldn't understand. But if Dr Kester thought Merritt needed a lecture on weather versus climate, he resisted the urge. Not a man to be baited.

'That it does,' Dr Kester said after a pause. 'That it does. You want to take a turn? I'm about to go up myself.'

Merritt looked at the cliff, not keen on trusting her life to somebody she'd just met.

'What will I see at the top?'

'Hopefully a bunch of sleeping bats and my assistant photographing them. Capturing a few for bloodwork. We'll compare the live ones to the others.'

'What do you do with them when you're done?'

Dr Kester looked like he might roll his eyes but resisted.

'We put them back how we found them.' Dr Kester cupped his hands over his mouth and made a cawing noise, halfway between a crow and a bullfrog. After a moment, the man at the top waved, turned his back to them and began his descent. He braced his legs against the top then pushed off, extending at least two feet into the air before his feet touched the surface again. Heights didn't bother Merritt, but the movement seemed reckless rather than precise. Whoever he was, the man enjoyed the thrill of being airborne.

'He's as smart as they come, though a pain in my ass sometimes. Too smart for his own good,' Dr Kester said as the climber touched the ground and unhooked his belt from the lime-green support ropes.

He unclipped his helmet and tucked it under his arm before approaching. He handed Dr Kester a sheet of handwritten notes then spoke directly to Merritt. 'You here about the witches?'

'See,' Dr Kester said. 'As smart as they come.'

Karl introduced himself and seemed willing enough to talk, though he kept glancing back at the rocks, making Merritt consider if there was something there she should see. Or maybe Karl was anxious to be back in the air.

'This town loves a horror story. The bloodier the better,' Karl said.

Merritt couldn't help noticing the resemblance between assistant and boss. Both athletic and windblown, one in his prime, the other in decline.

'Any truth to it?'

'Nobody's got hurt, as far as I know. A little vandalism. A few bonfires and screaming into the night.'

Dr Kester wandered off as they were talking, testing the support ropes then sliding into a harness himself. Merritt was a bit alarmed the old man intended to climb, but she tried to focus on Karl.

'The concern is always a turn for the worse.'

'What do you mean?' Merritt asked.

'Escalation. Kids getting bored with their spray paint.'

Karl followed Merritt's gaze to Dr Kester, who tested the rope again and double-checked his carabiner.

'You try to talk him out of it.' Karl excused himself and walked back the way he'd come. Sander lumbered to his feet and followed the men, his whine of concern piercing the air when the old man found a handhold and his feet left the earth. Merritt watched too, as he got smaller and smaller. From a distance, he could have been any age. Another Jack climbing a beanstalk in search of a little magic.

TWENTY-NINE

C harlene's parking lot filled up most nights, but it seemed busier than usual as Essa found a space. She crossed her fingers nobody would check her ID at the door, and she was too preoccupied with that worry to notice the protestors at first. But they were hard to miss. About a dozen or so people stood near the entrance with homemade signs, proclaiming drinkers went to hell and alcohol killed babies. Nothing creative. Words scrawled with black magic markers. A beer bottle with an X over it. They were chilling though, and Essa ducked her head as she moved past them.

'God watches you,' a man shouted at her, and Essa couldn't help but glance in his direction. She was relieved not to recognize him, but she knew the earnest expression. The man believed harassing people served some sort of higher purpose.

As if sensing her pity for him, the man moved closer, thrusting a yellow, photocopied flyer into her hands. *Support Resolution 9,* it read. *Make Thorngold Dry.*

The bouncer rushed Essa inside, not bothering to ask for her driver's license. He was more concerned with keeping the protestors from bothering customers, though it was a futile attempt, even for such an imposing figure. The man had a shaved head but a giant mustache. His arms were like two tree trunks, and Essa was surprised they grew men that large around here. All her brothers' friends were skinny as wet laundry. The preacher was the biggest man she knew, and this bouncer could split him in two. Essa liked the thought of that and even smiled a little as she walked inside. As expected, a few folks turned to stare at her – so out of place – but she ignored them and made her way to the bar.

She'd never been inside and didn't like the smell of stale beer. Her eyes watered from the cigarettes, but she resisted the urge to wave a hand in front of her face. She was practiced at not drawing attention to herself if she could help it. She smelled a little like formaldehyde after being at the lab all day, but nobody would notice that at least.

Dr Kester had complimented Essa on her new look, assuming she'd taken his advice on appearance to heart. He promised to make some calls for her, especially since her need to move was more urgent than ever. Essa didn't exactly know what 'make some calls' meant, but she appreciated the gesture. She'd dreaded telling him their snake notes had probably been lost in her house fire, but he'd barely reacted, saying they weren't needed anyway. Essa would check to see if the file had survived, but it seemed unlikely. She'd try to type a report from memory.

Once she found an empty stool, Charlene waved at her and walked over. 'Hiya, sweetheart. What can I get for you?'

'Can I get a Coke, please?'

'You bet.'

Essa felt relieved Charlene didn't pressure her to drink. She wasn't sure of the etiquette. She was unnerved when the man beside her snickered.

'Put that on my tab.' The man scooted closer to Essa, who turned away from his bloodshot eyes and stale breath.

'Not a chance, Pratt. In fact, you best be gettin' on home.'

'Aw, Charlene, love of my life. Can't treat a man like that.'

He mimed a knife through his heart, but Charlene was already swiping his credit card.

'Sammie, you mind getting my girl here a Coke? And some potato skins. Everything on the house.'

The bartender slung a towel over his shoulder, called the order into the kitchen then poured Essa's drink. He sat it down in front of her with a wink, and Essa thanked him. She knew him from high school but didn't expect him to remember. He'd been a couple years above her and played on the football team; drove an old red Mustang he'd restored himself. Nice enough, but oblivious like all the popular kids.

Pratt signed his tab and stumbled toward the door, seeming to forget all about Essa.

'Christ, Pratt! You better call a ride or you're not welcome back in here,' Charlene yelled.

The man shrugged and continued toward the exit.

'I need that like I need a hole in the head.'

Charlene came back over to Essa and leaned down, so it was easier to hear.

'I stopped by to thank you,' Essa said. That was partly true at least. She was also avoiding her brother. If she stayed out long enough, maybe Clyde would be in bed, and she wouldn't have to see him. She'd mulled over Juliet's advice about forgiving Clyde and decided she would. She really would. It didn't have to be tonight though.

'For what? Not letting you freeze to death.'

It had only been a few days since Charlene had found her on the side of the road, but Essa had all but forgotten about that. She'd meant Charlene's help while the rectory burned. How could she nearly freeze and burn to death in less than a week?

'Yeah, thanks.'

'You'll get used to the stàres.'

'Oh, I'm used to it. Whispers too. Poor little serpent orphan.'

Saying the words aloud made Essa feel sick, but she wasn't revealing anything Charlene didn't already know. She looked at her Coke all the same, unwrapping the straw.

'Oh, they're not looking 'cause they feel sorry for you.'

Charlene laughed and turned back to a customer who needed his Michelob refilled. The other bartender slid the potato skins in front of her. They smelled greasy and unappetizing, but as soon as she took a bite, Essa realized how hungry she was. She hadn't brought her lunch today, not wanting to use any of Juliet's groceries, so she'd had some peanut butter crackers from the vending machine. She ate two of the skins before even bothering to wipe her fingers.

'Good girl,' Charlene said. 'I can get you another order, if you want.'

Essa started to shake her head in response when the ghost of Sara Beth Booth squeezed past the bouncer and into the bar. Essa's sharp intake of breath caught Charlene's attention, and they both stared at the apparition, the girl clad in tight-fitting jeans and a black halter top. She wore makeup so heavy that her eyelashes looked like spiders, and for a moment Essa thought she'd risen from the dead.

'Oh, Amy June. What are you doing, child?' Charlene whispered to herself.

Charlene lifted part of the bar and walked toward the newcomer. Slowly Essa realized it was the victim's sister, a spitting image. Still, her heart beat erratically, and she watched to be sure the teenager was flesh and blood. A lull in the music made it possible for Essa to eavesdrop, and Charlene told the girl she had to go home, no ifs, ands or buts. Amy June looked on the verge of tears as she turned toward the exit, embarrassed to have been caught trying to drink underage. For a moment, Essa felt guilty, but she wasn't drinking, was she? When she returned, Charlene looked as sad as the high schooler.

'I'm a hypocrite with a capital H, I'll tell you that much. And if any fifteen-year-old deserves a beer it's that one. But with the damn protests, what am I gonna do?'

'What're they riled up about anyway?'

'It's not the first time my livelihood's been on the ballot. But it's the first time that nonsense has a chance of passing. Do they really believe people gonna stop drinking because the only bar this side of town's closed? No, they'll get themselves shit-faced at home. Or spend their paychecks in another county.'

'Why's it got a chance this time?'

'That hotshot new preacher deciding he can rule the world with a set of veneers. My teeth bite just fine. And they're real.'

The potato skins turned heavy in her stomach, and Essa put down the one in front of her mouth. Maybe she'd underestimated Pastor Micah's influence. Everyone else in town seemed to cast him as some kind of puppet master. But she'd made up her mind. It had never been an option for her, if she was being honest. She'd tried to imagine what it might be like, his hands on her neck and breasts and legs, but even in her imagination, she couldn't stomach the thought. Essa had no big dreams about losing her virginity – no rose petals and candles or anything – but she'd avoid being forced if she could.

'He made me an offer,' Essa said. Talking to Juliet had loosened something inside her. She felt bolder, that she shouldn't be ashamed to talk about it.

'A deal with the devil, whatever it is.'

Essa tried her best to explain what had happened with Pastor Micah. 'He didn't say the words though. That Clyde would be fine if I—'

'Screw him? Screw him. He didn't have to. This is how they get you, kid. Make you doubt yourself. Make you think you asked for it. Take it from me. I'm sixty years old, and men think they can get one over on me. I know you've been looking out for yourself a while now, so maybe you don't need this advice, but I'm givin' it anyway. You're number one, and don't forget it. Don't mean you have to be a jerk, but take care of yourself first, you hear me?'

'Yes, ma'am.'

'Yes, ma'am. You hear yourself? You're gonna get eaten alive.'

The words were harsh, but Charlene reached over and ruffled Essa's hair. 'It looks good, by the way. Suits you.'

'It's uneven.'

'It's original.'

Charlene walked away, and Essa dug in her purse for some dollars to leave as a tip. The bartender appeared in front of her, waving his hands.

'Charlene says on the house, she means on the house. Lest you trying to get me in trouble.'

He winked again, and Essa thanked him too. She'd spoken to more people in the past few days than she usually spoke to in a month. Juliet and Charlene both supporting her decision made her feel stronger. Maybe she wasn't being selfish after all.

She held her head a little higher as she walked toward the protesters. She took the flyer from her purse and handed it back to the man who'd yelled at her earlier. He tried not to take it, but she insisted.

'I'd hate for you to waste your time is all,' she said.

When Essa turned to her car, she noticed Amy June getting into a ride. The resemblance to her sister was uncanny. The headlights made it impossible to see who was driving the teenager home, and Essa felt a shiver up her spine, imagining all the ways girls get hurt. But she shook that thought away, glad somebody had picked Amy June up. Something about seeing the teenager turned away while she nursed a soda had cemented something Essa should have already realized. Essa wasn't a kid anymore, and she could stop behaving like one anytime now.

THIRTY

The signs made him flinch. Crude lettering and banal messages: *The Bible Beats Booze* and *Jesus Loves You, Hates the Drinks*. Alcohol, per se, wasn't the problem. Not opiates either. Not even weakness, though Lord knows, the county had its fair share of lily-livered drunks. No, the problem was lack of faith. Not having anything to believe in. And that kind of void? A person tries to fill it with something. Like pouring thimbles of water into the Grand Canyon. One glass, one pill at a time. And the void laps it up, asks for more.

Politics had never interested Micah much, but when a judge approached him about supporting the bill, he'd thought another ally on the bench might prove useful. And frankly, it had been easy enough to slip into a sermon, the sins of the bottle. The protestors didn't even know he'd planted the seed. They thought they'd spun up the mission on their own. Now look at them, parading around the only bar creek-side with placards and raised voices.

Mrs Kenner and her husband (gluttony and sloth, respectively), who did as she said most of the time. The two Thompson girls (both vanity) about to graduate from high school and start working full-time on the chicken line. Beverly Blake, the instigator he figured. Envy dripped from her mouth like blood after a kill. He could see it if he closed his eyes. But Micah had parked outside Charlene's for another reason entirely. His whole body burned to know what Essa Montgomery thought she was doing inside. She should know better.

He flipped through different scenarios, trying and failing to slot the girl into a category. Somewhere deep inside he believed if he could make sense of her, he'd control the beast she created inside him. Instead, she lured him out, baited and entrapped him. Essa had come to him, hadn't she? He'd left her alone all those years. This unholy feeling was none his fault. The girl had made him lose his faith. And he'd take it back.

Beverly knocking on his window didn't surprise him, though he hadn't been looking in that direction. He inspected her through the glass before acknowledging her presence. Mid-sixties and retired from teaching middle school. Her wrinkled face matched the pink peacoat buttoned to her chin. She'd pulled her dyed hair into a bun at the top of her head, and it looked like a wayward dinner roll. She knocked again, and Micah responded, rolling down the window and forcing a smile. The act came easily to him now.

'Praise be,' Beverly said. 'We was about to lose hope. You wouldn't believe the nastiness coming in and out of this place.'

Micah hadn't noticed anyone speaking to the group. Most ducked their heads, a little ashamed, and rushed inside. He'd noticed the teenager come and go. He glanced at the bouncer who stared at his car. No doubt his license plate number had been recorded, but it didn't matter. He was untouchable.

'These are lost sheep, sure enough,' Micah said, slipping into his show accent. 'And it's our job to find them.'

Beverly puffed up, pleased to see herself as a shepherdess. 'And that's the truth.'

'Who better than you to guide them? A woman who's dedicated her life to education.'

'That's right.' She licked her lips.

Micah pictured blood on them, which made him smile wider in genuine pleasure this time. They were sinners, the lot of them, but they were trying. He'd awakened something in this town, and far be it for him to coax that something back to sleep.

'Best not keep you, Miss Blake, from your calling.'

The woman nodded forcefully, dinner roll bobbing. 'Blessings to you, Pastor.'

Beverly walked back to the small group, and they crowded around her, waiting to hear the good word. He knew she exaggerated his message, but no matter. Charlene's was an eyesore – a clapboard building with dust-coated windows and a gravel parking lot. The air smelled stale, sad even. The town would do well to be rid of it.

His car engine hummed to life, the sound almost imperceptible, and he looked for Essa's Honda Civic, watching the exhaust leave trails in the cold. He pulled his car around, waiting until it didn't seem suspicious to follow her into the night.

THIRTY-ONE

Essa couldn't decide if she felt more like an astronaut or an archaeologist as she sifted through the remains of her home. At first, the sight disturbed her – the collapsed roof and charred furniture – but as the sky lightened, she found a rhythm, methodically filling a cardboard box with whatever could be salvaged. It wasn't much. A few plates, a photograph spared by its glass frame. As suspected, nothing remained of her mother's quilt or the dissection notes she'd hoped to find. Perhaps the whole operation should have made her nostalgic, but she was more fearful than anything, glancing in the direction of the New Hope tent every few minutes to make sure nobody watched her.

Only the sight of the burned oak tree choked her up. It had witnessed the Civil War, and Essa had counted on it to outlive her. She remembered one time when she'd climbed too high, trying to follow Clyde, and her father had shimmied after her. He'd made her get down by herself, but he'd kept a hand on her back or arm, ready if she should slip. She'd been angry with her father for so long that it bewildered her when the memories softened. Which version was true? Maybe both. The same could be said for her brother and her dual longing to be furious with him and to forgive him.

Giving up on what used to be the living room, Essa walked toward the oak, welcoming the rays of sun that rose over the creek. She'd come early to avoid the preacher, but she liked the quiet too. She could mourn if she needed to mourn.

As she drew closer to the tree, she noticed markings on the ground. At first, they seemed random, but soon shapes presented themselves. A seven-sided star with crudely drawn moons on four points. Essa looked around as if whoever had made them might be around. When she was sure she was alone, she crouched, reaching out for a corner and trying to smudge the star open so it didn't look as evil. She shivered, not knowing what the symbol meant but betting it wasn't something good.

The sound of tires on her gravel driveway made her whip around.

It was a patrol car, but Essa figured she had a right to be there despite the police tape. She shielded her eyes against the headlights and waited. She wasn't surprised to see Lieutenant Barnes and Sergeant Sallis emerge, talking to each other. They seemed to agree on something, and Sergeant Sallis hung back as Lieutenant Barnes approached.

'I'd say I'm sorry, but I bet you've had enough of that.'

'And I should thank you.' Essa knew she might have died if he hadn't pulled her out of the fire. It made her more embarrassed than grateful though. She was glad when Lieutenant Barnes didn't respond and instead came to stand beside her, whistling at the sight of the star cut into the ground.

'Now what do you make of that,' he asked in a low voice.

She watched him take out his phone and snap a few photos. Sergeant Sallis walked around the perimeter of the property, looking for something. Footprints maybe, but everything was frozen. Her own shoes hadn't left any tracks. It would have taken some effort to carve anything into the ground. Whoever left the marks must have been determined. Essa pulled the hood of her parka over her head but didn't feel any warmer.

'Could we talk here, do you reckon?' she asked, realizing the two officers probably needed a statement of some sort from her, and she didn't want to be late for work.

'If that's all right with you, that's fine by us.' Lieutenant Barnes exchanged a glance with Sergeant Sallis as she returned from her search, which made Essa wonder why they hadn't called her to the station. 'I hate to ask, but can we see what you removed?'

Essa bristled at the invasion of privacy, but if somebody had burned her house down on purpose, she needed to cooperate. It wouldn't look good for Clyde if she tampered with evidence. She handed the box over to Barnes and turned away, so she didn't have to see him paw through her only possessions. Instead, she kept her eyes on the New Hope tent, wary of any movement, even the wind.

'You lost anything valuable? I mean, of course, you lost things that matter to you, and I'm sorry about that. But anything worth stealing? Sometimes fires are used to cover up a theft.'

Essa shook her head without thinking. Her mother had been buried with her wedding band and gold cross necklace.

'I see.' Lieutenant Barnes examined a Harper's Ferry magnet

then dropped it back into the box. 'You did the autopsies on the copperheads, right?'

It wasn't a question Essa had expected. She didn't correct him that autopsies were for humans and necropsies for animals. What did it matter? Either way, you were cutting up something that used to breathe and think.

'Yes. Well, they wasn't all copperheads, but I know what you mean. A copperhead, a cottonmouth and two rattlers. Timber.'

'All native?'

'Not the cottonmouth, but their range stretches into Virginia a ways. Pretty easy to get in warmer months.'

'Where you think Granieri got the snakes?'

Essa was so used to Pastor Micah being referenced with his title that it took her a minute to understand he meant the preacher. Essa crossed her arms, and Lieutenant Barnes stood, noticing her reaction. His eyes were sharp as a hawk's, which made Essa tense in response.

'You know, I've thought that over, and I can't rightly say. It's a stretch, him standin' in mud, settin' traps and such. Some of the animals we get at the lab are black market. Usually folks want exotics. Cobras, mambas. But there's a buyer for everything.'

'You want me to put this in your car for you? We don't need any of it.' Lieutenant Barnes balanced the box on his hip.

Essa shook her head, and the lieutenant glanced at his partner again – she'd ducked under the police tape and was poking around the front porch.

'I hate to ask about something so personal, but where did your father get his?'

Essa wasn't sure what he meant at first then realized Lieutenant Barnes was still interested in the snakes. Why he wanted to know about the serpents of New Hope was beyond her. With anyone else, she'd assume morbid curiosity, but she sensed the lieutenant was after something else.

'Daddy was good with animals. Dogs and cats flocked to him like he was Francis of Assisi. He'd catch 'em. Go out with his bare hands singing some Merle Haggard song and, well, sort of scoop them up. He'd preach about how they were fallen angels, but he sort of liked them too? He treated them like pets, though he'd be the first to tell you they had about as much loyalty as a can opener.'

To be honest, she was surprised that her father had been bitten, not because she'd believed God would protect him, but because the snakes seemed to like him, they really did. Chickens, horses, guinea pigs. They all liked him. He never abused them like some of the other so-called 'signs-following' religious types.

'Your house title was in your brother's name,' Barnes said, interrupting her thoughts.

'I'm sorry?'

The shift in topic caught Essa off guard, and she reached out for the box for something to do. Barnes handed it over, and she held it to her stomach, looking at the photograph on top. Her dad, mom, brother and herself dressed up for Easter. After, they would have walked across their yard to the church. It had seemed so normal at the time in the way kids believe their realities are everyone's realities. And the truth rarely bursts into that illusion. It sneaks. It cracks a corner then seeps into the rest. When had Essa realized they weren't normal? Middle school, when a few girls had teased her. But more so after the deaths, when nobody teased her. Not even a taunt about her clothes. All the other students were unwaveringly polite, as if they'd been threatened within an inch of their lives to be nice.

'Clyde will get the insurance money, not you.'

'I'm sorry,' Essa said again, pulling her attention away from the memories. 'What's that about money?'

'Amalgamated Insurance. Monthly bills sent to the address of Juliet Usher.'

Barnes reached into his back pocket and removed a photocopy of the latest statement for $35. Her brother worked at a service station, fixing busted transmissions and changing oil. He did all right, but would he shell out over four hundred a year? For a place he no longer lived? Maybe he'd been looking out for her, she told herself. Or maybe he was hedging his bets in case things didn't work out with his girlfriend. She stared at the paper, trying to convince herself of some benign reason, make it mean anything but the obvious. That her brother had more than opportunity – he had a motive too.

THIRTY-TWO

The landscape matched her mood as it whipped by her window, icy and desolate. Essa liked seeing mountains in the distance, a bit like sentinels guarding their town, but once you found yourself in them, they became menacing, allies turned to enemies in a flash. The tree branches looked like they could snatch you right out of your car, steal you away like fairies coming after children. *Fairies and trees coming to life.* Essa tried to shake herself out of such foolishness. She didn't believe in fairy tales or witchcraft. The symbol by her oak tree worried her but not as much as the insurance money.

Finding Clyde seemed important, important enough to skip work for the morning. When she'd dialed his number, it had gone to voicemail, and Juliet had told her he'd gone hiking again. He rarely deviated from his favorite route, so Essa knew where to go.

The drive did little to calm her nerves. The water that usually trickled down the rock faces on either side of the highway had frozen into solid sheets, clinging to every nook and cranny. Truckers shifted to their lowest gears, making it necessary for Essa to pass, far too close to the edge for her comfort. She kept going though, crossing her fingers she'd have luck at the Cavern Trail. She hadn't been out there in years but remembered the way.

The parking lot wasn't full, but there were a few cars and even a family eating takeout on the bed of their pickup, bundled against the cold. She didn't see her brother's truck, but she got out anyway. He sometimes used one of the vehicles at his shop if his truck needed maintenance. The wind chilled her face, and she pulled back her hair to braid before remembering the shorter length. She tucked the strands underneath a black toboggan hat with gold sparkles that she'd borrowed from Juliet and headed toward the trailhead. When she got close, she tried calling again, but her cell phone didn't get any bars. She figured the same was true for Clyde and took a few steps on to the paved surface.

This part of the journey she could handle even if the concrete buckled from roots in a few places. There were no casual visitors, but a few athletic-looking figures zoomed past from time to time. Essa paused to enjoy the overlook when she arrived. Even in winter, the view was impressive, rows of blue hills spread out before her. Morning fog lingered, like a sleep spell had been cast over the state. She felt light-headed for a moment and took a deep breath before turning away. A lot of daytime hikers turned back when they got here, but she knew her brother would push forward, especially if trying to clear his head.

Three wooden signs announced the choices, including the mileage. She wished Clyde favored the route that was a 0.7-mile round trip, but she knew if he was nearby, Glenn Falls would be his destination. She decided to walk a half hour then turn back if she hadn't passed him returning.

Essa wasn't a hiker. She'd never been much of an athlete, dreading PE classes and getting picked last for dodgeball. Sometimes the teacher would take pity on her and let her 'manage', which meant keeping score and calling fouls. Essa never called any fouls, too timid around the other kids, but she didn't mind the tallies. The air burned in her lungs, but she had to admit it felt better to be outside rather than cooped up inside. Maybe Karl was right after all. She dreaded going into the lab where she'd have to ask her co-worker for his dissection notes since hers had been destroyed. He would give them to her of course, but the condescension on his face would make her feel worse than she already did. Dr Kester was doing so much to help her, and she'd let him down.

After about twenty minutes, she came to another small clearing and decided to take a break. Her legs and feet felt fine – she was used to being on them all day. But her heartbeat needed attention. She sat on a fallen tree trunk and took in her surroundings, surprised to see this view boasted caves and cliffs rather than mountains. She'd never gone this far down the path before, but knew once you got to the waterfall, you could climb to the cliffs. She squinted, thinking she might see a couple of people at the top but too far away to know for sure.

Pushing herself back up, she wandered off the path, ignoring the brambles that slapped against her jeans. There wasn't an official path, but she wasn't the first to venture that way either, based on the well-trodden grass and broken twigs.

Essa glanced behind her to make sure she knew the way back, wary of getting lost without any cell reception. But the way seemed clear enough, and she moved forward, holding a hand over her eyes for a better view. The cliffs disappeared for a few minutes, but when they came into view, she was even closer than she'd expected. She glanced at the top, disappointed to see it was empty. She'd have to turn back, and in the meantime, Clyde could have already returned to the parking lot.

Feeling defeated, Essa wondered if she would be better off following the gravel road up ahead to the highway, but she'd have to circle back for her car. Resigned, she took one last look at the cliff face before turning to go. A flutter of blue at the base caught her attention, and she peered toward the sight, thinking at first it might be a tent, but it was too flat on the ground.

Essa took a few steps back toward the brambles before curiosity got the better of her, and she walked toward the rocks. She thought somebody might have left a tarp behind, but when she saw boots, she ran toward the body.

Sleeping, she thought. *He could be sleeping.* Even as she tried to quell her panic, she knew the man wasn't sleeping. He was face down, blood pooling around his head, his right leg twisted at an unnatural angle. Essa skidded to a stop, the tip of her shoes already red. There was lots of blood, and Essa kneeled to check for a pulse because it seemed like the right thing to do, not because she believed he might be alive. *Please, God. Please don't let it be Clyde.*

Essa knew she should leave the body alone, but she pulled on an arm anyway, heaving the torso toward her, so she could see the face. The man's weight collapsed on her, and her knees slammed into the ground, then the body slid away from her. He was unrecognizable, his skull cratered from what she could only assume was a fall. But he was her brother's size, and she lay beside him on the ground, not caring about the mess, not caring about anything, convinced she'd lost her only family.

THIRTY-THREE

Essa stared at herself in the rearview mirror. She looked simultaneously like a deer and as if she'd killed one, her hands red from blood, her face stricken. A paramedic had given Essa a towel, but she'd folded it instead of using it and smoothed the edges again and again. The police officers had encouraged Essa to wait in her car out of the elements.

When Essa had stumbled on to the highway, a driver had almost hit her, but then, like a good Samaritan, called 911. He'd even waited with her. Essa could see the man now, standing on the shoulder, his hands stuffed into a camouflage sweatshirt too thin for the weather.

'Miss Montgomery, is there anyone we can call for you?'

Essa jumped, forgetting her window was rolled down. Then she laughed, a throaty sound that made Lieutenant Barnes turn away for a moment, mumbling 'shit' under his breath. Cracked. She'd cracked, but could they blame her?

'I could have saved him,' Essa said, and Lieutenant Barnes didn't respond right away, waiting to see if she would continue. 'You might as well lock me up.'

'Nobody's locking anybody up, Miss Montgomery. You want to tell me what you saw?'

'Barnes.' Essa focused. 'You're Lieutenant Barnes.'

When she laughed again, the officer stepped away, cell phone to his ear. At least somebody got reception out here. Sergeant Sallis hovered nearby, clearing her throat from time to time but never speaking. Both cops needed to work on their bedside manner.

'I really think that's a bad idea, sir,' Lieutenant Barnes said loud enough to be heard. Sergeant Sallis stepped in front of Essa to block her view, but she could still hear the lieutenant's angry voice. 'I'm not going to— Hello?'

Sergeant Sallis moved away, and Essa watched their whispering, not particularly caring about their conversation but not wanting to stare at herself in the mirror anymore either. It didn't matter. Nothing mattered. She hoped they would arrest her. Maybe she would tell them she'd pushed her brother over the cliff, mad about the insurance money. But no, Essa Montgomery had never been a liar, and she wouldn't start now.

Lieutenant Barnes walked back to the car and opened the door. Essa tried to climb out, but something held her back. Confused, she saw somebody had buckled the seatbelt. She must have buckled the seatbelt.

'Come with me, please.'

So this was it, she thought. She didn't even have to make a false confession. They would cuff her and book her, and she could die from heartache in a prison cell. But Lieutenant Barnes didn't touch her, instead heading down the gravel road, beckoning Essa to follow. She thought again about power. About how little she had and took a hesitating step after the officer. She took another and another until they were walking together, back toward her brother's body.

All the access roads in the area looked the same, in need of a few dump trucks full of gravel, potholes the size of wheelbarrows. The scenery around this one was nice. Mountains on the left and rock cliffs rising ahead. Essa didn't see any of it. She might as well have been walking through a snowstorm. For fifteen minutes, she followed the path she must have taken before but didn't remember. Then she saw the stretcher, a white sheet draped over the body. Essa stopped. Did they want her to identify the body? Here?

Essa watched Lieutenant Barnes approach the body. He lowered the sheet then recoiled at the face, smashed like a Halloween pumpkin, almost concave. Essa turned toward the grass, gagging. She wished she could vomit, but she hadn't eaten anything, and only a thin string of spit came out. She wiped her face with her bloody hands, turning in time to see Lieutenant Barnes push back the sleeves of the victim's coat. He turned the arm back and forth. Even from a distance, Essa could see what the lieutenant observed: unblemished flesh, no tattoos in sight.

It wasn't her brother.

The relief was painful and so sudden she gagged again before she could even turn away. She dropped to her knees, ready to pray, ready to rejoice. 'He performs wonders that cannot be fathomed, miracles that cannot be counted.' Job 5:9. Essa had her eyes squeezed shut when she felt a hand on her back, at first in her delirium mistaking it for the hand of God.

'I'm sorry for your loss, Miss Montgomery.'

Confusion replaced relief. Was she wrong? But no. It couldn't be her brother. The lieutenant had seen the arm, hadn't he? He knew it wasn't her brother. Essa looked up at the officer's young face. This was the man who'd arrested Clyde but also the man who'd saved her life, hauling her out of a burning building. Had he saved her to kill her? That's what it felt like, her disorientation, like being suffocated. Was she wrong, and her brother lay under a sterile white sheet, no longer of this world? No, death didn't erase the scars of the body, only the soul. Lieutenant Barnes wanted her to believe Clyde was dead. He wanted, for some unfathomable reason, for her to suffer.

'Thank you,' she said, letting Barnes help her stand. Thinking of what to say next as if she were in a play. 'Do you want me to identify the body?'

'No, no, nothing like that. Listen, I know this is the worst time to ask, but something must have been eating at your brother for him to make that jump. There's no use covering for him now.'

'Covering for him?'

For a second, she weighed whether she did know something that the officer didn't. Her mind had never felt so blank though, like a chalkboard washed with soap and water.

'OK, it can wait. I'd like for you to show me where you found your brother, how you might have moved him. Accidentally of course.'

Whatever game Lieutenant Barnes was playing, she didn't know the rules.

'Of course. Anything to help,' Essa said, watching her tone.

She walked back to where she'd left the trailhead, retracing her steps. There was the path she'd made through the brambles. There she'd seen the flash of blue jacket. There she'd held her brother, dead because she believed him dead, but now saved, praise be. She remembered how he'd felt in her arms and wiped her hands on her jeans. Who exactly had she found at the bottom of the cliff? Finally, she was asking the right question. Whose blood did she have on her hands?

THIRTY-FOUR

A dead hiker story wasn't at the top of her priority list, but the station had sent her out anyway, assuming she'd be interested in all things Thorngold County. Merritt straightened her blazer then checked her teeth in a handheld mirror, arranging her features in an expression of sympathy for . . . She checked her notes for the name.

'You're on in ten,' P.J. said with one eye closed, peering into his lens with the other. 'A little to the left.'

Merritt didn't like being told what to do by an undergrad, but she stepped to the side anyway, admitting to herself the kid knew more about filming than she did. A few inches, and the cliffs would be more visible, a stark reminder of nature's dangers. She'd prepared a neat little speech that included safety tips to employ in cold weather. P.J. held up three fingers, lowering them one by one then pointing at her as a small signal light glowed.

'We're coming to you live from the base of Cavern Trail, where behind me you can see the rocks that cost one explorer his life. Karl Wachter, a respected member of the Vintera Wildlife Investigation Laboratory team and an avid outdoorsman, has been identified as the victim of a ninety-foot fall. We spoke to his mother earlier who said he died doing what he loved best.'

P.J. gave her a thumbs-up sign to show they were cutting to footage of Mrs Wachter, whom she'd interviewed that afternoon. The wildlife lab had sent a generic statement, which she'd try to imbue with warmth. It was as colorful as a résumé, listing Karl's educational accomplishments and work contributions, but lacking in personal remarks. Merritt had only met the man once, but even she could have thrown in a remark about his impressive climbing skills. Impressive and reckless. It's the overly confident ones that get themselves into trouble, thinking they can scale Mount Whatever with a pocket knife and some energy drinks.

'Back in two.'

'Mrs Wachter's sentiments were echoed by his colleagues, who praised his work ethic and considerable contributions, saying, quote, he participated in over twenty-five investigations, many of which were successfully brought to trial.'

She hit 'twenty-five' hard, although she had no way of knowing if that number was impressive or average. She ended with her advice to trail visitors then let the anchorman back in Roanoke take over.

'And we're clear,' P.J. said.

Merritt pressed the earpiece to make sure there were no follow-up questions, but when the weather report started, she knew they were done for the day.

P.J. started packing, and Merritt approached the van to change her shoes. This place was turning her into a practical footwear kind of gal. It had been an eventful twenty-four hours as the local police department had scrambled to identify the man whose body had been found. Lieutenant Otis Barnes had responded in one-word answers to her texts, assuming – rightly so if she were being honest – she was hunting for information rather than flirting. Why not both? Had the man never heard of multitasking? Otis had confirmed they were going to arrest Clyde, but when she'd pressed him on why, he'd ghosted her. She suspected outside pressure, not new evidence.

She considered why, if Karl Wachter was such a dedicated employee, he'd been hiking instead of working. Or was the site part of the lab investigation on bats? When she'd pulled at the thread, nothing had come of it right away. No, the death had garnered attention because it was the third in Thorngold County to occur in a week. Not to mention two fires. The place might as well have been cursed. She imagined her tabloid colleagues were having a field day with their headlines. LOCALS ASK WHICH WITCH TO BLAME. WHEN THE MYSTICISM CLEARS, MURDERS LINGER. DETECTIVES ARE ESP-EEVED AT CRIME SPREE. Or something equally tacky, Merritt figured. Her best guess? There was nothing occult about these deaths.

Merritt was more and more convinced the preacher had something to do with the fire at his church. It wasn't wishful thinking. Why else would he set out to scare her away? Nonetheless, she hadn't been able to rustle up any evidence of wrongdoing. Well, not illegal wrongdoing at least. Abandoning your wife and child wasn't exactly winning any Boy Scout badges. But Merritt had something like a plan forming. She just needed opportunity. Or to create opportunity.

'You got everything you need?' P.J. asked, sliding his bag into the back.

Merritt stared at the satellite on top of the WTGX van, glad it worked so far out in the wilderness. Although she wasn't that interested in Karl Wachter, there was something to be said for a live broadcast. Even recorded footage would be better than nothing. She'd go above her supervisor's head, she decided. She'd get what she wanted. Merritt Callahan didn't need luck, only a little time.

'You bet.' She mulled over the wisdom of roping in the kid then decided to hell with it. 'I may need a favor though.'

P.J. gaped at her like an eager puppy, ready to learn a new trick. And she had new tricks to teach.

THIRTY-FIVE

'Give half to Essa, that's all I'm saying.'

Juliet watched her fiancé pace around the kitchen, stopping occasionally to take a swig of his beer. He wasn't drunk, but he would be in an hour or two if he didn't stop. Clyde drank to spend time with friends, not to black out. It was one of the things she liked about him. But he wasn't himself. Desperate like a cornered rat – wounded, scared and wild.

'You think they're going to hand over that insurance money, Clyde? They think you burned the place down. Both places.'

When she'd gotten pregnant, Juliet had come as close to despair as she'd ever been. They always used protection, but sometimes condoms broke, and the universe had a cruel streak. But she'd decided she was smart enough and Clyde was hard-working enough to make this little family work. She knew, as clearly as she'd ever known anything, that he would never leave her. It wasn't only love, though they loved each other. He was a man who believed in responsibility. But something had gone wrong. No, not something. Everything.

'Just promise me.'

Juliet could see he was upset, and she sympathized with him. He'd been stupid though, picking a fight with that fraud. She half-suspected Granieri had burned the place down himself, out of spite. And now Clyde thought the insurance company was going to hand over $25,000? She wanted that money as bad as anyone, but it wasn't going to happen. Getting money from Clyde's sister made a lot more sense. Never mind that she was starting to like the girl. All the more reason Essa should help.

'I promise, but you need to be realistic.'

'You know I got my feet right here on earth, baby. Always.'

He crossed over to her and kneeled beside her chair, putting down his beer and taking her hands in his. When he gazed at her, there was that pull. She'd never felt that with anyone else, like a magnet being drawn to its match. Sometimes she wished she loved somebody else besides Clyde. Or better yet, nobody at all. But as he stared at her with his hazel eyes, framed by those girlishly long lashes, she couldn't help but lean forward. He responded by kissing her lightly, and she tasted his breakfast cereal underneath the tang of alcohol.

'She'll be a good aunt.' Juliet didn't want to fight. Clyde was touchy about his sister. 'You don't believe that yet. Not really. But she will be.'

Clyde rubbed her swollen fingers as he teased her. She'd removed all her rings, even the garnet engagement ring, and missed their weight. Clyde might have his feet on the ground, but she needed to be tethered lest she blow away.

They both heard the bell chime in her living room, and his expression clouded.

'I want to work,' Juliet said before he could interrupt. 'What else I got to do? Lie around eating us out of house and home?'

She kissed him again, trying to hide her wince as she stood. Her back and hips ached constantly now, but never more so than when she changed positions. She'd started off her pregnancy worried about things like breastmilk versus formula, and now she could almost laugh at how absurd her concerns seemed. She hadn't researched baby forums for moms with incarcerated partners. Maybe she should start one.

These dark thoughts followed her into her workspace where she found a regular, Trace Poinicker, fidgeting with her tablecloth. Since giving up drugs two years ago, Trace moved all the time, hardly able to sit long enough for a reading. But Juliet admired his determination. She'd figured he wouldn't make it the first time he'd shown up. It was one of the few instances where she'd flat-out lied. 'I can see that you'll find success,' she'd said, feeling only a tiny bit guilty. But somehow her words had come true. So far at least. She'd willed them into existence maybe. Now that was a bankable power.

'Looking good, Trace.' She sank into her own chair across from him. Clyde had moved an armchair to the table, so she could work more comfortably. The effect was casual, but nobody commented.

'You always say that. I look like I got run over by a semi, but I'm alive.'

'Your momma all right?'

'Mean as ever.'

The joke normally didn't bother her, but Juliet cringed a little. 'You got something special on your mind.'

Trace paused, looking around the room. He'd been there at least thirty times before, so Juliet wasn't sure what he saw.

'January.'

'That a person, or you mean the whole month?'

Trace ran a hand through his thinning hair. He smelled nice, like he'd put on cologne the night before, and it lingered, not too strong.

'It seems like everybody's crawling through mud, under barbwire and such. And it doesn't seem worth it.'

Juliet picked up her cards and shuffled them, being careful not to tear any. The set was getting old and would have to be replaced sooner or later. She knew the deck didn't matter, but she liked this one all the same. She'd grown attached to the pictures.

Sometimes when she worked, Juliet considered herself more of a therapist than a reader. She wanted desperately to know her own future – and the little one's – but it was enough to see glimpses of the present for strangers. She could look at someone and know they'd lost their job or wanted a divorce. She'd have a general sense of where they lived or whether they preferred mornings or evenings. It didn't sound useful, but she'd mention something specific about, say, a lost earring, and they'd trust her. Her job became lending a sympathetic ear, trying to guide customers toward their own insights. Sometimes it only took a little prompting, and sometimes she'd have to dig, poke around in the dark until she hit the right nerve. She'd been working with Trace long enough to know he had an existential streak. He didn't talk about himself much, more the universe. He should have been a professor of philosophy instead of a plant worker.

'Worrying about the end of the world again.'

'Looking for a greater purpose, I guess,' Trace said as Juliet offered him the deck. He cut the cards three times before handing them back.

Juliet's lamp flickered, and she frowned in the direction. *Not now, CeeCee,* she thought. *You hold your horses.* She nearly always pulled a trump card first with Trace. He rarely dwelled on minor issues in his life. She suspected he had his fair share, same as anybody, but he kept those to himself. The Empress card appeared, the first of a Zodiac spread, and Juliet nodded at the same time as Trace.

'All twelve months represented, darling. Not one better or worse than the others.' Juliet worried she'd interfered with the reading somehow since The Empress also represented fertility, but she pushed on. 'You worrying about somebody in particular maybe? Want to help?'

Trace nodded and started talking about a kid at his NA group who'd shown up high at their last meeting. His eyes filled as he described the boy, no more than sixteen with burn marks on his face from when he'd tried to make meth and failed.

Ah, mothering instincts, Juliet thought, questioning how the man survived carrying around so much empathy. No wonder he'd turned to drugs.

The lamp in the corner flickered then fell to the ground, smashing the bulb. Juliet jumped, and Trace shrieked, knocking over his chair in an effort to escape.

'Enough,' Juliet said to the empty corner. 'You give me a minute with Mr Poinicker, then I'll deal with you, sure enough. I apologize, Trace.'

But he'd already grabbed his coat.

'Never you mind. I'll come back when' – he hesitated, hand on the doorknob – 'when you're alone like.'

Juliet hated to charge her client for an interrupted session, but she needed the money. She threw out some advice, hoping it would be useful. 'Call the kid. If he wants help, he'll take the help.'

Trace heard her but had already hopped down the front stairs. Juliet closed the door behind him as wind slipped into the room. She wasn't surprised to see Aunt CeeCee when she turned around. The figure hovered beside the table, looking at The Empress card. Juliet could see her own breath.

'You owe me a lightbulb,' Juliet said, braver than she felt.

'The dead don't owe anybody nothing. That's the beauty of the great beyond.'

Aunt CeeCee held a hand dramatically in the air, enjoying herself. Her pink bejeweled pants sparkled despite the darkness.

'Why you here then? It get boring up there hanging out with clouds and such?'

Aunt CeeCee snorted. 'Oh, you'd like to know, wouldn't you? A little insight into heaven, and you could rake in more bucks.'

'I suppose the dead don't have to eat.'

'I'm here for you, you know. No need to be ornery.'

Aunt CeeCee's edges pixelated then came into focus again, and Juliet's stomach roiled. Unconsciously, she moved a hand to her stomach, protecting her baby from something. God help her if she had to deal with dead in-laws as well as real ones on a regular basis. Maybe she should order some sage.

'Deliver your message, and get going, will ya?'

Aunt CeeCee grinned, and her teeth were blue. Juliet shivered, seeing the dark gullet beyond.

'I can see why he likes you. Most men fall in love with their mothers, but Clyde? No, Clyde found someone who sticks up for herself.'

Juliet appreciated the compliment but moved farther away all the same, opening the curtain and letting in pale light.

Aunt CeeCee flinched, her feet and legs disappearing in the sun. 'A little bit of a bitch too. Good for you.'

'I can hold my own.'

Aunt CeeCee floated toward the low ceiling, part of her legs reappearing as they left the sun. 'That's what I've been telling everyone. Don't let me down.'

At that, Aunt CeeCee flaked away, and Juliet had her first and only premonition: Clyde being handcuffed and taken away. The image was so clear she felt dizzy, as if she were on an amusement-park ride. She could see the light reflecting off the metal chain. She could feel her own intake of air. Why had she asked for this? It was worse knowing Clyde might be sitting in her kitchen for the last time. She understood what Madame Clarita had been trying to tell her. Hope made getting up in the morning possible. It made step-ping outside, looking at the sky possible. Getting groceries, meeting a friend for drinks, saving for a rainy day. You needed hope behind the wheel, or you'd crash every time. Juliet felt something grip her stomach, almost like a hand twisting her intestines, and she sank on to the carpet, breathing in through her nose and out through her mouth.

The sirens didn't come as a surprise, but she waited until the contraction passed then hauled herself up. She couldn't control much, but she could say goodbye to the man she loved and the future she wanted.

When she stepped into the kitchen, Clyde looked almost serene, holding out his arms to her. She stepped into them and willed time to freeze. But clocks are merciless, and the knock came as she'd seen, wolves dressed like cops at her door.

THIRTY-SIX

Too many ghosts. There had been a time in Essa's life where she'd wished for them. The scent of her mother's shampoo, a caress from the wind. Now, she struggled to tell the difference between living and dead. She occupied this purgatory herself, a useless, waiting sort of place. Essa floated between worlds, haunted and hunted. And so she began with the kitchen, filling the dishwasher then hand washing all the cups and plates that wouldn't fit. She wiped the counters and swept under the refrigerator. A sticky film inside the microwave kept her busy for a good ten minutes. Essa knew how long the task took because she kept glancing at the clock, wondering when she would hear something about Juliet. Wondering if anyone would remember to call her at all.

After she scrubbed the bathroom, she walked into the bedroom, feeling nosy but wanting to make sure everything was set up for the baby. She stopped to pray again, figuring it couldn't hurt. Maybe God hadn't heard her the first dozen times.

The room smelled like her brother and made her homesick. All she wanted to do was sit on the floor and cry, but instead, she scooped up the clothes on the floor and put them in a basket. She would drive to the laundromat later if there was time. Anything to keep her mind occupied, to pull it back from the brink of collapse. Her brother was alive but arrested. Officially charged. A painful sort of relief, hardly a relief at all. Except at least there was a chance now, however small. Her anger at her brother had been replaced by anger at Lieutenant Barnes. He'd tried to trick her, let her believe Clyde was dead. He must have thought she'd been protecting her kin, but she couldn't muster up any understanding for the cop. At another time in her life – a week before even – Essa would have felt sorry for herself. But now? Now she was furious.

A small bassinet sat next to the bed, but the crib was in its original packaging. Essa dragged the box into Juliet's reading room, so she had more room to work. The darkness startled her. She hadn't noticed when the sun dipped, and now the hairs on the back of her neck rose as she fumbled toward the lamp.

When she flipped the switch, nothing happened, and a chill ran through her body. Only a broken lightbulb though.

She found a new one underneath the kitchen sink, but the dim glow did little to calm her nerves. She moved Juliet's table closer to the wall, knocking over the tarot cards, which scattered all over the rug. Her hands and feet weren't working like they were supposed to work. Would she ever feel like herself again, or was this her normal now?

Essa sank to her knees to scoop up The Fool and The Magician, The Ace of Cups and Two of Wands. Essa liked the strength card, a golden lion staring at his tamer. She tried not to read anything into The Devil card, although it was one of the few that had landed face up. She picked it up by a corner and shrieked when somebody knocked on the front door.

Essa crept to the peephole, not recognizing the face staring back at her. When she cracked the door, she kept the chain in place.

'Can I help you?' Essa asked, peering out at a woman in her late fifties or early sixties, smoking a clove cigarette.

'Juliet got time for a reading?'

'We're closed for the night.'

'That so? The sign's lit.'

Essa slid back the chain and stepped outside to see the 'Open' sign illuminated. She hadn't remembered to switch it off.

'You're right about that. Sorry for wastin' your time.'

The woman grunted in disgust and stomped off the porch, tossing her lit cigarette toward the bushes.

Essa watched her drive away then scooted back inside, happy to be out of the cold. She tried every switch she saw, but the 'Open' sign remained on. Resigned, she slipped on her shoes and parka before walking back into the night.

A car sped by too fast, and she trembled, well aware it was brutally dark outside. Clouds covered the moon, and there wasn't a lamppost for miles. The extension cord was easy enough to spot though, and Essa followed its length back to the house, pleased with herself for finding the outlet. She unplugged the thing then turned to see a tall figure standing near the front door, head covered by a hood.

'We're closed,' Essa yelled, hoping the man would leave before she got any closer. She didn't see any cars in the front parking lot, and her heart started to race. 'Maybe try back in a couple of weeks.'

The man didn't move, and neither did Essa. She searched for anything she might use as a weapon, considering if the extension cord might come in handy. There was nothing else around her feet. She slipped her hands into her pockets, finding only the Harper's Ferry magnet she'd grabbed from her home. She gripped it between her fingers and took a hesitant step forward.

'Can I help you with something?' she called, voice shaking.

Still the man didn't respond. Essa saw him turn toward her though, aware she was out there, vulnerable and alone.

She took another step then moved in the other direction, heading around the house and toward her car. By the time she got to the other side, the man was there though, staring her down. He was closer to her car than she was. Could she sprint back the other way, make it back inside? As she weighed her options, the man spoke, his voice loud but flat. All hint of a West Virginia accent gone.

'I see you have the place to yourself, Essa.'

Now it seemed obvious the man was Pastor Micah. Who else would emerge from the darkness? She could make out his sleek, silent car now. The revelation offered no comfort though, and Essa wondered again if she could make it back to the front door.

'For now,' Essa said. 'Not for long though. Juliet's got family coming.'

It wasn't a lie, though she had no way of knowing when that family would arrive or where they would stay. Essa wasn't sure she should have used Juliet's name. Her brother's girlfriend was hardly a secret, but she didn't want anyone else on the preacher's radar.

'I won't be long. I doubt if I should have come at all. You've done something to me.'

Essa disagreed but stayed silent while her heart hammered in her chest.

'I was sorry to hear about your brother's arrest. That makes things harder on us.'

Essa didn't like that he referred to them as 'us'. She didn't want anything to do with him. 'How you figure?'

'Surely a smart girl like you understands. For an arrest? They must have more than circumstantial evidence.'

Essa now trusted the Thorngold County Police Department about as much as she trusted a thornbush. She wouldn't put it past them to fabricate evidence if they didn't have it. That didn't mean she needed to agree with the preacher though.

'Guess you can't help me then,' Essa said.

Pastor Micah walked toward her, and she glanced around for a place to hide. Even in the dark, Essa could see the blue satin lining of the man's coat. His dress shoes crunched the frozen grass.

'I've watched you for years, peering out at me from behind your little lace curtains. So pretty for such an ugly house. You won't miss it.'

Had he framed her brother? She hated the tricksy way he talked, never saying exactly what he meant. She had to run everything through an internal interpretation machine.

'I'll be all right.'

'I could still help, you know.'

He stood a few feet from her now, and Essa took a step backward, shocked when he closed the distance between them and pressed his mouth to hers again. He tasted like hot pennies, and Essa gritted her teeth. She swung the magnet at his head, satisfied by the small sound he made. He moved back a fraction of an inch and paused. For a moment, Essa thought he might hit her.

'What is it about you Montgomerys that want my blood? I'm not going to hurt you, Essa. I might be in love with you.' The preacher touched his forehead, where a trickle of blood had appeared. He wiped it off with his fingers then caressed Essa's cheek, leaving a line of red. 'You ever seen an overdose, Essa? The delirium always takes me by surprise. Thinking there's a ghost in the room or a beast by the side of the road. They can't catch their breath. They can't breathe. Flopping like a trout fresh from the river. Vomit if they're lucky. Blackout if they're not. I've watched them die, Essa. People I care about and total strangers. It doesn't get any easier.'

'I don't know why you're telling me all this.'

'This whole town is traumatized. It's not only people like you who've lost. Everybody's either losing or lost themselves. Two sides of the same awful coin. I'm trying to make a difference here. I'm trying to straighten this place up. Then you come along and—'

'And what?'

'And I'm not sure what matters anymore. I'm saying it's not too late for us. Come see me tomorrow night. I'll make this all go away.'

THIRTY-SEVEN

G reta looked on disapprovingly, but the red-tailed hawk always looked that way, her little beak curved down in a perpetual frown that Essa found comforting. Reliable. Her life didn't seem particularly reliable these days. She'd never moved any specimens before, but Essa had wanted company in the morning, so she'd brought the bird into the side office nobody used. The 6' x 6' room didn't have a stitch of personality, not even a window. Gray cinder-block walls and a matching metal door. Someone else might have been claustrophobic, but Essa didn't have that particular phobia. In fact, if the walls wanted to crush her, she only hoped they'd make it quick.

'Right, Greta?' She adjusted the bird on the makeshift perch she'd created out of textbooks. She planned to recreate as best she could the snake necropsy report from memory and the photographs. Partly, it was desperation. Maybe they'd missed something that could help her brother. But also she felt guilty about losing the file in the fire, especially since Karl's notes were now missing too. His death would mean more work for everyone and perhaps shame at how they'd rolled their eyes at him from time to time. It seemed a little blasphemous to remember his sour moods. Instead, Essa made herself focus on how good he'd been at his job, and that couldn't be denied.

Essa had slept fitfully at Juliet's place after her visit from Pastor Micah, waking at every little noise from outside. The man had seemed more unhinged and more dangerous. His patience with her had run out, and she worried about how he would react to an outright refusal. Would he resort to violence? Was saying 'yes' her only hope of survival? Or her brother's survival? No, there had to be another way.

Around two, she'd gotten up and assembled the crib, the confusing instructions keeping her occupied for a few hours. Then she'd gotten dressed and driven to the lab. In a roundabout way, Pastor Micah had helped her snap back into herself, into survival mode. There was no time for a breakdown.

If you could get over the macabre nature of the subject – the charred scales and raw, red flesh – it was interesting what you could learn about a fire from the animal bodies left behind. Fires are complicated evaluations since so little evidence remains. Sometimes not even enough to determine cause of death, though the cause might seem obvious. But there was asphyxiation, cardiac arrest, oxygen deprivation. Essa could only hope the young couple hadn't been burned alive. She pushed that thought aside and refocused on the snakes.

They had fractured bones, caused from the high temperatures. The skin on their heads had split open too, as if they'd been attacked. But Essa knew the heat could cause those sort of lesions as well. No accelerants were discovered on the bodies. No kerosene, implying the deaths were accidental. No surprise there. Who would bother to kill the snakes before lighting the place on fire? The local news reported that gasoline had been tossed on New Hope's walls, explaining why the place had gone up so quickly. That had been the last piece of information to make her fully accept the fire wasn't an accident.

Essa typed her notes into the software program, being careful to check each line. She noted where her memory might be faulty. They often performed necropsies on animals that looked like they'd fallen asleep. Maybe a little blood on the fur or an anguished expression. But the snakes had been decimated. Essa would be lucky if she ever forgot. The hard part was trying to convey the specifics. She pulled the photographs up on her computer.

The tongues had clear burn marks, and there were black stains on the lungs. But the stomachs had been untouched, and Essa entered their contents again. There hadn't been much. A few undigested bits in the first rattlesnake. The pieces like toy whiskers. Odd those. When performing fire autopsies, the primary goal was sometimes to determine if someone had died before the flames got to them. That is, had they been killed then moved? Essa concluded that the snakes were byproducts not targets. A lot of people hate snakes, but not that much.

She leaned back in her chair, stretching her back. The work distracted her, and she was grateful an hour had passed. For a while at least, she could forget everything was so awful. Even if she got a job offer somewhere else, she couldn't leave Vintera right now. Not with her brother in jail and Juliet at the hospital. Pastor Micah

had scared her the night before. Why her? She'd tried to make sense
of his obsession. She wasn't vain enough to believe it was anything
particular about her. It was more a general need for power over
someone reluctant to give any. She was the serpent orphan and
wanted nothing to do with him.

Essa stood, looking down at Greta from above. She liked the bird
even when only the dull, brown feathers were visible. Her mom
had called red-tailed hawks 'chickenhawks' because of an enduring
belief they'd prey on your flock. It was mostly a superstition though.
Greta herself wasn't much bigger than your barnyard hen. A rooster
could give her a run for her money. The taxidermy specimens made
comparisons easier. If a smuggled tortoise arrived, you could see
what the shell should look like. How far the legs should extend.

Essa wandered into their display room, looking for the timber
rattlesnake she usually avoided. She'd never given it a name but
decided when she found it this time, she would. Caliban maybe.
Cal for short. The snake had been posed in a purposely fierce position – its lower body coiled, three-inch rattle in plain sight. It
extended toward the ceiling, showing its dun-colored belly. The
head turned toward the viewer, mouth agape, showing off its fangs.

Their four burned specimens would be incinerated eventually,
after the case closed. There wasn't enough left of them to keep.
Essa considered again if she'd learned anything useful from their
dissections. Dr Kester's dictated notes had been perfunctory. They'd
died because of the fires. No prior injuries visible, which was a bit
of a surprise. Serpents kept for church services were notoriously
mistreated. Not back in the heyday of the movement. Not when her
grandfather had founded New Hope. But the new places? Starvation
and dehydration to make them lethargic. Or drugs. Some removed
their fangs. Another trick was sewing shut their mouths.

Essa thought back to the thin, plastic strips she'd catalogued and
considered. There'd been no bites at New Hope since her father's.
And at the service she'd attended, the serpents hadn't so much as
hissed. At least from what she'd witnessed before having a panic
attack. Unlike neighboring states, West Virginia didn't have any
laws protecting snakes. Would anyone care about stitches?

She touched Cal on his nose, thanking him for his help, and went
to find the evidence bags. The storage room overflowed with cardboard boxes and airtight containers for the more important work,
the federal cases. New Hope would warrant a file at best.

They hadn't recovered much. She found the bag, though, holding it up to the light. A few bits of undigested bone, perhaps left over from a mouse the copperhead ate. And three sutures – she was almost sure – about two inches in length and knotted in the middle. Her heart sped up with something other than fear, and she darted back into the main office space. She waved at Gloriana and Sip getting their morning coffees, and they nodded in return. Since Karl's death, they'd been a sober group but more unified. The bat case had turned into something. Not anything occult – not anything related to the Mercury Order – but instead evidence in a chemical dumping trial. Eleven more specimens were being brought in, and it would be all hands on deck.

Essa found Dr Kester in his office. He kept a taxidermy companion as well, even more impressive than Greta. The bobcat sported a healthy, shaggy pelt and stared straight ahead. Like a painting, its eyes followed you though, wherever you went. Essa didn't feel right naming the cat. It belonged to Dr Kester. But it could be a Bianca, in her opinion.

'Yes?' he said, causing Essa to jump. She'd been hovering at his office door, unsure of herself. She was an assistant. Who was she to question her boss's conclusions? She had insider knowledge though. It's not like there were college courses on houses of worship like hers.

'I hate to bother you, but I'm near done with the New Hope report, and I thought of something.'

Dr Kester gestured for her to join him. Essa relaxed at his neutral expression. She walked forward with the bag and placed it on his desk, pointing to one of the stitches.

Dr Kester picked up his magnifying glass and peered down. 'Undigested plastic, specific material undetermined, about two inches in length.'

'I'm wondering if they could be medical sutures?'

Dr Kester looked at her, something like resignation in his face.

'It's uncommon here in the States, but not unheard of. Sewing up their mouths, so nobody gets bit. They starve to death, but that can take months. Half a year sometimes.'

Dr Kester squinted at her, making a little clucking noise of concentration. 'Terrible. Truly monstrous.'

Essa glanced at the bobcat then back at Dr Kester. His face froze as he made his own calculations.

'Not bad, Essa. Not bad at all.'

Essa's cheeks went pink from the praise. She'd figured something out. All on her own too.

'Should I update the report?'

'Oh, I wouldn't bother with that.'

Essa deflated as Dr Kester sank back into his chair and picked up the toxicology screening he'd been studying.

'Our job was to assist with the fire and murders.'

Essa started to object, but Dr Kester cut her off.

'It's good work, Essa. Truly. Sometimes knowledge is its own reward. And at least no snakes will be harmed for a while.'

Dr Kester's wistful tone twisted Essa's already overexcited heart. She couldn't bring herself to tell him about the Sunday service, how Pastor Micah had replacements and no intentions of shuttering his operation. Instead, she thanked her boss and took the evidence bag with her. She dropped it back on her own desk and tried to concentrate on the dissection report again. What was the point though? Men like Pastor Micah always got away with their cruelty. You make enough friends – you make the right friends – and enemies disappear. Judges, politicians, policemen. Pastor Micah had lined them up like planks in a fence. Essa Montgomery was a trespasser at best. When she saw it was noon, she grabbed her purse.

'You're no chickenhawk,' she whispered to the bird. 'You're a majestic predator. What would Greta do?'

Essa laughed at herself, remembering those 'What would Jesus do?' bracelets that had been popular when she was in elementary school. Abbreviated as WWJD to make them cooler. She dumped her purse on to the floor and dug around until she found two small, white business cards. She threw one in the trash but held up the other: Merritt Callahan, WTGX-Roanoke.

THIRTY-EIGHT

The guitar didn't need an amp, but the group liked the rock 'n' roll feel of their Friday-night meetings. Gene had talent too – there was no denying that. His fingers moved over the neck like they'd been possessed, a blur of movement that made his audience hoot and whistle. A few even danced around the grass, holding their gloved hands toward the tent's plastic pitch. At least a hundred people gathered each Friday night – from Vintera, yes, but also from neighboring towns and counties – and the makeshift accommodations didn't affect turnout in the slightest. If anything the crowd seemed more determined, more electrified. They could have attended NA meetings in other churches, basement affairs with lights that buzzed. Pastor Micah told them not to be ashamed of their sins but to fix them.

'We're all weak,' he said after the music ended and everybody found a seat. 'Sure enough, we're all weak.'

Nobody noticed the pause stretched longer than usual. They knew their preacher had a flair for the dramatic. They kept up their amens and closed their eyes, even the ones who'd never thought much about Jesus before Pastor Micah arrived in their town. At first, they'd thought he was another snake oil salesman trying to profit on their pain. They'd seen their fair share of those. But he had snakes without the oil, and something about his methods seemed to work. Men who'd taken oxy for years following a back injury in the mines – living on disability and waiting on the next refill, the next hit – found themselves wanting to dry out. Wanting to feel something besides hunger again. Housewives who'd tried meth for a way out of their blinding depression could go a week then a month then a year. Oh, the cravings remained, but that was Old Nick talking, and he could be quieted. More than quieted, he could be crushed beneath your heel.

Pastor Micah had trouble reaching the teens, which mattered for prevention. He'd be the first to admit that failing. But he'd made inroads at the local high school. And as the Friday-night meetings got livelier, so did the audiences. He kept the tone jubilant. A celebration of triumph. That night, the tent blazed with light. Every bulb checked and replaced if necessary. From a distance, it looked like a carnival, advertising itself. A beacon in the dark.

The pause continued as Pastor Micah tried to see Essa Montgomery's driveway from where he stood, velvet bag at his feet. He went so far as to shade his eyes, but still he couldn't tell if her car had returned. He knew the place was damaged too badly for the girl to stay the night there, but she might stop by, pick through the ashes for more mementos.

'But weakness doesn't define us, brothers and sisters. Without weakness, how would we test our mettle? Let me tell you a story.'

'Praise be,' Beverly Blake said, and Pastor Micah spotted her in the crowd, her striped pastel blouse dotted in sweat. They'd cranked the heat lamps, and the preacher felt powerful in the artificial air. His meetings stayed open to anyone, no addiction required, but they weren't meant for the Beverly Blakes of the world, the teetotalers and competitive do-gooders.

'Way back when I hung my hat in Biloxi— Y'all didn't know I was in Mississippi for a spell? Why, I'm a world traveler.' He held a hand to his heart, and the crowd tittered appreciatively. If they could turn their lights out, he could see about Essa. He could ask somebody to turn out the lights, couldn't he? On some pretense about not needing light to see God? God must be felt, trusted even in darkness. 'And I met a man by the name of Hoyt Chicken. Oh, and he was rightly named. God does have a sense of humor.'

'You know he does,' Gene called out.

'You know he does. And Mr Chicken ran a little grocery down there. Some boxes of cereal and dog food. One cooler at the back for your Cokes and such. You know the kind of place. Bet you can even picture the candy bars and gum by the register. Well, the shop did all right. Folks would wander in all day long, liked to gossip a little. Pass the time, you know.'

Pastor Micah pulled the microphone cord, so he could walk. He stepped off the platform but still couldn't see past the edge of his tent. The plastic windows made everything outside look melted or covered in petroleum jelly.

'One day, a woman stops by, one of his regulars, and tells him about a deadly virus that can be caught from butter. She'd read about it somewhere or another, and isn't that a shame? Dry cornbread, whew. I'd take the risk myself.'

Pastor Micah walked farther down the aisle as his audience laughed. He kept his talks brief on Friday nights, let the addicts testify more than him. As their numbers swelled, he found a little preamble helped everyone loosen up though. Nobody liked to talk first.

'But our Mr Chicken stopped carrying butter and ice cream to be on the safe side. One day the woman returns and says some lowlifes have been putting poison in sodas. So he stops carrying Mountain Dews and Dr Peppers and such.'

He stretched the microphone cord as far as it would go and decided Essa wasn't there. It was foolish of him to expect her.

'Well by now, you know folks were grumbling. A hot summer day and no Coke in the cooler? Then it was cereal then potato chips. The candy bars disappeared. Even the gum until eventually all Mr Chicken sold was batteries and lottery tickets.'

He'd find her. Nobody would notice if he left while people told their stories. Or if they did, they'd make excuses for him. He'd track her down. Essa couldn't escape him forever. Pastor Micah pivoted on his heel and walked back toward the stage, buoyed by the attentive stares.

'And so the place was deserted. Morning to night, nobody walked through the doors. Mr Chicken ruined his livelihood because of fear. Does that sound familiar?'

Affirmative murmurs rippled through the crowd, and Pastor Micah ascended the platform again. If he looked closely, the velvet bag writhed a little. A lively one.

'I hate to tell you this, brothers and sisters, but he lost more than his store. He was an easy mark, all alone morning to night, and somebody got the notion to rob Mr Chicken, and somebody shot him in the head.'

Pastor Micah let the gasps die down before he kneeled and untied the bag, letting the copperhead reveal its burnished body to the crowd. He didn't touch it but watched the snake as the crowd grew excited. He didn't always bring any to the Friday-night meetings, which made their appearance more effective.

'A gun didn't kill Mr Chicken though. Oh sure, it was the instrument. But men use all sorts of instruments. Satan, that old so-and-so, only needs one. Fear.'

Pastor Micah bent then hoisted the copperhead into the air, holding it up so even the people in the back could see.

'And to fear, we say, be gone. We'll have none of you tonight.'

THIRTY-NINE

T he river-side neighborhood looked enchanted, each house with its own rod-iron lamppost. Essa half expected to see a snowy owl perched atop one, waiting for a summons. They were too far south for those though, and the owl population had been steadily decreasing anyway. Before she started, the lab had worked an illegal taxidermy case, a man hunting, stuffing and selling them for thousands of dollars. It was a grim thought, but Essa was in a grim mood despite the explosion of stars above her head. It was the kind of clear January night she usually appreciated. Everybody else tucked inside. The whole world left for her to explore. But tonight she was on a mission. If she couldn't trust the police and she couldn't trust the clergy, she would have to trust herself.

Essa parked a quarter mile away in a little turn-off. The dark walk made her jumpy, but she'd worn better clothing than the last time she'd found herself along a gravel shoulder. Jeans and boots, her dark-green parka covering everything that might reflect light. She'd even tucked her hair into a camouflage toboggan hat she'd found in Clyde's closet.

Thankfully, Essa didn't see anybody parked outside of Pastor Micah's home. It dawned on her that the car she'd seen was most likely a police presence for security. To keep the preacher safe. What a perverted sense of justice. Pastor Micah's surveillance had been deemed unnecessary after Clyde was officially charged.

She checked her watch again. Eight o'clock. She was glad the NA meeting hadn't been cancelled. The makeshift tent remained up, and the weekly meetings were as popular as any rock concert. At least in Vintera. They sometimes ran into the wee hours of the night, so Essa would be safe. Pastor Micah wouldn't be home for hours. Even so, she felt on edge, as if she'd climbed too high up a cliff and now had to make her way down without ropes. She tried and failed not to picture Karl's face again, smashed past all recognition. His death had been deemed an accident, and Essa agreed somebody with his attitude wasn't likely to jump.

She went around the back of the house and climbed on to the deck. Despite it being a subdivision, she might not be noticed back there.

The sliding glass door had a lock easy enough to pick, even without any experience. Someone stronger could have ripped it open, but Essa dug out the bobby pins she'd brought and wiggled one into the keyhole. When it clicked open immediately, Essa decided to call that a sign. This was the right plan. She only had to see it through.

A light from the stove made it easy for her to examine the lavish kitchen. Granite countertops and high-end appliances. It smelled like hyacinth, and a fresh vase of the unseasonable flowers stood on the bar. Their overly sweet smell made her queasy, made her resent the preacher a little bit more, and she needed all the motivation she could get.

She closed the door behind her and stepped fully inside, trying to get her bearings. The last time, she'd only seen the foyer and a sitting room. The house sprawled, three thousand feet at least. But she doubted he kept dangerous animals in his bedroom. She searched for basement stairs. Instead, she found a door that could be mistaken for a pantry except for the lock. The deadbolt looked a lot more intimidating than the sliding glass door, and Essa's pin bent when she tried to use it. It pinged as it dropped to the tile floor, and Essa cringed. She scooped that one up and stuffed it into her pocket, hands vibrating. She shook them to calm down.

The lock wouldn't budge, but she wasn't giving up yet. There had to be another way inside.

She retraced her steps and walked back into the night, closing the door behind her. With a little luck, the preacher would assume he'd left it unlocked himself, wouldn't know anything was wrong for a while, perhaps not until Sunday morning. Essa crouched low and stalked the perimeter of the house, stifling a giddy noise when she found a small, low basement window. It didn't budge when she tried to lift it, and she took a deep breath, knowing she was about to cross a line. No turning back now, she told herself, and maybe that was true.

She shook off her parka and wrapped her hand, then slammed it into the glass before she could lose her nerve. The pane shattered, a piece slicing her cheek. She wiped the blood away with the sleeve of her sweater then used the coat to knock out what remained of the glass as best she could.

She squeezed her body through, flinching when something dug into her stomach. It hurt, but she kept going, gritting her teeth.

She rolled on to the concrete floor and stood quickly, hands extended into nothing. It was too dark to see anything at all, and she groped in front of her until her hands hit something hard. A familiar rattle started – a song of warning in the dark – and she jumped back, bile rising into her throat.

FORTY

Glancing in her rearview mirror, Merritt started to have doubts about her plan. The boy had fallen asleep in his car seat and looked a little like one of the Precious Moments figurines her mother had collected. His dark hair curled over his forehead, and his hands twitched occasionally from a dream. She wished his mother would fall asleep too, but Kimberly Granieri stared out the passenger-side window, lost in daydreams. A better person would offer to turn the car around, say it was OK to change her mind. But Merritt changed the radio instead to a more upbeat channel and turned on to Pine Tree Road. When she crossed a bridge over Tyson's Creek, she knew they were getting close.

'I've never attempted a coup before,' P.J. said from the back seat, and Merritt balked at his loud tone. She glanced again at the boy who stirred but didn't wake up. His fingers tightened around his blanket.

'It's hardly a coup,' Merritt said. 'We're reuniting a family.'

She stretched out a hand to Kimberly, who squeezed it half-heartedly, her gaze remaining elsewhere.

'I don't want to get him into any trouble,' the woman said.

'A conversation, that's all. Don't you want to see him again?'

Merritt knew the question was unfair, a twist of the knife. Of course Kimberly wanted to see her husband. She oozed heartbreak from every pore. But Merritt needed the kind of footage that would go viral; she needed a dramatic reunion. She wanted to see Granieri's face when she walked into the tent with his wife and child. She wanted to see him try to spin a whole family away. She wanted to win.

Her call with Essa Montgomery had been illuminating. Merritt thought the only good rattlesnake was a dead one, so the stitches didn't bother her. But she wouldn't turn up her nose at the development either. She'd be the leading expert on all things New Hope. A guest on CNN maybe. She could make a documentary. P.J. would work for cheap, she figured. She hadn't approved or disapproved of Essa's decision to break into Granieri's home – at least not verbally – more interested in the reason why it had to be tonight. The preacher hosted a meeting at New Hope every Friday, drawing a crowd. A ready-made, attentive audience. As soon as she'd hung up on Essa, Merritt had driven to Charlotte, North Carolina. Her dress was wrinkled, and sweat pooled at the small of her back from being in a car so long, but it would be worth it. Wouldn't it?

The New Hope tent came into view, a bright square against the velvet background of night. It eclipsed everything else around it, including the charred home and rubble of a former church. Kimberly tensed beside her.

'I've heard the Friday-night meetings are more like revivals. Music and dancing. Zach will love it,' Merritt said.

P.J. snorted, and Merritt wished she could kick him in the shins. She shot him a dirty look in the rearview mirror.

'We should wait until it's over to go inside,' Kimberly said.

Merritt didn't respond right away, knowing that would spoil her vision.

'Of course – whatever you think is best,' she said as she pulled over to the road's shoulder. The parking lot was full, and she didn't want to get stuck there if she needed to leave in a hurry. 'It's pretty cold out though. I'm not sure it's safe to wait out here on such a dark road.'

Kimberly mulled over the warning as Merritt exited the car and headed toward the trunk. She watched as the woman pulled her sleepy son from his car seat and slipped his arms into a puffy coat. The boy was awake now but groggy.

This is going to work, Merritt thought. She would make it work.

She smoothed out her dress as best she could and pulled on the matching blazer. She moved to let P.J. grab his equipment, the young man practically bouncing with excitement. She'd picked him up at his dorm on the way back from Charlotte. Kimberly had questioned if a camera was necessary, but Merritt had assured her anything she wanted struck from the record would be struck from the record. If she crossed her fingers behind her back, nobody would be the wiser.

'Ready?' Merritt asked brightly, heading toward the gravel parking lot where she'd be able to walk more steadily in her heels. Kimberly was dressed casually, but she'd taken the time to fix her hair and put on makeup. A pretty, faithful wife. She was going to pop on film, as if pulled from central casting for the part. Micah

Granieri didn't deserve her, and maybe she'd wake up and see that some day. Maybe tonight. Maybe Merritt was doing the right thing for the wrong reasons. It wouldn't be the first time.

Their little band of four approached the tent opening, and Zach perked up. He squirmed to be let down, and Kimberly let him.

'Are we going to a party? Will there be cake?'

'No cake, sweetheart, but I packed snacks.'

Kimberly held Zach's hand while rummaging in her purse for a fruit rollup. Zach seemed satisfied, and Merritt ignored the pang of guilt in her stomach. She didn't mention Kimberly's desire to wait outside but instead opened the makeshift door as if the matter had been decided. They filed into the back, and Merritt gestured for P.J. to start rolling. He was already hoisting the camera on to his shoulder though, and Merritt nodded in approval. A quick study, she'd give him that.

A man she'd never seen before stood at the microphone talking about how he'd woken up one morning in the middle of a deserted parking lot, not remembering how he'd arrived but knowing he had to change his life.

Amens rippled through the crowd. The man was fully clothed, but his earnestness made him seem naked. Exposed.

'This was a mistake,' Kimberly whispered, but she craned her neck to see over the crowd, trying to catch a glimpse of her husband. Only a few people standing at the back noticed they'd walked inside.

Merritt glanced at the people on stage, disappointed not to see Granieri. She wanted P.J. to get a clear shot of his face when he saw the wife and son he'd abandoned. The wife and son he'd failed to mention to his adoring followers, the ones who tried to set him up with their daughters or flirted themselves.

'Stay put. I'll have a quick look around.'

Zach asked what they were doing there, but Merritt had already moved away by the time Kimberly answered. Merritt walked to the left side of the tent, scanning each row as she made her way to the front. She was too conspicuous for people not to notice her, but she didn't care. Her heart started to pound as she got to the front and turned around. He wasn't anywhere to be seen. He wasn't there. *Oh god,* she thought. *Essa.*

FORTY-ONE

Essa imagined hell might feel like this when you arrived – heat, pain and fear swirling into a kind of dizzying cocktail. Her limbs went numb, but somehow her feet moved forward. When her forehead brushed against something, she screamed then slapped a hand over her mouth. A string. Only a string. She pulled on it, and a bulb buzzed on overhead, bathing the room in orange. She could see the plastic boxes now, each one with a venomous snake peering out. The rattlesnake she'd bumped didn't seem happy. It raised its triangular head as best it could in such a confined space, lidded eyes assessing. Essa looked back, as scared as she'd ever been in her life. Black spots filled her vision, and she sank to the ground, putting her head between her knees for a second.

She took a few deep breaths and practiced the grounding technique she'd been taught by her high-school counselor. What could she see? In the corner, an empty terrarium. What could she hear? The low hum of the lightbulb and an occasional rattle, like dice rolling around a cup. She could hear a snake that wanted to be left alone. Smell? She couldn't place it. Some combination of bleach and mold maybe. Unlike the rest of Pastor Micah's house, the basement was unfinished and unimpressive. Touch? The cool concrete in contrast to the heated room. And taste? She'd always struggled with that one, but her mouth was sour as if she'd eaten cabbage. She rose to her knees then wobbled to her feet.

Essa moved toward the boxes, ignoring the first rattlesnake and looking for a more docile animal. She found a copperhead flicking its tongue and moved away. That one wouldn't do. She found another rattlesnake curled up, its head tucked into a corner, and tapped on its container. When it didn't respond, she shook the box slightly, and it uncoiled a little, raising its head. Bingo. She could see the fresh sutures, and her heart squeezed.

'You'll be all right, little one.' Essa carefully slid the box toward her, hoping the latch held. It was a high-stakes game of Jenga. The container was deep and awkward to carry, but Essa pressed the side against her stomach, wincing when it touched her new cut.

She turned back toward the window, head jerking toward a movement along the baseboard. When dark scales slid forward, she
fumbled the container, regaining control before it hit the ground. A
cottonmouth stood between her and her only escape.

She'd always had trouble telling cottonmouths apart from water
snakes. They both sported dark olive or brown skin, the pattern
difficult to distinguish. Up close, water snakes have vertical stripes
along their mouths, but if you're that close, you're too close. This
specimen was easy to identify though, because its jaw hung open,
exposing an expanse of white inside and two long fangs. When it
hissed, Essa took a step backward obediently. She gulped air and
prayed, hoping God would understand, yes, she'd gotten herself into
this mess, but she hadn't meant to test her faith. Her father sprang
to mind, how he was always so good with animals, how she was
better with the dead ones.

The snake hissed again, its body settled except for the head. She
took another step back, her heel finding the stairs and making her
stumble. The cottonmouth lashed at the air in response, and Essa
took a couple of steps up. The door at the top remained locked, but
at least she was farther away for the time being.

The snake retreated but stayed below the window, its coiled body
ready for a fight. Essa searched for something to throw, her eyes
finding the empty terrarium. Could the snake be pregnant? That
could explain its aggression. The reason did little to calm her though.

Essa pushed through her panic and took a cautious step toward
the tank, cringing when the cottonmouth moved, ready to spring.
Awkwardly, she shifted the plastic box to her right hip then scooped
sand from the bottom of the tank. Her first throw only made the
animal mad; it jerked its body back and forth then sank back into
its defensive stance. Essa tried again, and the snake moved a few
inches before settling.

They're more afraid of us, she told herself, scooping more sand
and flinging it. Her heart beat painfully inside her rib cage.

When the snake stretched out, she aimed for its tail, which caused
it to move even farther from the window. The motion would have
been hypnotizing in another situation. Uncoil, coil, uncoil, coil.

After a last toss, the snake retreated to a corner as far as it could
go, and Essa crept toward the only escape, keeping the snake in
sight. Then she had a terrible thought. If she left the light on, Pastor
Micah would know right away somebody had broken in. Without

the light, he might not discover his snake was missing until morning at the earliest or even Sunday. Her instincts told her to run, save herself, but the rattlesnake's lethargic body told her it must be starving and dehydrated. She could save this one at least. Essa reached overhead, tugging the string and plunging them into darkness.

With a few quick strides Essa reached the window, conscious the cottonmouth was only a few feet away, and shoved the box through the opening, pushing it as far as she could. Then she placed her hands on the frame and pulled herself up, ignoring the glass that dug into her palms. She could almost sense the snake inside moving below her, but she kept crawling, her body halfway to safety.

The bite didn't surprise her. In some ways, she'd been moving toward this moment her whole life. She screamed nonetheless as the fangs pierced her jeans and sank into her calf. And then she was free, collapsing on to the frozen ground. She scrambled forward, expecting to see the snake crawling toward her, but after a few seconds, when nothing happened, she stumbled to her feet and picked up her kidnapped specimen.

Essa could see two puncture marks in her pants, and she knew there was blood underneath. Less than on other parts of her body but more deadly. She limped toward the cul-de-sac, hurrying. If she could make it back to her car, she could stow the snake and call an ambulance. A quarter mile. Five minutes. She put one foot in front of the other.

FORTY-TWO

'I know you're in there. I can see your disgusting toes underneath the door.'

Merritt Callahan knocked again on Otis's apartment door, slapping her open palm against the wood. She should have been nicer, but nice didn't come naturally, and Merritt felt as panicked as she'd ever felt. If something happened to Essa, would it be her fault?

When Otis unhooked his safety chain and opened the door, he was standing in only boxers, his hair disheveled and eyes red. He looked like he hadn't slept in days. Merritt glanced behind him to see his bed covered in papers and photographs.

'This is a pants-on situation, Lieutenant. The sooner the better.'

Merritt turned around to give Kimberly an encouraging smile, hoping the expression didn't look like a grimace. Zach remained surprisingly docile, scared maybe, and P.J. looked like he was on the adventure of a lifetime. Merritt could picture him regaling his friends with the tale back at his dorm. One for the yearbook.

'Ma'am,' Otis said to Kimberly, nodding politely in greeting then retreating to pull khakis over his underwear. 'A little warning would have been good, Merry. You don't get cell reception?'

Merritt regretted telling Otis her childhood nickname, even if it did match his decor, but at least he hadn't asked her to leave. Yet. She had a pretty big favor to ask.

'What's all this?' Merritt gestured to the mess on Otis's bed. He pushed the papers into a pile, hiding his work.

'Are you an elf?' It was the first time Zach had spoken since they'd left the New Hope tent. Kimberly put him down, and the boy walked over to a plastic reindeer, inspecting the bells. 'You're not short. Elves are short.'

'Santa's an elf. He's not short,' said Otis. The man and boy stared at each other, unblinking.

'That's true,' said Zach, conceding the point.

'This is important, Otis. I need you to call it in.' Merritt didn't have time for bonding rituals.

'Call what in?'

Otis handed Zach the remote, and Kimberly helped him find a channel with cartoons. The woman was confused, not sure why Merritt was so upset. She'd asked to go home more than once, but Merritt couldn't let her leave yet. Basically, she'd kidnapped a woman and child. That was a concern for another time though.

Merritt never rambled, but the words cascaded out of her. How she'd met Kimberly and liked her immediately. How she'd wanted to reunite the Granieris. She sold her version of events as best she could. Otis looked more and more suspicious rather than charmed.

'How sweet. Merritt Callahan, do-gooder extraordinaire. So what's the problem? Granieri's not at his meeting. This can't wait until tomorrow?'

Merritt took a deep breath, trying and failing to stay calm. She picked up some of the papers Otis had assembled. Autopsy reports and interview notes. She could have kissed him. He still didn't believe Clyde was guilty. Maybe there was a chance.

'The Montgomery girl might be in danger.' Merritt glanced at Kimberly before continuing. 'She may have been planning to break into the preacher's house. She wanted proof of some sort. Of animal abuse.'

Merritt lowered her voice at 'animal abuse' so Zach wouldn't hear. Kimberly made a strangled noise low in her throat.

'Were we supposed to be a distraction?' the woman asked. 'Were you using us?'

'No, nothing like that.'

Otis gave her a look that said *everything like that,* which Merritt ignored.

'It's that I knew your husband would be at New Hope because Essa told me. That's all, I swear. I didn't even think about her stupid plan. But what if he finds her? Who knows what he'll do.'

'Wait, what animal abuse? The snakes?' Otis asked.

Merritt nodded pointedly at the boy who'd climbed on to Otis's bed and was swishing the papers around.

'It's ugly,' she said.

Otis went to his nightstand and picked up a blue file.

'These are the necropsy results. There's nothing in here about animal abuse.'

'Nothing about sutures?'

Kimberly walked over to the bed and sat beside her son. She

seemed subdued for being tricked by Merritt. More disappointed than angry the night hadn't turned out how she'd wanted. Used to being mistreated.

Otis flipped back through the pages, showing Merritt the notes on burns and smoke inhalation. Photos of the exteriors, then closeups of the organs, including the stomach.

'Is there a list of contents?'

'Only digested bone,' Otis said.

'We don't have time for you to play Sherlock,' Merritt said. 'Call it in.'

'You think anybody at the department's going to listen to me? I'm on the thinnest of ice. I'm on water basically. And I'm no Jesus.'

Merritt wouldn't beg. Instead, she stood quietly until Otis's conscience got the better of him. She knew he wouldn't leave the Montgomery girl in danger.

'You all right here for a while?' he asked Kimberly. 'There's a Chinese place that delivers.'

'We'll have to be, won't we?'

'Be sure to use the locks,' he said. 'All the locks.'

Merritt wanted to give the woman some sort of pep talk, but cheerfulness – even fake cheerfulness – failed her. She watched Otis open the top drawer of his dresser and pull out his shoulder holster and Glock. Zach watched him too, *Paw Patrol* no match for a real-life cop. Otis put his badge in his coat pocket then took it out again, grabbing his walkie-talkie instead.

'I'm breaking a few rules,' he said to Merritt, perhaps wanting her to know how much he was risking.

Laws, Merritt thought. Not rules. But she didn't correct him.

FORTY-THREE

The velvet bag moved on the seat beside him, and Pastor Micah cracked a window, letting the icy air whip inside his car. The snake stopped after a minute or two. He was surprised the copperhead had lasted so long, and he admired the will to live, he really did. He didn't bother defanging copperheads or stitching them up. Compared to rattlesnake venom, theirs was mild. Still dangerous, sure, under the right conditions, but nobody had died from a copperhead bite in West Virginia for years. No, it was enough to withhold food and water until they gave up the ghost.

Essa's car wasn't parked at Juliet's place or at Charlene's. Pastor Micah even looked at the lab before turning toward his home. It wasn't logical – the notion that she might be waiting for him – but when had logic guided him since the girl came into his life? She'd possessed him, but there would be an end to his suffering. He could feel her, pulling him toward her in the dark. He didn't even mind the cold, and he rolled down his own window. His eyes burned, and the houses blurred into one another.

After a while, the creek-side neighborhood disappeared, and he started the stretch of wilderness that led to river-side. Not for the first time, he considered how abandoned Vintera felt at times. Forsaken. But he'd been called to guide them back. If Essa belonged to him, there'd be no getting rid of him. He'd be one of them, a shepherd bringing the serpent orphan back into the fold. He knew he'd created his own mythology, but it was a mythology nonetheless. There was power in belief.

He fantasized about Essa waiting for him on his front porch, celestial light above. Her skin would be cold to the touch, her mouth warming under his. He'd take his time, try not to scare her. Micah lost himself so completely in this fantasy that he didn't notice the body when he passed it. About a mile after, his thoughts shuddered back into reality, and he wondered what he'd seen on the shoulder. A bundle of clothes including a familiar olive-green coat. He shivered and rolled up his windows as he pulled over. Tricks. His mind playing some sort of terrible joke. It couldn't be.

Pastor Micah had little experience with panic, but his breathing became shallow as he pulled back on to the road and headed back the way he'd come, creeping. Still, he almost missed her, sprawled on the gravel. He stopped and bolted out of his car.

Essa lay face down, her legs curled as if she'd been trying to crawl. At first, he thought she was gurgling then realized the sound came from his own throat, his own fear. He kneeled, placing his fingers against her neck, relieved to find a pulse. He moved to turn her over when he noticed the neat puncture wounds in her jeans, the fresh blood around the holes.

He looked around, seeing a familiar plastic box, a dark shape inside, and his fear turned to fury in an instant. *What a little bitch.* She'd stolen from him. Taken from him. As if she hadn't done enough, robbing him of his sanity.

He pulled out his phone to call 911, the pieces clicking together. If she lived, the girl would tell the police about his basement. He'd lose his congregation if they knew he maimed the snakes, maybe serve a little time even for keeping dangerous wildlife. He'd lose everything he'd worked so hard to gain. But he loved her, didn't he? Hadn't he thought of her every day for years? Wasn't this love? He could scarcely breathe.

Pastor Micah couldn't wait any longer. Somebody was bound to drive by. He looked around, surprised to see a turnoff he'd never noticed before and Essa's car parked out of sight from drivers. He used his foot to roll her still body farther away from the main road, then he opened the lid of the container. The snake was unresponsive, but after a good shake, it raised its head and slithered out into the night. Pastor Micah climbed back into his car and drove away in the other direction.

FORTY-FOUR

The painkillers dulled her sense of reality, and Juliet already wanted off them. She'd tried skipping a dose, though, and found she couldn't move an inch without a hot sort of searing pain in her stomach, as if she was being branded. The row of stitches in the shape of a grin irritated her. She'd been told not to lift anything, but what was she going to lift in her hospital room? Her mother had gone to tidy up the nursery before Juliet and Aster came home. Aster Usher Montgomery. Though Juliet still called her Starfish.

Juliet leaned up in bed, ignoring the outline of Aunt CeeCee in the corner. The ghost had arrived as soon as her mother left but had been blessedly quiet. More watchful than anything. Juliet thought she might well be a hallucination this time. Regardless, she didn't want an 'I told you so' from an incorporeal being, not even one her own mind had created.

Juliet swung her feet to the floor, unsurprised to find it icy but surprised to find she liked the sensation. With only a small grimace, she pushed herself to stand. Essa hadn't dropped off the hospital bag Juliet had packed for delivery, but she wasn't angry at the girl anymore. It was as if all that built-up resentment had slipped away as soon as she'd seen Aster's face. Essa had been somebody's daughter too. And she was left alone in the world. *But not alone now,* Juliet thought, determined she'd offer Clyde's sister – Aster's aunt – a permanent place to stay. It wasn't the life she'd imagined, but she could see it working out somehow.

It was a short walk to the NICU, where Juliet stopped in front of the windows to stare at the three babies inside. Aster was bigger than the other two, almost full-term, and the doctors said she was responding well to the antibiotics.

A nurse noticed her and gestured for her to come inside, unlocking the door. 'Wash your hands, hun. I'll get her for you.'

Juliet didn't pay much attention to the soap bubbles on her skin as she watched the nurse scoop up Aster and adjust the swaddle. The nurse rocked side to side while Juliet lowered herself into the chair available for parents, not even noticing the twinge this time.

Then Aster was in her arms, her eyes closed in sleep, her mouth moving slightly, searching. When Aunt CeeCee kneeled beside them, Juliet made herself ignore the ghost or vision, not wanting to look insane. But somehow she felt calmer even as the temperature in the room dropped.

The nurse rubbed the arms of her cardigan. 'I'll just be a sec.'

She stepped into the hallway. Juliet could see her through the glass, consulting with a doctor. She'd ask when Aster could come home as soon as she returned.

'You said something had to fall apart.' Juliet glanced at Aunt CeeCee then lowered her gaze back to her perfect baby. 'This feels like something coming together.'

'Uh-huh. I told you we can't predict the future, no more than you can.'

'Then why warn me?'

'Same reason you left that protection mark on the ground in front of little Essa's oak tree. Always best to be prepared. Human plans so rarely work out.'

Juliet thought back to her vision of a cozy home with help from Aunt Essa and occasionally her mother. Her friends stopping by. Aster asleep in the corner during readings. Her heart tightened, trying to read between the lines, understand this new warning.

'A seven-sided star for the seven days of creation. I thought it would suit Essa,' she said.

'It does, and that's the truth. Might even make a difference when she needs it the most.'

Something about Aunt CeeCee's tone made Juliet tear her attention away from Aster's perfect face. She tried to read the ghost's emotion, but it was a sensation unlike anything she'd experienced before, in some ways even more intense than what Madame Clarita had shown her.

'You saying Essa needs protection now?'

'We don't feel things the same way as you. What's fear when you're already dead?' Aunt CeeCee said, her tone as gentle as it had ever been.

'Spit it out. I don't have patience for riddles.'

'I'm saying, I've done what I could for you girls. And I hope it's enough.'

FORTY-FIVE

The robin's call sounded human, like a man trying to get his wife's attention while she gardened. It trilled, a few notes up then down, and began well before dawn. Not a species to join a chorus so much as start one. The gentle whistle met Essa where she lay, sprawled on a gravel road, her head and hands beneath her own car. Her eyes opened to darkness, and the pain followed. Every part of her body ached, including her palms as she tried to push herself back and failed, collapsing to the ground with a ragged inhale. Had she died? Was she dead? The rocks felt real enough, and she could smell tar. She winced but pushed again until she could roll over and sit up. Nothing had ever felt so much like a dream, especially when a watery form of Great Aunt CeeCee swam in front of her, waving. Essa almost waved back, but the image vanished.

She wasn't dead then. And the lid of Pastor Micah's box had been knocked loose, no rattlesnake in sight.

'Damn.' Essa cringed at her own language. She should have been praising God instead of cursing him. The cottonmouth's bite must have been dry, no venom, her reaction nothing more than a panic attack. A laugh bubbled up from her sternum and burst into the air, startling the birds nearby. They took off into the air as Essa convulsed hysterically, holding her sides. *They shall take up serpents,* she thought, *and they shall recover.* What sort of faith was this?

It took her a few minutes to catch her breath, but she wiped her eyes, stifling a few last laughs. She rolled her jeans to examine the bite marks, which were swelling, but like you might expect from a cat scratch. She didn't pause to inspect her other injuries but climbed to her feet, letting her eyes adjust. The sky had turned gray. She'd somehow made it back to her car but not inside it, and as if she needed to feel more grateful, she sent up a small prayer for not freezing to death. But it would all have been a waste of time if she couldn't find the rattlesnake. Dehydrated and starved, it couldn't have crawled far.

Essa took a ginger step toward the woods, squinting at the ground.

She made a small circle around her car, then expanded it. When she was in high school, a little boy had gone missing from the playground, and volunteers had come to help the police force, including her entire senior class. They'd cancelled school, allowing every adult and almost adult to spread out alongside professionals and their hounds. Round and round they'd gone, widening the circle with each pass. They hadn't found anything, but the story had a happy ending of sorts. The boy's father had taken him. The kid had been found unharmed at a Six Flags in Maryland, returned to his mother within a day.

As the sky grew brighter, Essa became paranoid, worried Pastor Micah might come for her, might be watching her now. Every snapped twig made her pause, but she focused on the task at hand. She was cold, hungry and tired. She needed medical attention, but something made her keep looping.

She was about a yard into the nearby woods when she heard the rattle. Fear and relief flooded into her body at once, almost taking her back down. But she walked toward the sound, spotting the animal. Unlike her taxidermied version back at the lab, this one looked pathetic, its body barely moving, much less coiled. It shook its tail in warning, but Essa could almost see it as an old dog, happy its owner was there. She kneeled, expecting her heart to pound, but instead it squeezed again in sympathy. Her hand moved slowly toward the animal as it half-heartedly ducked away from her then tried to strike. She lifted the body into her arms and cradled it.

'We'll get through this.' Essa maneuvered the snake back into the box and closed the lid. She put the container in her back seat and said one last prayer for her car to start, knowing she'd asked for a lot of favors recently. The engine caught though, and Essa let out a whoop of satisfaction. She put the car into gear and pulled out on the highway, torn between calling Merritt right away or going to see Dr Kester. A few days ago Essa might have called Lieutenant Barnes, but she didn't trust him. She wanted desperately to take down Pastor Micah, and if he noticed the break-in, he'd get rid of all the other evidence. There'd be nothing except for what she'd stolen. Maybe Dr Kester could save the animal. It hadn't done anything to deserve this kind of treatment. Stitches. She couldn't imagine anything more barbaric.

She checked the time and saw it was almost six o'clock. She drove toward Dr Kester's house. She'd never been there, but she knew where he lived, way out in the country where he could commune with live animals before dealing with dead ones.

As she drove, the sky lightened, turning to a brilliant blue. She passed her own house on the way, knowing she'd never be able to move back inside. Her bedroom was gone and half the living room. It stood though, unlike New Hope, which was a pile of ash and rubble. She hoped that meant something. She hoped that meant she'd survive too. The white tent looked like an emergency medical facility, a triage center. She might pull it up herself, stake by stake, if Pastor Micah left town. She might like that. She might like that a lot.

It seemed appropriate that deer grazed in Dr Kester's yard when she arrived. Three of them, and they froze as she stepped out into the morning. Some people called them overgrown rats and argued to extend the hunting season. With their big brown eyes and long legs, Essa would call them little miracles, but she was feeling inspired. Proud of herself even.

She opened the back seat and pulled out the box, carrying it toward the front door. The gash on her stomach hurt, but she hardly noticed the sting. She stopped to appreciate the Kester house with its stone facade and peaked roof. Smoke even rose from the chimney on top, a sure sign they were awake despite the hour. Their yard was overrun by weeds, and beyond, the woods swallowed everything. Essa could be happy in a place like this.

She wasn't sure how long she'd been standing there when Dr Kester stepped outside in his robe, followed by Sander, who looked impressive from a distance, his giant frame covered in clean but patchy fur. The guard dog let out a low growl, but Dr Kester calmed him with a touch. Essa wanted to remember that moment forever.

'Essa?'

Dr Kester sounded as worried as she'd ever heard him. She must look bad, and the paternal concern was too much for her. She tried to make a joke, something about the other guy, but her voice caught in her throat.

Dr Kester clucked compassionately and walked toward her in his house slippers. When he got closer though, he recoiled seeing what she carried toward him. 'What in God's name do you think you're doing?'

'It's hurt,' Essa forced out. 'Can you fix it?'

Dr Kester's unruly hair blew in the wind, his eyes equally wild. His face turned from pink to white as he stared. For a moment,

Essa thought he might refuse. She'd thought this was the natural thing to do. Well, not quite natural, but the right thing to do, saving the animal. Her emotions had turned toward embarrassment when Dr Kester finally took the box from her.

'I thought—' he started then cut himself off. 'Never mind.'

His wife appeared at the front door, her flannel nightgown no match for the January morning.

'Wick,' she called. 'Everything all right?'

As they drew closer, Essa could see the woman had goosebumps along her arms. They favored each other, Dr Kester and his wife. White hair and red faces. Dr Kester's was pale, though, as he walked inside. Essa noticed his shoulders sagged, and she deflated in response. Maybe nothing could be done. The feeling of triumph seeped from her body.

'Monsters being monsters,' he said to his wife as he passed by her and into their kitchen.

It had a small hearth with a fire burning inside. An old Winchester shotgun hung above as decoration, and Essa felt a little as if she'd stepped back in time. She saw a few of the jadeite pieces she knew the Kesters enjoyed collecting and a brass tea kettle on the stove.

'Same as it ever was. Best get out some parchment paper.'

Mrs Kester scurried to the pantry, finding two boxes and bringing them to the dining-room table. As she spread them out, covering the wood, she snuck glances at Essa. They'd never met before, and Essa wished that the circumstances were better. That she wasn't covered in blood.

As if Mrs Kester could read her thoughts, she mentioned a bathroom down the hallway. Essa glanced self-consciously at her cut palms and limped in the right direction.

The sight that met her in the mirror was even worse than she'd expected. She touched a cut on her forehead.

'Towels in the closet,' Mrs Kester called, and Essa jerked back, wiping the blood on her pants. Dr Kester murmured something in response, but she couldn't hear him.

When Essa opened the closet door, she found a deep, cold space filled with linens and knickknacks. She spotted a bicycle missing both tires and a shelf full of jigsaw puzzles. She pictured the Kesters working them on the weekends.

She grabbed a navy towel and started to close the door when her eyes fell on two antique gasoline canisters. Essa paused, second-guessing herself. A lot of prepared people kept gas cans and extra oil around, especially in the country.

Essa walked deeper into the space, clutching the towel to her chest. Even though she was half expecting them, the lighters shocked her. Had Dr Kester burned down New Hope? Had he burned down her home?

She recalled his efforts to get her a new job. Could he have been trying to get her out of town? No, he had no reason to want her gone. And he'd helped her. For years, Essa reminded herself, reaching toward the canisters. Empty, they lifted into the air, and she put them back as quietly as she could.

Essa pulled out her cell phone, distressed to find she didn't get any reception so far out. But when she tucked it away again, she almost laughed at herself. She was being paranoid again. She was tired and dirty and not thinking straight. Dr Kester was an honorable man, passionate about making the world a better place for animals of every fur and feather.

Back at the sink, she ran water and splashed it over her face, using soap to clean the cut. She lifted her shirt, wincing when blood made it stick to her skin. There wasn't much she could do about those injuries, so she washed her hands instead. *For animals of every fur and feather,* she thought, freezing. *And scale.* Would he have burned down the church to shut down Pastor Micah's operation? Keep him from hurting any more snakes?

When she walked back into the kitchen, Dr Kester had administered some sort of sedative to the snake and held a magnifying glass over the animal's mouth, a sharp set of scissors in the other. Mrs Kester sat in a nearby chair, her eyes closed.

Essa lowered her voice so as not to wake her.

'I can hold the glass for you,' she said, her voice shaking. She wasn't scared of Dr Kester over a few cans of gasoline, was she? Her mind scrambled to justify the lighters she'd found. It was a catchall closet. She'd probably find buried treasure if she hunted long enough. Nonetheless, she hung back.

Dr Kester noticed the change in her demeanor and leaned up. She tried to meet his gaze, but before she could help herself, she glanced away.

'I hoped it wouldn't come to this.' Dr Kester took a step toward her. 'I am sorry about your brother, truly. I didn't want anyone to get arrested. It should have looked like an accident. Would have been deemed an accident if that blowhard hadn't gotten involved. Stirred up trouble. What's the devil without a captive audience?'

Essa felt faint and told herself now wasn't the time for another panic attack. Not that her internal pep talks had ever worked before, but she had to stay calm. She'd been thinking about the fires – about the teenagers – but Karl's face swam into her mind. The way she'd been able to see the bones and cartilage of his nose. It now seemed obvious to her – Karl must have found something during the dissection he'd performed. His arrogance would never let anything go, while Essa could be cowed into submission. At least, Dr Kester would assume as much. He saw her as a lost sixteen-year-old, trying to disappear behind a mop. And getting rid of Essa's necropsy notes had been as easy as striking another match. Dr Kester wouldn't kill her though, she figured. Not right in front of his wife. Essa glanced again at Mrs Kester whose head had rolled to the side. She breathed so heavily that it sounded like snoring.

'Telazol,' Dr Kester said. 'I'd never use anything that would hurt her.'

Dr Kester took another step toward Essa. His attitude still read as paternal, but Essa kept her eyes on the kitchen shears. She watched as he tightened his hold. Tears sprang to her eyes, which made him pause.

'I could give you Telazol first, if you'd like.'

The offer sounded so gentle, so compassionate that for a moment Essa didn't understand what he meant. When the information sank in, she darted to the front door, aware Dr Kester followed. She reached the knob before being pulled back. The grip on her arm hurt, and when she yelped, Dr Kester hesitated. Essa took advantage of the moment to kick him in the leg as hard as she could. Her boot connected with the fleshy part of his calf, and he dropped her arm. She yanked the door open and ran into the yard, scattering the deer.

She glanced at her car then the woods and took off sprinting for the trees. They wanted to push her back, the tangled branches scraping at her face, and the roots tripping her feet. The bright day disappeared, and after a few seconds, she could hear Dr Kester crashing behind her, knowing the place better than she did. Her lungs burned as she scrambled farther into the dark, and the blood in her ears drowned out everything else. Her heartbeat. All she could hear was her heart pounding.

When she stumbled and fell, her knees slammed into the earth, and she rolled in pain. She scooted backward, looking around for a place to hide, looking around for anything that might be useful. A flash of white a few yards away had her climbing back up and sprinting again as best she could.

The trees seemed to come alive, as if they moved right in her way. She ducked under branches, somehow remaining upright as she half ran and half limped through the woods. The morning sun scattered light over the ground, making it slither and slide. Every once in a while, full sun would hit her in the face, and black spots would swim into her vision.

A noise to her left made her scurry in the other direction. She no longer had a sense of where she was in relation to the house, but she came to a clearing and skidded to a stop, her feet a few inches away from a drop-off. She inched forward and peered over the edge, her stomach sinking at the long way down. She wasn't up as high as Karl had been, but she was too high to survive such a fall.

When she turned to leave, Dr Kester walked into view, holding his side in one hand and the shotgun in the other, Sander beside him, the large frame and bared teeth making him look more menacing than an old dog had any right to look.

Essa raised her hands in the universal sign of surrender. Wind whipped behind her back, as if trying to help her, move her away from the ledge. But when she took a step forward, Sander growled, and Dr Kester leveled his shotgun at her.

'A fall will hurt less,' Dr Kester said. 'Instantaneous. These old guns have a mind of their own.'

'I know you meant to help,' Essa said in response, her heart trusting Dr Kester while her mind worked to override the affection she had for him. 'Same as you always done. Helpin' animals that can't help themselves. I understand. It's that . . . I want you to know is all. What you do matters. I should have burned New Hope down myself the day my mother died, saved us both a lot of trouble. But the thing is – there were kids inside, you know?'

Essa's throat felt scratchy, trying to project. She'd never made a speech before, but it seemed like the right time. The mention of the teenagers bothered Dr Kester – she could tell.

'I hate those foolhardy souls got mixed up in all this. But they shouldn't have been there anyway, right? That was none my fault.'

Essa tried to agree with him but couldn't force the lie out. She stared straight ahead instead, trying to imagine some creative way to save herself.

'They made a sacrifice,' Dr Kester continued, with more confidence. 'A small sacrifice to save countless animals from abuse. From torture, Essa. You of all people should understand. That church had to go. That pastor has to go.'

A small sacrifice? Essa didn't think their families would see it that way. Dr Kester had twisted himself up into knots, trying to justify his actions. He'd twisted himself up into such a tangle, there was no getting that mess loose again.

Essa tried to keep talking, say anything to stall for time, but she was too horrified to muster up even a word. She thought this might be the end, that God had protected her from the cottonmouth bite because she had a purpose. Yes, she could see now: her death would exonerate her brother. The police couldn't dismiss two colleagues dying in the same way as accidents. And maybe that was for the best. What did she have to live for besides herself? Now Clyde, Clyde was starting a family. Essa would get to see her mother again. And in heaven, she'd forgive her father. She forgave him now, she realized. Faith – real faith – was the greatest comfort she could know. A peace settled over her, and she closed her eyes.

The sound of a gun firing didn't surprise her. She didn't feel pain. She didn't feel anything at all except for the wind on her cheeks, cold but tender. She spread her arms and leaned back, time slowing down. Her happiest childhood memory swam before her, and she saw Tyson's Creek from the top of their oak tree that she'd climbed by herself for the first time. The foliage a red so vivid the leaves seemed more like rubies. Her father and brother stood on the ground below her, shielding their eyes to watch her. Fearless. They'd both called her fearless, and she remembered that sensation, reveled in it. She'd never felt that way again until this moment, and her heels tipped back.

The arms around her waist startled her, and she found herself slammed to the ground. At first, she thought Dr Kester had changed his mind, but when she looked over, she saw his prone body nearby, blood seeping out of a hole in his side. Confused, she realized the arms belonged to a woman in a dress much too thin for the weather and shoes much too tall for the forest.

'Miss Callahan?'

'Oh, thank God.' The reporter rolled off Essa, hand over her eyes, breath uneven. 'I thought we were too late.'

FORTY-SIX

Essa sat up, trying to make sense of everything she saw. A camera watched her from the shoulder of a young man. Merritt told him he could stop filming, waving him off as she gulped air.

'That was wicked.' The kid looked at Merritt Callahan as if she were a superhero. Lieutenant Barnes holstered his gun and checked Dr Kester's pulse.

'Alive,' he said, and Essa felt relieved even though the man had tried to kill her.

Lieutenant Barnes lifted his walkie-talkie, asking for assistance and reading off GPS coordinates. Essa saw him reach for his cuffs then hesitate. He slipped them back into his pocket but didn't take his eyes off Dr Kester. Not following the rules but not being stupid either.

'Miss Montgomery, you all right?'

Essa thought about her answer, how she'd been ready to die. She heard Juliet's voice in her head as clearly as if she were sitting next to her future sister-in-law: *You're thinking about making yourself into a little martyr.* She didn't know how Juliet had known, but she'd been right. Essa had failed, and she was glad for it.

'Fine besides owing you for my life,' Essa said when it seemed like the lieutenant was waiting for an answer.

'Pretty sure I owed you one.'

Essa started to dismiss the comment but decided he was right. He'd lied to her about Clyde. He'd accepted her suffering as a byproduct of his investigation. And it hadn't even helped him.

'Pretty sure you did,' she said, letting Merritt help her up. Lieutenant Barnes sent them and P.J. ahead, and they wove back through brush and trees. They reached the Kesters' driveway in time to see paramedics bringing Mrs Kester out on a stretcher. The woman's eyes were open, looking around, but heavy from the sedative.

'Merritt figured it all out,' the kid said, barely able to contain himself. 'Beats the hell of me how, but she knew. We went to that preacher's house, but nobody was there. And the basement—'

P.J.'s energy flagged, and he turned almost gray.

'I hate snakes, I have to tell you, but seeing them like that,' Merritt began then stopped too. 'Dr Kester would care, that's all. And frankly, I don't believe in coincidences. If he hadn't killed Karl Wachter, I never would have thought about it.'

Merritt's dress was wrinkled and had a tear in the side from where she'd tackled Essa. Otherwise, the woman could have stepped off a movie set. Even her lipstick looked fresh. Had she reapplied during their walk back through the woods? Essa didn't know much about reporting, but she knew if they'd recorded everything, Merritt Callahan could be a household name soon.

Nobody seemed in much of a hurry, that's what Essa noticed next. Sergeant Sallis even sat in a rocking chair on the front porch, pushing herself back and forth. Essa had been running since the night before, every limb weary. She wanted to slow down too, but it wasn't over yet.

'I'll see about the snake,' she said as if she needed to explain herself.

'I can kill it for you.'

Essa blanched. She hadn't even noticed when Lieutenant Barnes arrived. Two uniformed officers carted Dr Kester out of the woods, his body slung between them like a buck. Essa noticed the lieutenant squeeze Merritt's hand.

'"Behold, I send you out as sheep in the midst of wolves; so be shrewd as serpents and innocent as doves." Matthew 10:16,' Essa recited.

'If you say so,' Merritt said.

Essa shrugged. As she passed Sergeant Sallis, she thanked the officer for coming as if she were receiving guests at a wedding. In some ways, she felt like a bride, crossing a threshold into a new life. She didn't know what that life would be, but everything had changed now.

'I don't like to see the wrong man hanged is all,' the woman responded.

Essa walked inside the cabin, not liking to picture her brother on the end of a noose. A cop in latex gloves carried out the gas canisters, lighters already in an evidence bag. They were going to get it right this time. Clyde would go free.

Everybody ignored Essa as she walked back into the kitchen and toward her rescued rattlesnake. It was still sedated but awake now, the twin of Mrs Kester. Dr Kester had started to remove the stitches, and three sat on the linoleum countertop. Essa felt calm, no pounding heartbeat or sweaty palms. Fearless. She picked up the magnifying glass to get a better view. The removed sutures had left ugly red welts.

'We gonna do this or what,' she whispered and gripped the snake lightly behind its head. She didn't want to impair its breathing any further, but she didn't want to get bitten by a disoriented animal either.

With a knife she sawed at the remaining bands, her mood lightening with each pop. She could see the fangs now, but they didn't bother her. It was as if she'd floated above herself, a saintly version ready to step in if anything went wrong. Her protection.

But nothing went wrong, and Essa finished her procedure without incident. She put some water on a plate and let it drink, its forked tongue darting in and out like a cat. Since there weren't any frozen mice around, she picked up her charge and placed it gingerly back into the plastic box.

She looked to see Lieutenant Barnes, Sergeant Sallis and a couple of other law-enforcement agents shaking their heads. P.J. had his lens trained on her, and Merritt rushed to assure her they wouldn't run anything without her permission.

'Well, if that wasn't the damnedest thing I've ever seen,' Sergeant Sallis said.

'Maybe one of y'all could call Hovatter's for me? They'd know what to do,' Essa said, trying to deflect attention from herself. The zoo was closed to the public this time of year, but they'd have veterinarians on staff. Hopefully a herpetologist.

The ambulances left while Essa was giving her statement. It wasn't a straightforward story, but she didn't lie about breaking into the preacher's house. If they wanted to charge her with trespassing, they could. Somehow she doubted her transgression would make it into the final report. Essa promised Merritt a real interview after she had a chance to clean herself up.

When she stepped outside, snowflakes greeted her, christening everything they touched. Within the hour, Thorngold County would be blanketed in white. For the first time in many years, Essa noticed how pretty her hometown was. Fields and creeks and mountains in the distance. As she drove back to Juliet's, Essa imagined the daughter who would grow up with two loving parents, and she said another prayer, one filled with thanks rather than requests. Anything seemed possible. Not elsewhere, but right there in Vintera, now that she had faith in herself.

A YEAR AFTER THE FIRE

The figurine looked like something you might find in an antique shop, dirty and ignored on a back shelf, surrounded by porcelain cats and metal toy cars. Essa had never seen one in this shape, a three-inch goblet that would hold a thimble's worth of water. Small elephants were popular in the ivory trade. Human faces and necklaces. Her textbook showed confiscated roses. But this? She let her magnifying glass hover over the oddity. It would have to be crushed up to determine whether it was made from illegally hunted elephants or legally hunted sea lions.

'Best guess?'

Essa turned toward her newest hire, a girl who'd dropped out of the local high school. Esther Ruth cleaned the lab in the mornings, but Essa usually sent her home before five. She locked up herself. Some habits are hard to break, and she liked to talk to Greta and sometimes Cal without being interrupted.

'Toxicology's not my specialty. We'll speak with Sip when she gets back from vacation.'

'Thought it might be nice to have a case without blood and guts for once.'

Esther Ruth had nearly passed out the first time she'd watched Essa cut into a specimen, but she'd grown more curious than repulsed over time.

'Maybe someday we'll solve the case of the missing yarn, but not today.'

Essa had been surprised when the lab's board of directors had made her interim director, assuming Sip and Gloriana would balk. Instead, they'd been happy not to deal with paperwork. They focused on investigative work while Essa stuck to the forms and dissections. Her minor celebrity status didn't hurt. Video footage of her saving the rattlesnake had gone viral. They called her the rattlesnake whisperer. It was a step up from serpent orphan at least.

Essa walked through the taxidermy room to her office. She'd had the fluorescent lights replaced with new bulbs, which made the specimens look less like hunting trophies and more like models.

Their local taxidermy guy had come in and repaired them as well. Everything shone a little brighter than it had under Dr Kester. They all missed his expertise, though they never mentioned him by name and would never see him again. Back-to-back life sentences.

Enough time had passed that they sometimes reminisced about Karl. The year had softened their memories, his overbearing personality more a source of humor than irritation. Gloriana had proven to be an untapped resource with an almost photographic memory. She could recall cases going back to the founding of the lab. Not to mention zoological details. She'd noticed a missing gallbladder from an ocelot that had helped prove the animal had been kept in captivity.

The budget kept Essa up some nights, wondering if one day she'd wake up to shuttered doors. But worrying about salaries and benefits felt like an appropriate worry, not like dead parents and abusive preachers.

After Merritt Callahan's breaking story, Pastor Micah had paid a fine for keeping illegal wildlife. A slap on the wrist. But his name was dirt in Thorngold County. He'd moved back in with Kimberly and Zach. The woman deserved better, but to each her own. New Hope closed for good. No more summer tent revivals. No more Sunday-morning services. The community missed the Friday-night recovery meetings, but a few NA groups had popped up to try and fill the gap. The land around them had been sold, but Essa and Clyde had held on to their little parcel. One day, they'd build there, make a cheerful home for Aster Montgomery. Her brother had given Essa half the insurance money and refused to hear otherwise. She'd bought a car seat and put the rest into savings. She had everything she wanted for the moment.

The knock on her door didn't surprise her, and Essa smiled to see Juliet holding Aster on her hip, takeout bags in her free hand. The child had chubby red cheeks and giggled when she saw her aunt. The happiest baby Essa had ever met.

'Her first word's gonna be Greta,' Juliet said as Aster reached toward the stuffed hawk.

'Better than snake.' Essa took her niece. The child clung briefly then reached out again for the bird. 'Aunt Essa knows what to get this love bug.'

'You wouldn't dare.' Juliet pulled out napkins for their weekly lunch date. The women never seemed to tire of each other even though they'd lived together for a year. Instead, they both felt as if a void had been filled. Aunt CeeCee hadn't visited lately. Juliet said that the ghost's unresolved business was complete. She'd brought them together. Essa hated to admit she wanted to see her dead aunt, but she had a real-world family now.

'I know where I can get a deal on taxidermied squirrels,' Essa said.

'And I know a good trashcan.'

Juliet finished unpacking their meal, tossing the extra ketchup packets on to the middle of Essa's desk. Sometimes they ate out, but Essa preferred their makeshift picnics where Aster could crawl on the carpet when she got tired of being held. At first, Essa had used the unclaimed, windowless office even after her promotion. After a while though, she'd realized there was no reason not to move into Dr Kester's old space. She'd never noticed before, but she could stare out her window and see the Alleghenies in the distance. They changed every season but would be there long after she'd departed the earth and joined her ancestors. Sometimes her mind drifted in that morbid direction, but other days? Other days, she unwrapped a hamburger and helped plan a zoo-themed birthday party for one spirited, beloved little girl.

ACKNOWLEDGMENTS

When I was a junior in high school, I went on a field trip to the Alabama Shakespeare Festival in Montgomery where I saw a production of *Measure for Measure*. I had never read the play before, which is perhaps why I was shocked at the plight of Isabella as well as swayed by her passionate pleas for mercy. Decades later, I can recall how I leaned forward in my seat, rapt. *Measure for Measure* remains my favorite Shakespeare play and certainly doesn't need to be reimagined, yet here we are.

Some of the research for this book was completed while working on my essay collection *Snake*. I would like to thank again all of the conservationists and herpetologists who were generous with their time. The documentary *Holy Ghost People,* directed by Peter Adair, influenced Essa's backstory. I gleaned important insights into tarot from a class taught by Holly Buczek as well as *The Wild Root Tarot: Wherein Wisdom Resides* by Mark Ryan and John Matthews. *The Fortune Telling Directory: Divination Techniques to Unlock your Fortune* by Isabella Drayson helped with Chapters 12 and 19. And for anyone interested in animal forensics, I recommend *Animal Investigators: How the World's First Wildlife Forensics Lab Is Solving Crimes and Saving Endangered Species* by Laurel A. Neme. All mistakes are mine of course.

I am deeply grateful to my wonderful agent Michelle Richter for championing this book. It has been a dream to work with everyone at Severn House, including Rachel Slatter, Tina Pietron and Laura Kincaid. This book is better because of early readers Lucia Gadja and Cathy Dee, who helped me think more deeply about the characters. I wrote many of these pages while sitting across my kitchen table from my friend Matthew Pennock. As always, I am thankful for the encouragement and friendship of Ricardo Maldonado. Our sporadic workshops with Elaine Johanson and Stephanie Anderson lighten my heart. I am so lucky to have such supportive friends, including Kristen Linton, Katie Meadows, Toral Doshi, and Emily Mitchell.

The crime-writing community amazes me, and I appreciate the

encouragement of Alex Segura, Kellye Garrett, Steph Post, Tara Laskowski, Daniela Petrova, Con Lehane, Ellen Clair Lamb, Kathleen Barber, Radha Vatsal and so many others. Thank you also to Tayt Harlin, Emily Fragos, Whitney Brough, Nora Walsh, Dorsey Rickard, Courtney Allen, Maryanna Powell, Davin Rosborough, Eric Hupe, Elizabeth Lindsey Rogers, Barbara Thimm, Meakin Armstrong, Dana Chamblee Carpenter, David Burr Gerrard, Loula Heffner Parks, my brother Chris Shiflett and his family plus aunts Alice Wright, Beth Roggeman and Phyllis Faulkner.

My parents Kevin and Paula Wright encouraged me and my writing from as early as I can remember, and they have my endless gratitude. I also want to thank my husband Adam Province whose presence calms me, no small feat. Our little family has grown by one, and nobody and nothing in the world – not even Shakespeare – inspires me as much as Arthur.